Open Marriage: An Erotic Trilogy

I0668040

Also by **ANNE DREA**

Confessions of a Surrogate for Celebrities

Open Marriage: A.S.E. Sports Agency (Book 2)

Open Marriage: Behind the Scenes (Book 3)

Open Marriage: An Erotic Trilogy

By Anne Drea

ISBN: 978-0-9855988-6-0.

Open Marriage: An Erotic Trilogy

By Anne Drea

Anne Drea

1

Stacy

We met at a bar.

He was wearing black slacks, a black linen shirt, and instead of the traditional black loafers I would have expected, he had on camel-colored gators. I thought that set him apart, gave him an edge, and it immediately made me want to get to know him better. I was in a bold and frisky mood, so I sent him a drink. When he received it, along with the hand-written message I had sent via the cocktail waitress, he raised his glass in acknowledgement of the drink, but he did not immediately come over. Normally, I am a southern belle, but tonight I decided I would be "that woman" and I allowed myself to be the pursuer. I watched him as he flirted with the other women. I watched as they shamelessly flirted back with him. All the while he watched me watching him, and I decided that I was enjoying this game we were playing.

At some point I decided to take it up a notch.

I went out to the dance floor and started to dance seductively. This whole show was for him, and he knew it. I had already changed clothes after work, and instead of my conservative navy blue pencil skirt and blazer, I was wearing a short and tight little black dress that showed off my natural double D's, even as the dress accentuated my tight ass. My ass had always been my secret weapon, and I wielded it tonight like a sword.

I worked my ass around and around and grinded it up against the first man who had the nerve to dance up on me on the dance floor. I moved it around his dick until I felt its stiffness, then I abruptly left the dance floor to get a drink. But really I left to reassess my position in this little cat and mouse game we were playing.

When I got to the barstool and looked over my shoulder, I saw that I had Mr. Man's full attention, along with the attention of about five other men. This time Mr. Man sent me a drink. Instead of raising my drink to him as he did me, I declined it and sent it back. I had decided that I wanted to be pursued. I declined the next three drinks that were sent to me from three different men, all the while rocking on my barstool as if I was grooving to the music. But really I was letting Mr. Man get a glimpse of how good I would ride his dick when given the chance.

Luckily, the chance came quickly.

I saw him approach me out of the corner of my eye, but I pretended not to notice. I was prepared to play coy and extend this little game of cat and mouse, but a quick glance at my watch let me know that enough time had passed and I needed to speed things along. When Mr. Man approached me, he smelled as good as he looked and I was instantly wet. I was so wet that my thong was plastered against the swollen lips of my pussy. I wanted this man now.

He leaned over and whispered into my ear, "Can we dance?" I countered and whispered back, "Can we fuck?" He leaned back, almost in shock, as if taken aback by my boldness. Yet I could see the shift in his pants, as if his dick had responded to my request, and I knew he was down even before he did. He led me out of the bar.

I could see his confusion when he glanced back at me, and I knew what he was thinking. As he held my hand leading me out of the bar I knew that he could feel the huge 4.5 carat, cushion cut diamond and platinum wedding ring sitting on my left hand that signified my marriage commitment to another man. I could sense that he wanted to ask me if I was married, but that he didn't want to know the answer. Or rather, that he already knew the answer, but didn't want to ask the question, for fear that he might remind me of what he assumed I had forgotten. Or, perhaps what I didn't want to remember. I could see it all over his face, and in the bulge of his pants, that he didn't want to ruin his luck. So he didn't ask the question, and I didn't supply the answer.

When we got to his SUV he asked, "Your place or mine?" I looked at the spaciousness of his Lincoln Navigator and said, "Neither." Then I opened his truck and entered the backseat. I could see Mr. Man begin to thank his lucky stars. I must admit I was making this very easy for him. It's just that I had to be home by 2 a.m. That was the rule, and I had already wasted enough time with our little game of seduction in the bar.

When Mr. Man got in the backseat, his dick was hard as stone, and as much as I wanted to feel it throbbing inside of me, I couldn't resist the urge to taste it first. I used to hate giving oral sex, but now I loved the taste of a new dick. It was like exploring an unknown flavor of ice cream with a blindfold on. The taste and the texture would all be new and that drove me crazy. When I'd had my full, and Mr. Man was on the brink of cumming, I pulled away and allowed him to come back down as I prepared his dick and my pussy for the next part of the evening.

When his rapid pant had decreased to a steady breath I slid my wet pussy over his dick and mounted it, tightly clinching the lips of my pussy over the head of his dick. He moaned with delight, and a small tear escaped out of the corner of my eye. I didn't usually allow guys to go in raw – as in without protection -but I was pressed for time and something about this one made me feel deliciously reckless.

I started to establish my rhythm, and I could swear I heard Mr. Man exclaim that he loved me. That's when I knew I was giving him the good stuff. Not to be outdone, Mr. Man clamped his big hands around my hips and began to slam me down real hard on his dick. The sex was so fucking good that I wanted to keep it going for a while, but when he reached down and began to tease my clit with his thumb while steadily slamming me down on his dick, I couldn't help myself and I began to cum all over him. Within seconds he came too and I could feel the warmth of his cum spread inside of me and come dripping back down the sides of his dick and out of my pussy.

We sat there for a while, just enjoying the silky wetness all around us, both of us throbbing, panting, smiling. Until finally I spoke. "I gotta go" I said. Mr. Man looked at me like he had lost his first love. I was touched by his sadness to see me go, and definitely wanted another taste of this fine, handsome stranger, so I gave him my business card. Not the business card that listed me as an attorney in a prestigious law firm, but the one I'd had made for occasions such as this, with my "alternate name" and my google phone number so that we could keep in contact while I maintained my confidentiality.

I stepped out of Mr. Man's car and declined his offer to walk me to my car. When he had driven off, still looking back in his rearview mirror, I pulled out my travel size mouthwash, gargled and spit. I removed my panties and tossed them into the nearest dumpster. Then I headed home.

When I got home I decided to park on the street so that the garage wouldn't wake my husband and children.

I opened the front door, disarmed my alarm, and crept slowly up the stairs.

My house smelled of sweet goodness, and I could tell that my husband had baked some cookies with the kids.

I stepped into my children's rooms and watched them sleep for a moment, and then I slowly closed their doors being careful not to wake them.

I tiptoed down the hallway into my master bedroom.

On the left side of the bed, his side of the bed, lay my beautiful husband, sound asleep.

I removed my clothes and stepped into the shower. I stood there in the water for several minutes savoring the hot water as it slid down my body. I allowed it to remind me of the evening I had spent with the tall handsome stranger I'd met at the bar. I remembered how he'd touched me and made me cum, and I felt myself grow moist again. I hurriedly finished my shower, resisting the urge to pleasure myself and obtain one final release. Done with my shower, I rinsed off, put lotion on my body and slid into bed, naked, with my husband.

Feeling the warmth of my body, my husband nestled up next to me and whispered, "Did you enjoy your night?" I whispered back, "Yes." He then asked, "Will you be seeing him again?" I sighed, "I surely hope so." My husband gave me a soft peck on the cheek, and off we went to sleep.

My name is Stacy. I am a happily married mother of two, and yes, I'm in an open marriage.

2

Frederick

It is Saturday morning. I usually awake early so that I can get some yard work done. I know how Stacy and the kids like to sleep in on the weekend, so I hope to get all the yard work done while everyone's still sleeping. I like working in the yard. It helps me to think. I grab my gloves and the manual grass cutter and set to work. I use the manual cutter because it's so early and I don't want to wake the neighbors. I tackle the front yard first. After cutting the grass, I trim the hedges, and apply new mulch to the flower bed. Moving on to the backyard I cut the grass, edge around the trees, and spray Stacy's vegetable garden with her special "mix" that she swears makes the vegetables grow so big. Considering that Stacy's vegetables are the most delicious I've ever had, I don't question her special "mix." I just do as I'm told.

When I am done with the backyard, it is still fairly cool outside, so I quickly wash both Stacy and my cars. I want to get them done before the sun rises and that infamous southern heat makes its debut. After washing both cars I am done, and I head upstairs to take a shower. When I am done showering I start breakfast. The kids and Stacy are still sleeping, but I know it won't be long before they smell my buttery pancakes frying, and my bacon sizzling.

Sure enough, the minute the coffee starts brewing, I can hear footsteps. They are Stacy's. She peeks her head in the doorway and gives me a big, beautiful, though still sleepy smile, and my heart catches. Stacy and I got married when we were 22, and even though we have been married for 11 years, my heart still skips a beat when I see her. To this day, she is the most beautiful woman I have ever seen. She has the softest skin and the biggest, most expressive eyes, and they can just as easily communicate "I love you," as they can "Don't talk to me right now." I think her eyes are what drew me in when we met back in the sixth grade. I was the new shy kid in a big private school, and she was the spitfire that came right up to me and said, "You're pretty short to be a sixth-grader, but you can come and sit at my table so you won't be by yourself." Then she turned around, and without waiting for a reply from me she began to walk off. When she turned back and realized that I was not following behind her, she stood and waited. She set those big pretty eyes on me as if to say, "I'm not leaving without you, so let's go" and off I scurried behind her. She literally had me at, "You're pretty short...."

Over the years Stacy grew even more beautiful and always had guys following behind her. I was always "just a friend." I had grown a lot taller, and girls mostly always told me how cute I was, but I never could get Stacy's attention. That is, until the year I came home from basic training. By then I had a six-pack and was all muscle, and Stacy couldn't keep her eyes off me. Funny enough, at that time I had a girlfriend, so Stacy found herself in the "just friends" category. But we grew closer, and soon our friendship became so obviously more, that my girlfriend became uncomfortable with Stacy and I hanging out. She gave me an ultimatum, telling me to choose my friendship with Stacy or my relationship with her, and although I didn't want to hurt my girlfriend, I knew I couldn't let Stacy go. Well, needless to say, I chose Stacy, and we were married the following week. Now, 11 years later, she is still able to melt my heart and make me feel like the luckiest man alive.

Stacy walks into the kitchen and lays her head on my shoulder. My wife is not much of a morning person, and she doesn't talk much before her cup of coffee, so this is her way of saying good morning. She is wearing a short white silk robe that reaches the middle of her thighs, and as she stands there beside me, I allow my hand to move up her robe and caress her ass. My wife is not wearing underwear and I am instantly aroused. I had already been inside my wife once this morning. I couldn't resist making love to her after she slipped into bed, naked, following her night out. She had fallen asleep, but I couldn't resist her naked body against mine, and I had slid myself inside her while she was still asleep. Stacy had cum within minutes, with me cumming right behind her. Still, I cannot get enough of my wife, and I entertain thoughts of lifting up her robe and bending her over our kitchen counter. That is, until those thoughts are interrupted by our seven year old daughter, Hannah, who sleepily walks into the kitchen rubbing her eyes and holding one of her teddy bears.

Other than her mother, my daughter Hannah is the only person who can make my heart skip a beat. She walks right up to me and extends her arms. I pick her up, and she nestles her head into the crook of my neck. As she rests her head on my shoulder, she sucks her thumb. She only sucks her thumb when she is comfortable, and I instantly know that she is not planning on getting down any time soon. My daughter might look like me, but she has her mom's personality and is able to communicate a thought with only a look or a gesture. Briefly I realize that this is probably a skill that all women possess. I know that my girls have perfected it.

Stacy pours herself some coffee, still silently beautiful, and my little angel rests comfortably on my shoulder. As Stacy sips her coffee, she begins to move the plates of food into the dining room. Right before the table is set, my six year old son, Henry, bounds down the stairs with the energy of a freight train, wearing a red and blue cape with a matching red and blue eye mask declaring that he is a "super-hero, spy-kid, crime solver." My daughter and wife giggle and I just shake my head. That is my boy. Funny enough, he looks like his mom, but he is all me – full of energy and restless enthusiasm. I have no doubt in my mind that my son has been up probably as long as I have, but stayed in his room assembling his super-hero outfit. I am also pretty sure that if I go into his room I am going to find a matching fort.

When the table is set, and my son has successfully orchestrated his "big reveal" we sit down to breakfast. I look around at my family, and I realize as I do every single day that I am incredibly blessed. As my wife wakes up and becomes the "Chatty Cathy" that I am used to, and my daughter alternates between smiling at her little brother and rolling her eyes at him, and my son regales us with tales of saving villages from one-eyed monsters and cafeteria ladies, I send a silent prayer up to God, thanking him for my family. I am a lucky man.

After breakfast I prepare to leave. I am in pharmaceutical sales and every Saturday I drive the three hours to our state's capital to meet my crucial contacts. Unlike for a lot of traditional Monday through Friday nine to fivers, Saturdays for me are a big workday. Stacy told me that she is taking the kids to the movies today and then they are going to the mall to get new school shoes. After that they are going to do some grocery shopping and stop at the library to check out their books for the week. Like Stacy and I, our children are avid readers and it is a family ritual to go to the library once per week to check out our favorite books.

I kiss the kids and Stacy goodbye, letting them know that I will be back tomorrow morning. While the kids walk out the front door, I pull Stacy to me and give her a long deep kiss, while rubbing her ass. I love Stacy's ass. I have always loved a woman with curves, but Stacy's ass takes the cake. It is simply amazing. So is the rest of her.

After walking my family to the car, I stand there and watch them drive off. When they have driven off I go back inside to pack my overnight bag. I grab my dark gray suit, my dark gray loafers and a few changes of dress shirts and ties. I also grab my dress socks, and a box of condoms. I am meeting Serita tonight, so I definitely don't want to forget those.

During the three hour drive I listen to my jazz CD's. When I am done grooving, I turn to my rock station to keep myself alert for the drive. When I pull into the capital city, I immediately go check into my hotel. There, I change into my suit and one of my dress shirts and off I go to my meetings. Five hours later, I have met all my contacts, including a few new ones, and am adjourning my final meeting over dinner. When we are done with dinner, I shake hands, enjoy a little small talk, and make plans to follow up with the gentlemen in three weeks. Once they are in their cars, I walk back into the hotel lobby and sit at the bar, waiting for Serita.

Within 20 minutes I hear a pair of heels begin to approach the entrance to the hotel's bar, and without even seeing her I know that it is Serita. I have never seen Serita in anything other than six inch heels, and I wait anxiously to see if it is indeed her, and what shoes she is wearing. I want to see what shoes she's wearing not because I love women's shoes, but because Serita always wears her stilettos to bed. Sex with Serita always involves props and one of the best ones are whatever heels she decides to wear. There is nothing like an ass-naked woman in nothing but a pair of six inch heels. My dick grows hard just thinking about it.

Sure enough, Serita turns the corner and sees me. She smiles seductively and my dick shoots up straighter, and harder. Serita is wearing a short blue dress with a deep v-neck that shows off her incredible tits. Her heels are also blue and spiky, and as I expected they are very, very high. I smile knowing that they will be a part of what we do later. She approaches me, leans down and kisses me full on the mouth. She has the softest, fullest lips and I can't wait to slip my dick between them. Serita sits down beside me and removes her bag from her shoulder.

I take a moment to soak in her beauty. Serita is exotically gorgeous. She is multiracial and is equal parts Brazilian, French and Japanese. I like exotic women, and Serita definitely fits the bill. As Serita reaches for her drink, her hair cascades forward and brushes my arm, and I think instantly of pulling it and fucking her from behind. Like my wife, Serita has a nice ass and I love to hit it from behind.

I clear my throat to refocus my attention back on what Serita is saying. She notices my distraction, and knows me well enough to know what has me distracted, so she smiles at me. When she is done with her drink, we head upstairs to my room, hand-in-hand.

When we enter the room, Serita drops her bag and gives me a passionate kiss. I push her against the wall, and grind my dick against the front of her dress as she wraps her right leg around me. I grab her left thigh and hold her pussy in place as I move slowly across the front of it. The friction of our clothes against her throbbing clit makes her hot and horny, and impatiently she tugs at the belt of my suit pants. We kiss, and although I know Serita would love it if I just ram my dick into her pussy, I make her wait.

Right there, beside the front door of the hotel room (because we haven't made it pass that point) I kiss her mouth, then her neck. I move downward and kiss the top of her breasts. When her breath catches, and her head goes back and her mouth opens, I insert my finger into her mouth, while taking her breasts first into my hand, then into my mouth. I suck her nipples, flicking my tongue against them and I insert my other finger into her pussy. It is so wet that my finger slides in with ease.

By now Serita is breathing hard, and she is trying to squeeze my fingers off by tightly squeezing her thighs as I softly finger-fuck her. She has arched her pussy towards me so hard that it pushes me back. I apply just as much force to push her back on the wall. She is grinding so hard against my finger at this point that it takes effort to remove it from inside her pussy. But I do remove it, as I trail soft kisses down her belly towards her navel. Serita's belly button is pierced, so I take the barbell into my mouth and gently roll my tongue around it. Serita half-moans, half-groans and before she can react I travel down farther, to the point where her other lips meet.

I gently flick my tongue out, and caress the swollen bulb of her clitoris. She jerks and gasps and I put the length of my tongue between her legs and lick the lips of her pussy from the back to the front, like an ice cream cone. Serita is so wet that her juices sit on my tongue like sweet water. I swallow them, enjoying the taste of her, and I lick her pussy again.

When she saunters down to the floor, I use that opportunity to hike up her dress, remove her thong, which sits wet in my hand like a used paper towel, and eat from her pussy like it is my last meal. I alternate between licking between the lips of her pussy and flicking my tongue, side-to-side, across her clitoris. When she says something to me in French, it sounds so fucking sexy that I grunt and begin to tongue-fuck her. The whole time I am eating her pussy, I am softly rubbing her sensitive nipples with the tips of my index finger and thumb. She lets out a soft "Oh, shit..." followed by a harder "Fuck!" and my mouth fills up with her juices as she cums in my mouth. I swallow it all, and turned on but her wetness, which is leaking onto the floor, I pull down my pants and enter her pussy.

Her eyes open wide when she feels me enter her wet pussy, raw. We usually use condoms (because Serita is not on birth control) but the wetness of her pussy makes me hungry to feel what the inside of her might feel like. Right away I am thrusting so hard that it jerks Serita's body upward, making it appear that she is running away from me. This turns me on even more, so I fuck her harder. Serita groans, and bites her lip so hard that it draws blood. Her eyes are shut tight, and she hangs on for dear life as I fuck the shit out of her.

Abruptly she moves me out of her pussy, and turns over, giving me full access to her ass and permission to fuck her from behind. I aim to slide my dick back into her pussy. But because her pussy is so wet that her juices slide down into the area around her ass, I accidentally slide my dick into her ass. She jumps a bit, and looks back. So I try to move my dick back into her pussy. But she stops me and slides my dick back into her ass, and begins moving back and forth. Her asshole is so fucking tight! It takes everything I have not to fuck her hard. I have no idea if she has ever had anal sex, so I don't want to go too hard or too fast at first. But after a few minutes of going slowly, and moving my dick in and out of her and around and around in her ass, she starts to buck faster and wilder, so I increase my speed and go deeper. I begin to move faster and harder in her ass. At one point I grip her ass on both sides and ram my dick so hard into her ass that she yelps. The sensation of the tightness of her ass and her screams are too much to handle and I cum inside of her ass.

When the throbbing has subsided and I have emptied myself inside her, we both collapse onto the floor. She is on her stomach and I am on mine, with my right leg strewn across the back of her legs. We lay there for a while, until we both drift off. When I awake two hours later she is still asleep on the floor, snoring softly. In that moment I think she is so beautiful. I go to wake her, and she only shifts and goes back to sleep, so I decide to carry her to the bed. She is still sound asleep. I chuckle to myself about how out of it she is and go back to grab her bag, which is still beside the door where we had fucked. I grab one of the handles, but miss the other one, so that when I go to lift her bag the contents spill out.

As I bend to retrieve the bag, I notice a picture that has fallen from Serita's wallet. In the picture is a photo of Serita and what looks to be a carbon copy of her. The young girl in the picture looks to be about three years old, and appears to be in a giggling fit sitting on her mom's lap as the picture was taken. Inadvertently, I wonder who took the picture. The thought appears so quickly that I barely notice the slight twinge of jealousy that accompanies it. I wonder if the person who took the picture is the child's father. Was it an old lover of Serita's?

I dismiss the thoughts floating around in my head and chalk my jealousy up to not wanting to share Serita's pussy with anyone else. I mean it is so good, it makes a man want to own it. I knew these were all inappropriate thoughts, so I outwardly shake my head from side to side in an attempt to inwardly clear my thoughts of Serita. The deal that my wife and I struck was that the other partners in our lives would be for sex and nothing more. I certainly don't want to have any personal thoughts of Serita, nor of "owning" her pussy. As was the agreement, I would hit it when I came to town and wouldn't concern myself with what or who she did when I wasn't around.

After putting her purse next to her side of the bed, I take a quick shower, and because I am feeling nervous about the direction my thoughts have gone in, I decide to head back home. Even though it is the middle of the night, I feel wide awake and know that my music will keep me great company as I drive the three hours back home. I leave a note for Serita, letting her know that I have left the room for her and that I will see her in three weeks when I come back into town, and then I pack my bags and leave. On my way out I request a wake-up call for the "guest" in my room, and order some room service to be sent up 30 minutes after the wake up, and then I hit the road.

I start my drive out listening to my rock. Within an hour or so, I switch to the smoothness of my jazz, and let it float me all the way back home. A couple hours into my drive, my thoughts shift to Serita. What is surprising though, is that instead of thinking about Serita's round ass or her delicious pussy, I find myself thinking about her daughter, and what it might be like to spend an afternoon with them. Those thoughts scare the shit out of me, so I take my jazz CD out, turn back to my rock station, and crank up the volume to drown out my thoughts. I jam all the way back home and to my wife.

3

Stacy

I love Sundays. It is my favorite day of the week.
Sunday mornings are the only mornings I wake up
chipper, and without the need for my usual cup of
Joe to get me going. I love Sunday mornings
because it is the one day of the week that both
Freddy and I are home, not working, and able to
spend some time with the kids. We also get to
spend some time together. Freddy is snoring softly
beside me as I slip into my robe and slippers. I hop
out of bed, kiss Freddy on the cheek while he's still
sleeping, then I tiptoe out of the room so that I
don't disturb him. I peek in on the kids who of
course are still sleeping, then head downstairs to
fix breakfast. Whereas on Saturdays Freddy gets up
and fixes everyone breakfast, on Sundays it's my
turn to do my thing.

When I get into the kitchen I turn on the radio and
listen to some gospel as I make my French toast
batter. I am humming along and whipping up my
secret ingredients. Freddy got in really late last
night, and was exhausted, or else he'd be up with
me sitting at the kitchen counter while I prepare

my famous French toast. I dip the bread into the mix, and lay them gently into the skillet, as I also set the table so that everything will be done before my family wakes up. When the first slices of French toast are made, I yell up the stairs for everyone to come down. It is a few minutes before I hear the heavy steps of my husband walk from room to room waking up the children.

Despite having just woken up the kids, the first person down the stairs is my husband. He is truly a beautiful man. As he walks toward me, I take a moment to cast an appreciative glance at his body. His hair is tousled from sleep, and his eyes are smiling in a sleepy, yet sexy way. My husband's build is lean. He is 6'1, with long legs and strong arms. His chest is chiseled as a result of hitting the gym five days a week. He is wearing boxers with an old college T-shirt, and it makes him look boyish. In this moment I am so in love with this man. He walks up to me and wraps me in his arms and I close my eyes and just nestle there.

We are interrupted by a loud "Mommmm!" The screech is coming from my daughter as she tries to untangle herself from a net that her little brother has thrown over her as he attempts to catch "The Hannah Monster." I untangle my daughter, scold my son, and usher them both down the stairs in time to catch my husband standing beside the sink nibbling on a folded slice of French toast with an amused smile on his face, ankles crossed, watching me wrangle the kids. I get the children seated, while giving them a look that says, "Not another word." I then go over to my husband and walk him to the table by holding his hands as they are wrapped around my waist.

We walk that way to the table and when I notice that the kids aren't paying attention, because they have resumed their argument, I brush my ass across the front of his boxer shorts. It gets a rise out of him and he moans softly before sitting down at the table and hiding his erection.

As we eat breakfast, in between talking to our children about school and their upcoming projects, we cast lustful glances at each other and I know what both of us are thinking. A quick glance at the clock dashes our hopes for a morning quickie, however, when we realize we only have 45 minutes to finish breakfast, get dressed and get to church.

We arrive at Grace Church 15 minutes late, and I hate to be late. Freddy and I quickly enter the church and are warmly greeted by Ms. Floretta and Ms. Candice, while Mrs. Swift frowns at us from behind her glasses. Ms. Floretta and Ms. Candice have been best friends for 53 years. Both are considered spinsters, having never gotten married or having children. They are roommates in a home they bought together, and are always together. If they are not at the church serving on the usher board, then they are at the church gardening. But they are always at the church. They are two of the nicest women you'd ever want to meet.

Mrs. Swift, on the other hand, is the meanest old lady you'd ever want to know. She is also an usher and is always at the church, like Ms. Floretta and Ms. Candice, but unlike Ms. Floretta and Ms. Candice she never has a nice word to say and is always either gossiping about folks or harassing them. We greet all the ladies as we hurriedly pass by, and although Ms. Floretta and Ms. Candice cheerfully say good morning to us and hand the children mints, Mrs. Swift reminds us that church started 15 minutes ago. Despite my desire to remind Mrs. Swift that I am grown, I instead apologize for being late and rush off. I swear, if that woman was getting some from Mr. Swift she'd be a whole lot happier.

Grace Church is a nondenominational, multicultural church and we've been attending it for 12 years. As a matter of fact, it is the church that Freddy and I were married in. When Freddy and I were dating, we visited a few churches and neither of us felt a real connection. But when we visited Grace Church we felt an instant warmth. We both knew we had found our church home. We liked that Grace Church was nondenominational. Freddy was raised Catholic and I was raised Baptist, and we found it easier to go to an all-inclusive church instead of trying to make one of us "convert" to the other's religion. At the end of the day we both felt like it was our relationship with God that was important, and not the title of our religion.

We are ushered to our seats just in time to hear the choir stand and start to sing. The singing gets me going. I stand and start to clap my hands and sway to the music. Several other church members start to stand and sway as well. Pretty soon we are all warmed up and ready for the sermon. Pastor Flemmings stands up and starts to preach about temptation.

I glance to my side, noticing that Freddy is all ears and that my children are busy doing what they do to keep themselves entertained until church is over. My son Henry is drawing what looks like some sort of superhero hot dog (he later explains to me that it was an airplane) and my daughter Hannah is reading. I smile inwardly at my children, squeeze Freddy's hand and blush when he winks, and then I start to pay attention to the sermon.

Pastor Flemmings preaches about not getting caught up in temptation. About resisting our flesh and being aware of the ways in which the devil will try to get in to take over a family. As he talks about boredom being the devil's playground, my mind starts to drift and I begin to think about how Freddy and I started out.

Freddy's dad had been in the military, and was stationed in Okinawa, Japan. When Freddy's dad got stationed back in the U.S., he started school at the school I was attending. Our teacher had told us a couple days early that a new student would be starting in our class and that he was moving from Japan. Since he was moving here from Japan, we all thought he was going to be Japanese. All the students were really excited to see the new Japanese student.

When Freddy arrived, in the middle of the school year no less, he was nothing that anyone expected. He was short and scrawny, and more importantly, he was not Japanese. Since he was nothing special, everyone ignored him. At lunch I watched him grab his lunch tray and go sit by himself. I felt sorry for him. Even at a young age I remember thinking that it couldn't have been easy for him being the new kid in a new school in the middle of the school year.

I had always been pretty outspoken as a child. My family joked that it was because both of my parents were attorneys. I decided that I would befriend Fredrick. I walked over to him and told him to come and sit with me and my friends, then I walked away. Truthfully, it never occurred to me that he wouldn't do what I said (I have a bit of a bossy nature). So when I turned around and saw that he hadn't followed, I said it to him again and he came. When we got to the lunch table I introduced him to my friends, and although they were hesitant to welcome the new guy right away, within a week of sitting at our table, he became good friends with my friends.

When Freddy's family moved out of base housing into a house three doors down from mine, Freddy and I became good friends. We stayed that way for several years until the tenth grade when Freddy asked me out. Freddy and I had been friends for three years at that point and I was beginning to think of him like a brother. His was the first ear I whispered into that I'd had my first kiss, and his was the shoulder I cried on when I had my first heartbreak.

I'd had several boyfriends, and was quite popular with boys when we were growing up. Whereas Freddy was always single. I'd had a few girls tell me that they thought Freddy was cute, but he never seemed to give them the time of day. I was beginning to think that Freddy liked boys. So, imagine my surprise when Freddy asked me out to the spring dance. At first I laughed thinking it was some kind of joke. But then I saw how serious Freddy was. I stopped laughing and thought about it. Even though Freddy was handsome, he simply was not my type. I had known him too long, had told him too much, and just didn't see him that way. But I didn't want to hurt his feelings by turning him down completely, so I agreed to go to the dance.

I made it clear that I was going to the dance as his friend, nothing more. But what I didn't tell him was that I was planning to hook him up with my best friend's sister. I would introduce them at my house, before we got to the dance, and hopefully they would hit it off. On the night of the dance, I had my best friend and her sister meet at my house one hour before the dance. Freddy was coming to pick us up at 7 p.m. in his new car that his dad had bought him three weeks before. His dad had surprised him with a brand-new Nissan Sentra, and I was the first person that Freddy had shared the good news with. He took me for a ride to the mall and we celebrated his new car over ice cream. Although the Nissan Sentra wasn't the fanciest car in the world, it was his first car, and we were both super excited. Freddy having a new car meant that we would always have a ride to the mall, to the movies, or to the park. Freddy had even let me drive his car! Although we made sure not to let his dad see.

One hour before Freddy was to arrive, my best friend Lisa, and her sister Valerie came over to my house. Lisa was wearing a royal blue floor-length, A-line gown, with a side slit, and she looked great. But Valerie took the cake. She was gorgeous in a silver, above-the-knee, baby doll dress, and although I had cute breasts, hers were slamming in that dress. Even I couldn't stop looking at them. I complimented her, and secretly gloated at how appreciative Freddy was going to be when he saw Valerie and realized that I was hooking him up. I wondered if he would even let me drive his car again.

I brought the girls up to my room while I finished slipping on my shoes. I was wearing a classic little black dress with peep-toe pumps, and I was also looking really cute. I hoped Damien thought so too because I was hoping to catch his eye and get him to ask me out. Damien was too cute and was also smart, and I thought he would be a great prom date and an even better catch. Damien was a Junior and I was only a Sophomore, but I had already been asked to the Junior prom twice. Still, I was holding out for Damien to ask me. Even though he didn't know it, I was secretly giving him until tonight to ask me before I went with one of my backups.

Promptly one hour later, at 8 p.m., Freddy rang my doorbell. He was always prompt, courtesy of having a military dad. My dad let him in so that us girls could make an entrance. Lisa went down first, followed by Valerie. I couldn't see Freddy's reaction to Valerie because I was still upstairs, but I hoped he'd be pleased. Then I began my descent.

Let me be honest about something first. Even though I didn't have romantic feelings for Freddy, I kind of liked that he liked me. If nothing else, it was an ego boost to watch him eye me appreciatively, so I just knew Freddy would gawk when he saw me come down the stairs. With that sentiment in mind, I began my descent down the stairs.

When I got to within Freddy's eyesight, I was dismayed to find that he was still looking at Valerie. Maybe looking is an understatement. He was actually staring at her to the point that when I came down the stairs I actually had to clear my throat to get him to notice me. He looked up, saw me, gave a distracted smile, and resumed his visual admiration of Valerie. I was surprised that I was feeling a bit jealous. I didn't want Freddy, but I guess I did want the attention.

After taking pictures, and noticing Freddy and Valerie sidled up next to each other, we were on our way. I had planned to ride in the front seat since Valerie didn't really know Freddy yet, but that plan was dismissed when I saw Freddy walk Valerie to the front seat, open her door and help her in. When in the heck had Freddy become a gentleman?! I sat in the back seat upset. I didn't like it one bit that Freddy was ignoring me and all into Valerie. Didn't he see that she had a big forehead? So what if she had massive boobs? Hello, I had a pair of those too. Well, maybe not those exactly, but I did have a pair.

When we got to the dance, Freddy and Valerie spent the whole night talking, dancing or smiling at each other like fools. I was so busy watching them that I didn't have time to pay attention to Damien when he came over. The whole time he sat there talking to me, I was like, "Huh? What did you say? I'm sorry, can you repeat that?" At one point he must have gotten frustrated and walked away, but I was too busy to even notice that. I only knew that he'd walked away when I saw him standing near the punch table, when I thought he'd been sitting next to me. Well, I'd had enough, so I decided I was ready to go. I made up a lie about not feeling well and asked Freddy to bring us home.

The whole drive back, Lisa was talking animatedly about some boy she'd met and Valerie and Freddy were sitting in the front seat holding hands. Boy, I couldn't get out of that car fast enough! Freddy dropped Lisa and Valerie off first and I sat back and watched him lean over and give her a kiss on her cheek after he'd walked her to her door. Then he got in the car and grinned all the way back home.

When he pulled up in front of my house, I silently got out of the car and began to walk toward my door. As he waited for me to get in the house safely, I heard him call out to me. I wasn't sure why, but that made me happy. I thought maybe Freddy was going to apologize for ignoring me all night and being a really bad friend. But all he did was thank me for introducing him to "Val." I grunted a "You're welcome," and went inside. I was grateful this dreaded night was over.

The next week I avoided Freddy. I was trying to make sense of how I was feeling. I didn't know why I was feeling jealous, but I was. I reasoned it was because I had been Freddy's friend for so long and had been his #1 girl, and now someone else was taking my place. I tried to tell myself that that was all I was feeling, but deep down inside I began to speculate that maybe I liked Freddy more than what I was letting on.

After about two weeks of avoiding Freddy's calls (which were much less frequent than what they had been), I finally agreed to see him. He picked me up in his car and we drove to the movies to see a comedy he had wanted to see. We were hanging out in the arcade when I decided that I did not want another girl to be as important as I was to Freddy. I wanted him to myself. I told Freddy this with nervousness in my voice, and to my surprise he picked me up and hugged me. He admitted that although he had feelings for Valerie that he had loved me for a long time and wanted to be with me. Then he leaned down (because he was six inches taller than me) and gave me a kiss.

In that moment, swept up in the feelings of being in Freddy's arms and his #1 girl again, I realized two things. The first is that, when he kissed me I felt like I was kissing my brother. There were absolutely no fireworks or sparks whatsoever. The second thing was that Valerie had seen the whole thing. She and her sister were walking past the arcade at the exact moment that I was getting kissed by Freddy and they had seen the whole thing. Apparently, she and her sister were also going to see that comedy flick.

Valerie let out a sharp gasp, dropped her bucket of popcorn, and ran out of the theater with her sister behind her, me behind her sister, and Freddy behind me. When Valerie got to her car and stopped running, she turned around to face us, and I was met with her tear-stricken face and her sister's angry glare. Valerie looked from me to Freddy and back again, and Freddy was the first to speak. With his head down, he told Valerie that he was so sorry to hurt her, and that he was sorry she'd seen us kiss, but that he was in love with me and wanted to be with me. Then he apologized again.

I stood there in total shock. I had thought he was going to try to reclaim Valerie. I was actually hoping that he had felt the emptiness of the kiss and was running to tell her it meant nothing. But I guess it had meant something to him. I guess he had felt something. Before I could say a word, Valerie hopped into her car. Her sister, my former best friend, hopped in behind her after telling me not to ever call her again, and Freddy put his arms around me in a show of support. In one short day I had lost a best friend, broken someone's heart, and gained a boyfriend that I didn't want. It wasn't my intention to take Freddy from Valerie (or maybe it was) and now I was stuck with him as a boyfriend, when all I'd wanted was for us to be great friends again.

Over the next month I tried to "date" Freddy, but it felt awkward every time he tried to put his arms around me, or kiss me. I had told him secrets. I had shared crushes with him, and now here I was supposed to be romantic with him? It was just too weird. Plus, aside from loving Freddy in a friendly kind of way, I just didn't feel anything romantic. Still, because I had taken him from Valerie I felt obligated to play along.

Then Valentine's Day came and Freddy presented me with a beautiful heart necklace that I knew must have cost a fortune, and I just couldn't play along anymore. With tears in my eyes (because I really didn't want to hurt him, but knew that I would) I told him that I didn't love him romantically and only wanted to be friends. At first he thought I was joking and leaned over to give me a kiss. When I pulled back, he saw then that I was serious. Without a word he rose from my sofa (we had been at my house) and began to leave. I ran behind him and tried to give back his necklace, but he wouldn't take it. He told me "It's yours. I want you to have it." Then Freddy walked right out of my house and out of my life.

I saw Freddy over the next couple of years as we became Seniors in high school. It was hard not to, being that we lived three doors away from each other and attended the same school, but we were never friends again. I think it was too hard for both of us. I think Freddy was embarrassed that he had put his heart on the line and I was ashamed that he might have thought that I had played with his emotions, so we just eventually stopped talking.

Freddy and I had both started dating other people by then. I saw Freddy on a few dates with a few different girls and I had begun to date Damien. Then I stopped seeing Freddy around the way after we graduated from high school.

After a few months of not seeing Freddy I stopped by his house and asked his mom where he was, and she told me he had enrolled in the army. He would not be home again for several years. I was a bit saddened by the news, but not too much. We had not been friends for a couple years by then, so although I wished him well and hoped he'd be safe, it was not a big deal to me. I was also on my way out of state. I was beginning college in the Fall.

4

Stacy

Fast forward four years. I had moved back home for the summer after finishing my B.A. in Political Science/Pre-Law and would be starting law school in the Fall. I had planned to spend the summer de-stressing, shopping, and hanging out with old friends from high school, if they were still around. I basically wanted to spend my summer doing a whole lot of nothing, to get rested for what lie ahead in law school. One thing I was going to do, however, was get back in shape. I still looked good, but I had managed to gain about 15 pounds while away at college, and although they all seemed to go to my boobs, I still wanted to tighten everything back up.

On one of my morning runs, I saw the most beautiful specimen of a man outside washing his truck. As I jogged up I took a moment, or two, to take in his chiseled chest, narrow hips, and tight ass as he leaned over to wash his truck. I darn near jogged into Mr. Wagner's trash can because I couldn't take my eyes off the stranger. The reaction I had to him was primal and unlike anything I had ever experienced before. I had always been something of a sexual prude, quite conservative, and had only had sex with one person my whole life and college career. That person was my boyfriend Damien. He had been my boyfriend from my Junior year of high school all the way to my Sophomore year of college, and he was my first and only sexual partner. We broke up when he dumped me for a cheerleader at his school. He didn't tell me that part. That part I found out from Facebook-stalking him.

Anyway, it was shocking to me that this stranger made me so wet and that my first reaction was to want to have sex with him. I was even more shocked when the stranger turned my way and I was able to see that it was none other than Freddy. Except this Freddy didn't look like high school Freddy. This Freddy was Frederick the man, and he was sexy as hell.

Freddy had always been tall, but Frederick had filled out nicely. His chest and abs were defined and his arms were thick and hard. Like a horny teenager, it made me wonder what else was thick and hard. He had a light trail of soft-looking hair going down the bottom of his abs and disappearing into his shorts. I wanted to follow that trail of hair with my hands. Without even seeing myself, I knew I was blushing because of my thoughts.

When Freddy called my name and I jogged over closer to him, I couldn't even look him in his eyes. I was worried that he'd see all the freaky thoughts that were going on in my head. Freddy was excited to see me and wrapped his arms around me as I stood there frozen, like a deer caught in headlights, feeling the solidness of his dick against the top part of my belly. When he let me go, I just stood there wobbly. He looked concerned and I played it off like I was just a bit dizzy from my run. He told me to stay there, then he strolled into his mom's house to get me a bottled water.

I wondered why I hadn't noticed that the sexy-ass stranger had been standing in front of Freddy's old house? I watched him walk away enjoying looking at his ass in those gym shorts. What was happening to me? Who was this pervert that I was turning into? I had never even been into men's asses, but Lord have mercy I was into his. When in the hell had Freddy become so damn fine? Did I miss something all these years? Maybe I was ovulating. Maybe that's why I was having these thoughts.

I watched Freddy jog back out of the house and I realized I was holding my breath. Why was I acting like such an F'ing idiot? I had never been awkward around guys before. Even though I hadn't given it up a lot, I had always had guys interested in me. I just tended to be a bit picky. But I had never had this reaction to other guys before. As I stood there talking to Freddy I realized that I was in love. Maybe I had always been. Ever since we were young, Freddy had always held a special place in my heart. I realized now that even then I had loved him. It hadn't been a romantic love then, but now I was feeling it, hard and deep. I was totally in love with Freddy!

I listened to Freddy tell me about being in the army and everywhere he had traveled. I heard him tell me that it had been the best and worst decision of his life. Freddy said being in the army had made him strong and responsible, but had required so much. We stood out there for hours with him telling me about all the friends he had lost in the war, and me telling him about college. Even though my experiences weren't nearly as exciting as his had been, he listened intently as if I was the most important person in the world. As corny as it sounds, my heart skipped a beat. I stood there talking to him with my heart filling up with so much love. I actually had to swallow to suppress the love that was boiling out of me. I debated telling him that I loved him right then and there. I wanted to scream it from the rooftops. But then I remembered how I had already broken his heart. I remembered how I thought I felt something before, only to realize I hadn't felt anything at all. So I didn't tell him that I loved him. What I did instead, as hard as it was, was tell him that I had to go. I told him it was great to see him doing so well, then I gave him a hug, and walked away.

I couldn't explain why, but there were tears in my eyes as I walked away. I brushed one of them away very quickly and I lightly jogged the three doors down, back to my house. When I got inside, I locked the door, and grateful that I was home alone, sat right there on the floor behind the locked door and cried. Not even two minutes later I heard the doorbell ring. I quickly dried my eyes, stood, and opened the door. There stood Freddy. In that instant I played out a scenario in which he was coming to the door to say that he still loved me and wanted to be with me. I imagined that he would wrap me in his arms and confess his love for me, as I confessed my love for him. But that is not what happened.

Instead of confessions of love, Freddy invited me to the movies that evening with him and his girlfriend and a few of their friends. My heart actually physically hurt when I heard him say girlfriend, so much so that I clutched my chest for a brief second. When Freddy noticed me grab my chest, he looked at me quizzically and I lied and said that it had been a while since I had been jogging and that I was still catching my breath. I told him that I would love to come to the movies with him and his friends and meet his girlfriend. He told me what time the movie was starting, what time they would be by to pick me up, gave me another quick hug and left. I went up to my room, lay across my bed crying, and fell asleep.

I woke up a couple hours later, with about 30 minutes to get ready before it was time for Freddy to pick me up. I wasn't much in the mood for a movie, or for being around Freddy and his girlfriend, so I didn't bother dressing up. I took a quick shower, threw on a pair of jeans, a yellow v-neck tank shirt, and a pair of brown wedge sandals, then I went downstairs to wait.

Mom and dad were back by then and were sitting on the sofa watching a movie. I hadn't really noticed it before, but I suddenly realized how in love my parents were. How strong a bond they had. As they sat on the sofa watching TV, my dad had his left arm around my mom's shoulders and his right hand was over hers. Both of their feet were up on the same Ottoman and mom had her right foot over dad's left foot. They sat there so intertwined and so comfortable with each other, and I realized for the first time what my parents had. I imagined as I looked at my parents, that that was what love looked like.

Before then I had never given it much thought, but now I hoped that I would one day be lucky enough to find what mom and dad had. Even though Damien and I had been together for years, and I had loved him, I had never really thought about marriage. I didn't even know if I ever wanted to be married. I had only thought about a successful career as a lawyer. But all of a sudden, mere hours after seeing Freddy, I knew that I wanted to be his wife.

I also knew that this time I would not interfere. This time I would not break his heart, even though not telling him how I felt was breaking mine.

I told my parents that I was going to a movie with Freddy and his friends. Even though I was an adult and didn't have to tell them where I was going, since I would be staying in their house for the summer, I felt I owed it to them to let them know.

They told me to enjoy myself, dad told me to be careful, and then they went back to their movie, actually snuggling in even closer to each other this time. I chuckled softly to myself at about the same time that the doorbell rang.

I opened the door to see Freddy standing there looking beautiful. Beautiful is not a word used to describe a man but that's exactly what he was. He also had on a yellow shirt. It was a button-down with khaki cargo shorts, and brown slippers. He was wearing a brown baseball cap over his head, and he looked so effortless and gorgeous. He gave me another quick hug, and I wondered if he felt the chill that ran through me every time he did that. We then walked out to his truck together.

I got into the backseat and had to squish in tight next to two guys and a girl. In the front seat was a dark-haired woman whose face I couldn't see, and next to her, driving of course, was Frederick. We drove to the movie theater with everyone chatting, and hopefully not noticing the glances I threw Freddy's way. When we got to the movie theater I was able to see Freddy's girlfriend up close. She was even more beautiful from the front. She had dark olive skin and long dark hair, with a slender figure and light brown eyes. Her name was Cordi, and she looked as exotic as her name. She looked to be a mixture of Spanish, and based on her accent, Italian. They had met on the base where Frederick was stationed. She was not in the Army, but she worked for the Army, and she and Frederick had been together for two years. The two guys there were Mike and Jay, and they were old friends of Freddy's from the neighborhood. The other girl there was a friend of Cordi's, and her name was Marisa. She also worked at the same base as Cordi and Frederick.

We all hung out in the arcade, and I wondered if Freddy remembered the last time we had been in the arcade together. That had been the time when he and I had kissed and Valerie had seen us. That was also the last day that I had been really good friends with Freddy. I looked over at him and saw him looking at me and I wondered if he was thinking the same thing. I wondered if he missed the friendship we used to have. I wondered if he ever longed for us to have it back. I watched he and Cordi play a game together, and although my heart ached, I decided that I would at least have Freddy as a friend. I was not going to do anything to ruin our friendship this time. I would accept what I could get from him, even if it wasn't his heart.

After that night at the movies, I hung out with Freddy and his girlfriend and their friends several more times. We went skating, we went bowling, we went out to restaurants, and we went to the local bar and played pool. Freddy and I also hung out sometimes ourselves. He had begun to jog with me, and slowly but surely those extra pounds that I had picked up dropped away.

One day we went fishing, and although it was obvious that nothing was biting (we managed to only catch a branch), we spent hours out there just laughing and talking like old times. We were out there so long that Freddy actually missed his lunch date with Cordi. When he called her in the truck to explain to her what happened, she didn't seem too upset. They rescheduled for later in the day, and then he and I had lunch instead.

The second time we were out and he missed a date that he had scheduled with Cordi, she did seem a bit upset, but she seemed to also understand that he was simply catching up with an old friend. Her patience began to run short, however, after it happened a third time. Freddy and I had been out jogging, and we decided to take a new path. The new path led us to a clearing nestled behind some trees. In this clearing was a body of water with turtles and ducks everywhere, and it was so picturesque that we decided to hang out there for a bit. I dared Freddy to jump in, he'd double-dared me to do the same thing, and before you knew it, we were both playing in the water.

When we got back to his house several hours later, soaking wet and laughing hysterically, we were met by Cordi, who had been sitting in her car for hours waiting for Freddy. Apparently they had made a date to have breakfast together, and he had forgotten. I felt bad and apologized to Cordi, but her patience had worn thin with me as well. She rolled her eyes at me and turned her back to me. I walked back to my house stopping only to turn around and watch Freddy and her having an animated conversation.

I felt bad that I had caused some strife between them, and I told myself that the next time I saw Freddy I would apologize. Although we had seen each other nearly every day since that first day we went to the movies altogether, it took a few days before I saw Freddy again. When I went over to his house to check on him and ask where he'd been, he confided in me that Cordi was no longer comfortable with the two of us hanging out together. I apologized again, told him I understood, and started to walk way.

When I got to the edge of his lawn, he called me back to his house and told me that he didn't want us to stop hanging out. He said he respected his girlfriend's wishes, and because of that we would no longer be able to hang out as much, but that he still wanted us to continue building our friendship.

I have to admit I was so happy to hear that. We continued to hang out. But it was done under wraps. For example, every time Cordi would call I would have to be quiet in the background. Freddy never told me to be quiet, but I could see the look of concern on his face whenever she was on the other end and he was with me. We had not done anything inappropriate. We had not kissed or gone beyond friendship in any way, but I think we were both feeling guilty that we were sneaking around to hang out with each other. I think Cordi also began to suspect that we were still seeing each other. Whenever he and Cordi were on the phone, the conversation seemed to be tense. On more than one occasion when he got off the phone with her, he was very quiet after.

One day the shit hit the proverbial fan when we arrived back at his place to find Cordi sitting in the driveway. I didn't bother apologizing this time, because I knew she was not going to want to hear it. I hopped out of Freddy's truck and began to walk back to my house, trying to keep as low a profile as possible. But Cordi had other plans. She called my name. I tried to ignore her at first, because I didn't want any drama, but then she called my name again, louder this time. By the third time she called my name, she was screaming, so I slowly turned around.

In an instant she was standing face-to-face with me, with her hand around Freddy's wrist. She had pulled him over to us. She stared at me intently before she spoke. Then she did the unthinkable. She told Freddy to choose, between the two of us, right then and there. I couldn't believe she did that. I thought it was totally unnecessary. I could see that it embarrassed Freddy, because his cheeks started to develop a slight red tinge. I was embarrassed too. I was embarrassed because I knew that Freddy would choose her, and I knew that she knew. So it was obvious that all she wanted to do was put me in my place. Because I didn't need to hear his answer, and because I didn't want to give Cordi the satisfaction of seeing me be rejected, I turned and began to walk away. Then I heard him say the words that would forever change our lives. I heard him say, "I choose Stacy....I'm sorry. But I love her."

My heart reacted to his words, even as my head sought to make sense of what he had just said. Had he really just said he chose me? Had he really said he loved me? My feet kept moving, walking towards my house. As if they had not believed the words, as if they wanted to protect me from getting hurt. I walked into my parent's house, shut the door, went upstairs and into my childhood bedroom. I sat on the edge of the bed. It was almost like an out of body experience. I felt like I was actually watching myself processing what had happened. I was trying to make sense of it. It wasn't until I sat on the edge of that bed for well over an hour that my mind finally registered what my heart had heard. Then I sprang into action.

I ran out of my bedroom, down the stairs and out the door, back to Freddy's house. I shakily stood on his doorstep and rang the doorbell. I noticed that Cordi's car was gone, but Freddy's truck was still there. He came to the door with his eyes cast downward, almost as if he was afraid to look at me. Was he unsure of how I felt about him? Did he not know how much I loved him? Here I thought I'd worn my heart on my sleeve, I thought every time he looked at me he'd be able to tell how much I loved him, but he didn't know.

I looked at Frederick, so beautiful, so manly, but still so insecure. His vulnerability made him even more beautiful to me. My mind kept shouting "I love you! I love you!", but no words came from my lips. All they wanted to do was kiss him. So that's what I did. Right there on his parent's doorstep I wrapped my arms around him and touched my lips to his, and my body began to explode.

I was floating and drowning all at the same time. The intensity of his lips against mine made my knees weak and I began to sink to the floor. It was like I couldn't support my own body weight. Freddy pulled me into his parent's house and lay there with me, as we began to kiss some more. We lay there kissing on the floor, until the woman in me took over. Although I had not been very sexually experienced at that point, it was like my body knew exactly what to do.

I rolled on top of Freddy and began to remove his shirt. I had decided I was going to make love to him right in the foyer of his parents' house. In my mind, I didn't care if they were home. They could have even been watching. I was not going to stop making love to Freddy, no matter what. After I removed his shirt I began to kiss his nipples. I kissed them slowly at first, then I sucked on them gently. When I heard him moan and felt his penis growing under me, I started to suck on them.

Empowered and emboldened by his response, I removed my shirt at the same time that I began to trail kisses down his body. My nipples hardened as they brushed against his body. That turned me on even more. When I got to the trail of hair down his lower abdomen, I stopped right there and kissed it. I had been longing to kiss him there since that first day when I saw him standing outside washing his truck. He had closed his eyes by then and his breathing was labored. I was enjoying the effect I was having on him. I was enjoying it so much that I decided to do something I had never done before. I slid Frederick's pants down and began to kiss the tip of his penis. When I heard him gasp I kissed it some more and then started to run my tongue along the side of it. I felt so powerful, so womanly. So I took it a step further.

I slid Freddy's penis into my mouth and tasted it. It tasted a little like bananas, and I loved bananas. I started to suck it more, then I twirled my tongue around the tip of it. By then Freddy was calling my name and I was on a roll. I started sucking harder and taking more of it in my mouth. As I sucked harder and took him deeper into my mouth the taste changed and became a bit salty. It also got wetter. Freddy was moaning profanities by then, trying hard to restrain me and stop himself from cumming. He got the best of me, flipped me over and started to kiss my breasts and suck my nipples. I arched my back, already feeling the wetness ooze from my vagina and moisten my thighs.

I wanted him inside of me so badly that I couldn't stand it. But Frederick had something else in mind. He lifted my skirt, and when he had it around my waist, he moved my underwear to the side. Damien had done this a million times so I knew what was coming next. I tried to move his head because I had never been that crazy about Damien giving me oral sex. I think he liked it more than I did. So I tried to remove Frederick's head, but he was persistent. He held my hands in his and started to slowly kiss along the edge of my vagina. The sensation was ticklish so I began to wiggle a bit. But when he got to the center of me and started flicking his tongue across my small bud, my body went limp.

The feeling was so sweet and so full that it was all I could do to stay there on the floor. He expertly moved his tongue all around that bud, first across it, then up and down. It was driving my body crazy. Damien had never done that. My body began to quiver and shake and before I could even comprehend what was happening, a sensation erupted in my stomach and surged all the way up to my heart and exploded. My body shook and convulsed and I was not in control of what was happening. What in the hell was that, I wondered. I'd had orgasms before. But none like that. That orgasm, if that's what that was, seemed to originate from the floor. It grabbed a hold of my body and wouldn't turn me loose.

I lay there convulsing, not even realizing that Frederick had gotten up off the floor and gone to his room to get a condom. When he came back I was still convulsing, trying to come down from the high of that powerful orgasm I'd just had. Between my legs were so sticky, and the warm wetness seemed to intensify the deliciousness of what I was feeling. When I opened my eyes I saw Freddy leaning over me, looking at me so lovingly. He whispered, "I love you. I always have, and I always will." When I tried to speak, he put his finger over my lips and told me I didn't need to say anything. He said the fact that I was there with him was enough. He then entered me so softly and sweetly that it felt like a dream. I had to keep blinking to remind myself that I was not dreaming. That I was there with him. We started to move together in unison, and within a few minutes Freddy came softly. He moaned out an "I love you so much" and then he held me tight as he emptied himself into the barrier between us.

When we were done, as I lay there in a blissful state of love, spent energy, and silky wetness, I was overcome with love. Yes, the sex was great, and Frederick was beautiful, but it was more than that. I realized that Frederick had been more than my best friend and that although we had gone our separate ways for a few years, our hearts had remained intertwined, forever connected to each other's. I realized what I had known all along, even during that dreadful first kiss. I realized that I loved Freddy – mind, body, and soul. I loved Freddy with all my heart. And right there on the floor, half-naked, laying in Freddy's parents' foyer, I said it. I told Freddy that I loved him and wanted to be with him forever.

The next week, despite my leaving for law school within a month, and despite never having discussed where we'd live and what we wanted out of life, we were married. We've been together, happy and in love, ever since.

I snapped myself out of my walk down memory lane just in time to hear the sermon ending. As I wiped my eyes, I realized that to others who were looking it would have appeared that I was moved from the sermon. But the real reason I was crying was because I had been reminded of how blessed I was to have Freddy in my life. He made me whole then, and would forever. I was never surer of anything else in my life.

5

Stacy

The early years with Freddy were great. We were married in a small intimate ceremony. By small and intimate, I mean it was myself, Freddy and our pastor. We said traditional vows at Grace Church, but then said our own personal vows right there at the lake, by that clearing we had found earlier, and then went to a fast food restaurant for dinner. Because we were newlyweds, and wanted some privacy, we didn't want to stay with either Freddy's parents or mine during the final month of summer before we moved back to where I would be attending law school. So we stayed at the extended stay hotel.

The room consisted of a small kitchen with a two-burner stove and a full-size refrigerator, a bathroom, a small bedroom, and a living room area consisting of a sofa and a flat-screen TV. The room was not big but it had everything we needed to enjoy a month full of love and togetherness. And sex. We had sex all over that room. We did in the living room, on the sofa, on the coffee table, on the floor in front of the sofa, up against the refrigerator. We did it with me bent over the two-burner stove, in the shower, over the sink, in the bedroom, in the closet, in the hotel's pool, and even in the utility closet when the door was accidentally left open. Freddy dared me and I double dared him and we wound up getting it on in that utility closet.

Those days with Frederick were some of the best sex I've ever had. But they were also the best days I've ever had. Frederick worked from 6 a.m. to 2 p.m. stocking shelves at the local home improvement store, and I spent my days getting my school supplies and material together for law school. I made index cards, organized notebooks, and ordered some of the books I would need. Then when Freddy got off at 2 p.m., we would go to lunch, or to the movies, or to play pool like in the old days. Or we would simply take walks. Or we'd jog together.

Even though we had known each other for so many years, and were able to relish in the old memories, we still learned so much more about each other. I learned that Freddy had dreams of becoming an entrepreneur. I had never known that. I learned that Freddy wanted to live in an RV so that he could travel the world. Freddy was both ambitious and impulsive, and had a real zest for life. He said the Army had brought that out of him. It had made him weary of restraints and control, and hungry for travel and excitement.

Although Freddy always knew that I was smart, he learned that I was a bleeding heart and that my goal was to open my own law practice following law school, so that I could help young people in trouble turn their lives around. He also learned that although I was always very popular in school, that I was still very shy and timid. I think he enjoyed pulling me out of my shell in the bedroom. In the bedroom there was nothing Freddy wouldn't do. There was nothing he wouldn't try.

During those first few years, Freddy and I had every kind of sex there was to have. We had oral sex, Tantric sex, and sex with toys. We didn't have anal sex because neither of us were interested in it. But we acquired a porn collection that would have made most people blush. We had fun-filled days and sex-filled nights.

But things weren't all rosy. We still had to get used to living with each other. I was something of a slob, leaving shoes on the floor, mascara in the soap dish, blush in the bathroom sink, and dirty dishes in the kitchen sink. Freddy, on the other hand, was organized to a "T." Everything had to be in its place. To say he was so leery of being controlled, he was awfully controlling as it pertained to keeping our place nice and neat. I had heard that most marital arguments concerned men being a mess, but it was just the opposite in our case. When I came home from a jog I had to remember to put my running shoes in the closet, and not leave my sports bras on the bathroom floor after a shower. Whereas Freddy had to learn just how emotional I was. I would cry at the drop of a hat. Whether it was a romantic movie, or a sad story on the news, or even just a really good book, it took almost nothing to reduce me to tears.

On that same vein, I also loved to be touched and caressed and held. If I felt that Freddy hadn't given me enough kisses and hugs, then I'd be really sad or moody. Poor Freddy wouldn't know what was wrong with me. He soon learned that I couldn't sit on the sofa without cuddling next to him, and that I couldn't fall asleep unless I was in his arms. Regardless of the adjustments we had to make, we made them willingly, and never once regretted getting married so quickly. In fact we often joked that we wish we'd done it sooner.

When we moved away for me to attend law school, things got a little bit more hectic. My school schedule was crazy busy and we had almost no time together. Freddy was working all the time to keep us afloat, because I was not able to work while attending law school, and his busy schedule gave us even less time together. On those rare occasions when I could take a break from school work, and Freddy was off from one of his jobs, instead of going to the movies or out to eat like we used to do, we were more than happy to stay home and take a nap. Also, of course, have sex. But we got through it.

I finished law school in three years and passed the bar on my first try. I also got an early job offer from my second choice law firm. Even though it wasn't my first choice, I was super happy to get the job offer because it was still a prestigious law firm. I was even happier because they had offered me the job several months before I was even due to take the bar exam. Around the same time, Freddy had gotten a great job with great pay as a pharmaceutical salesman. He was a natural at it, and had already been promoted within his first six months on the job.

With Freddy as a pharmaceutical salesman making six figures, and me due to start at that law firm within the next several months, life was looking good and smelling sweet. Our plan was to live in a small but nice apartment, make a lot of money, and pay off my law school loans within five years. We knew we would have to sacrifice, but we were looking forward to reaping the benefits of living debt-free after those five years were up.

After those five years were up and we had paid off all of my law school loans, we planned to buy a luxury RV, and travel the world, with Freddy and I as entrepreneurs. Freddy was going to write books and conduct national and international seminars on achieving success in the workplace, and I was going to open up my own law consulting firm. We would spend our days traveling the world, doing what we loved by day, and making love by night. Then, five years after we had lived on the road and seen the world, we would start a family.

We planned to have one child, that way we could pack him or her up and bring them on the road with us. By the time the child was older, we planned to buy a home somewhere in an exotic location, and raise him or her in a nontraditional way. We would homeschool our child on the beach, or have tutors that traveled with us internationally. Our child would live life to the fullest, as would be. We had it all planned out.

But you know what they say about making plans. The day after I passed the bar, three months before I was due to start work at that prestigious law firm, I found out I was pregnant. The pregnancy was not planned and it caught Freddy and I by surprise. Yet we were very excited. Freddy was more excited than I was because he has an impulsive nature and kind of liked that it just happened, without us planning it. He said it was meant to be. Although I was scared, I was excited at this new development in our lives. I had always been a go-getter so I knew it wouldn't slow me down. If anything I figured a child would make me work harder to achieve success even sooner. I planned to take a job at that law firm and continue on with Freddy and my five year plan.

But then I got sick. I started to bleed six weeks into my pregnancy. When I went to the doctor they could not figure out why I was bleeding. I was told I'd had a "threatened miscarriage" and to "take it easy," and keep my stress at a minimum. I inwardly laughed at that. My stress was always at full blast. I was a lawyer after all. Still, I took the doctor's advice to heart because I wanted to protect my child, and I made plans to only take a few cases when I started my new job in the next six weeks. But then I started to bleed again, and this time the blood had clots of tissue in it. When I looked down in the toilet and saw it, I had thought for sure that I'd had a miscarriage and I began to cry. Freddy ran into the bathroom, saw the blood, and as best as he could, tried to console me as we rushed to the emergency room.

The good news was that we had not miscarried, the bad news was that I was put on bed rest. My doctor strongly advised against me starting work in the next several weeks. Even though I had been scared about the blood I had seen, when I realized we had not lost the baby, I went back to my stubborn ways and decided that I would, in fact, take that job. On the day we were due to be released from the hospital, I started to bleed again, and that's when I took it seriously. With disappointment, and tears in my eyes, I called the law firm and explained to them what had happened. I told them that I would be on bed rest for the duration of my pregnancy. Surprisingly, they said they would hold the position for me for one calendar year. They told me to have my baby and to come back when the baby was six weeks old.

I was delighted! The time passed quickly, and despite those earlier complications, I went on to have a pretty smooth pregnancy. In July of the following year we had a beautiful baby girl whom we named Hannah. Despite having wanted to wait until we had paid off our debt before buying a house, we went ahead and bought a beautiful home in the suburbs. We brought our baby girl to that house, and I spent the whole six weeks of my maternity leave holding, rocking, and kissing her. I was absolutely loving being a mom.

The only part I did not love about being a mom was the 50 pounds I gained while pregnant. The most I had ever gained was 15 pounds while in college, but I guess while I was inactive and on bed rest those 50 pound had just crept up on me. My usual B to C cup breasts had turned into double D's, and my 26 inch waist had gotten much wider, as did all the rest of me. I did not like the way I looked in the mirror, but I didn't worry because Freddy still thought I was hot, and I knew that as soon as I started working the weight would fall off.

After that initial bleeding had stopped for good, and we were cleared, Freddy and I'd had a pretty active sex life during the pregnancy. After we'd had our daughter we were told to wait six weeks to resume sex, but we didn't. We had sex within one month of having our daughter, and six weeks later, exactly two weeks before I was finally to begin working at the law firm, we found out that we were pregnant again. This time we weren't excited. We were actually scared. We were worried that we had gotten pregnant too soon after the first child. We worried about the bleeding. I worried about whether I'd be able to go to work. I worried about what another pregnancy would do to my body. Heck, I had already gained 50 pounds. I was scared to see how much more I would gain with the second pregnancy.

When I found out I was pregnant again I frantically called Freddy at work. I didn't tell him over the phone, but I did ask him to come home. When he came home, looking worried that I had called him so frantically, probably thinking it had something to do with our little baby, I told him the news. He gave me a hug, and even managed a smile, but I could see the worry in his eyes. I made an emergency appointment with my OB/GYN, and within the next couple hours we were sitting there in her office. She confirmed my worst fears. Not that I was pregnant - because that wasn't a fear so much as it was reality - but that I would have to be on bed rest again. My doctors had never identified where those random bleeding episodes had come from. They did not want me to take the chance of them happening again, and maybe losing the baby this time. My pregnancy was classified high-risk. And this time when I called the law firm to tell them the "happy" news that we were expecting again, they did not offer to hold the job for me. They offered their congratulations, and informed me that when I was ready to enter the workforce that they would love to receive an application from me. And that was that.

All of a sudden, for the second time in the course of a year, all my hopes and dreams were being put on hold. Again. But I was a trooper. I had never let anything hold me back before. I was not going to let anything hold me back now. I got through my second pregnancy with no complications and no problems, except for the 60 extra pounds I gained. My double D's were now G's, and I had long since stopped wearing anything other than sweatpants around my waist. But still I had a beautiful baby boy, whom we named Henry. Now that we had a pair – a girl and a boy - we were done, so I convinced Freddy to get "fixed" so we wouldn't have any more pregnancy surprises.

But my new mommy body was definitely a surprise. Between my two children I had managed to gain 110 pounds. To be honest, I hated my body. I loved and respected that it had brought two lives into the world, but I didn't recognize it. The new body I had was that of someone's mom, two people's mom actually, and I despised it. But Freddy didn't. Freddy made me feel so sexy. Even though I was overweight, he would grow hard watching me take a shower, and he would delight at sucking my size "G" breasts. He even got jealous when my size "G" breasts caught the attention of other men. I never saw anyone looking. Indeed I would've wondered what they'd found attractive about my massive mommy boobs, but Freddy swore they were every man's fantasy, and that every man was looking. I loved that he still got jealous. I loved that he still found me attractive.

Even though I was now a housewife, in my heart I knew I was still a lawyer. I appreciated that I had the privilege of being able to stay home with my children while they were young. But I knew that no matter what, I would always be a lawyer, and that no one could take that from me. I would just simply wait until my children got older, and when they did I would join a law firm. Or maybe I would skip that step and start my own.

I settled comfortably into our lives. I was proud to keep our home clean so that Frederick would be comfortable when he came home from work. I was proud to have a hot meal ready for him when he came home. He worked so hard, and he alone was chopping at the burden of my law school debt, so I worked hard to make sure he knew that I appreciated what he did for our family.

I loved being home with my children, and that I was able to see every milestone, able to give my children all the attention they needed. Although being at the house all day didn't help with getting the weight off, I had managed to lose all but 40 pounds, and I knew it was only a matter of time before I lost the rest. All in all, I was happy with our lives. Our lives had not gone according to Freddy and my plan, but in my opinion it had turned out even better than what we could have hoped for. Because even though within five years we had not paid off all of our debt, we had two beautiful children. We also had a love that was even stronger than before. During those first five years I had everything I could've wanted. I wouldn't have asked for more. But then Freddy began to change.

6

Freddy

The day after our six year anniversary, my company made an announcement that they were being bought and only a few employees would retain their jobs. Although a man is not supposed to admit fear, I was scared. Stacy stayed home with the children and had not practiced law in years, so my job was the only income my family received and without it we would lose everything. If I didn't have a job, my family wouldn't have a home to live in or any of the other things we needed to survive, like food and clothes. A man is supposed to provide. But if I didn't have a job, how would I be able to provide for my family? How could I be a stand-up man for them?

In an attempt to level the playing field, and give each employee an equal shot at one of the coveted remaining positions, my company gave each of us an impromptu review. The review would serve to let us know where we were strong and where we needed improvement. Before that day and before that review I had always been a good employee. I was never the best, but I was also never the worst.

Every year my review was good. It wasn't great, but it was good. It always said the same thing. I was the quintessential dreamer, so I always got good marks for my ideas and for being a visionary. On the other hand, my follow-through was not always up to par, and my reviews reflected that fact.

This review was different though. This review was honest and open and more forthcoming than the others had been. This review told it like it was from a company that was closing and thus had nothing to lose. I was told in plain words that I was seen as a non-substantive employee, meaning that I brought only ideas to the table and nothing of particular substance or value. I was told that dreams without action or a plan for follow-through were useless to a company and that I would have lost my job long ago if not for my people skills and charismatic magnetism. My saving grace, I was told, was the fact that I could sell anything to anyone but in an honest, non-salesman way. I was told that if I could become a stronger finisher, and combine that with my vision and ideas, then I could become a great pharmaceutical salesman.

I took that review to heart because I knew it was true. I had always suffered from a lack of follow-through. I've always had great ideas but I couldn't really remember ever finishing any of them. I would start a project at home and leave it so long that Stacy would call someone to finish it professionally. Or I'd start a book, only to leave the idea after a few chapters and move onto the next one. I had even wanted to own my own company, but for one reason or another, I had never done anything about it. Even in the military, although I had done really well, I had not made a career out of it, like many in my position would have.

I wondered if Stacy also saw me as a quitter. I had never thought of myself as a quitter before, but all of a sudden I couldn't get the word out of my mind. They had not said that I was a quitter, but the word quitter was playing over and over in my head. I wondered what had I accomplished in life? Sure, I had bought my family a home and bought a couple vehicles for us, but could those be considered an accomplishment?

That day when I got home, I couldn't wait to talk to Stacy. When we first got together there wasn't anything we could not talk about. Nowadays Stacy was pretty busy with the children, but I knew that she would give me a listening ear, and let me work through some of what was bothering me. When I arrived home and walked into the house, Stacy was in the middle of something with the children, so I sat on the sofa to wait. After about 10 minutes of whatever she was doing, she turned around and saw me sitting on the sofa, and lost it. She started yelling about me helping her and not just sitting there. I couldn't believe it. That was not what I was expecting to hear. Still, I got up, gave my little guy a bath, hung out with my daughter for a little bit, and just figured I would try to talk to Stacy again later.

But later never came. Stacy went from one task to another then another, and before I knew it, the time had come for us to go to bed. When we got into bed I rolled over to tell her that I really needed to talk to her about something. But she was already asleep. The next day at work I was in something of a funk. I wasn't my usual "charismatic" self, so I played it off like I wasn't feeling well, and took the rest of the day off. When I got home, Stacy appeared to be her usual self again, so I started to talk to her about my review from work. But as I was speaking, she kept interrupting me to tell me little things the kids had done all day. I listened intently, smiled when it was appropriate, but I was just so stressed out about work, that my heart wasn't really in what she was saying.

Don't get me wrong, I love my kids, and I love hearing about them, and the fun they had. But I also missed having adult conversations with my wife. I missed talking about her hopes and dreams and goals. I missed talking about us. I think that day was the first time I realized that there was no longer an "us". We were no longer Freddy and Stacy, we were simply Hannah and Henry's parents. I blamed the negative thoughts I was having about Stacy and me on the mood I was in. I knew I was feeling this way because of the bad news I had gotten at work. I tried to make myself believe that that was all it was.

When Stacy was done telling me all about how many times Hannah had gone to the potty, or what interesting thing was on Sesame Street, I excused myself and went to lie down. It wasn't until I had awoke a couple hours later that I realized that Stacy had not even asked me why I was home early from work. I realized then that the vivacious, feisty Stacy that I had always known had been replaced by a woman who was the mother of my children, and not much more.

The next day I didn't even bother going into work. I sent an e-mail that I was still out sick, then I got dressed as if I was going to work. Instead of going to work, however, I went to a coffee shop and had a light breakfast, and then I went to see an early movie. After the movie was over, I still had a few hours before I would've typically been home from work, so I looked for something else to do.

I had gone a couple towns over to see the movie so that no one I knew would see me at the movie theater in the middle of the day. As I was leaving the theater, I drove by an adult bookstore that was about five blocks up the road. On a whim, and because I was feeling so rebellious, I decided to go in. I perused the books, the movies, and some of the toys, mostly for entertainment. A few of the movies seemed like they might be really good, and a couple of them were totally out there, but I enjoyed looking.

I have to admit, I was getting a little bit aroused. After about 30 minutes of looking through the shelves, the guy behind the counter came over to me and let me know that there were private viewing booths in the back. I noticed then that he and I were the only ones in the shop. He asked me if I'd be interested in renting one of the viewing booths. After a few seconds of thinking about it, I told him, "Sure, what the heck." I picked out a movie that I was interested in, and he led me to the back, to one of the viewing booths.

I sat down in the booth, and within a couple minutes the movie started. In the opening scene, there was a husband and wife stepping out of a sports car and entering a beautiful home. When they got inside the home, right there on a sofa that I assume was theirs, were two guys and a girl fucking. One guy had the girl turned around and he was fucking her from behind. He was bent over her with his right hand wrapped around her hair and was pulling her hair back slightly as he tipped her head back. He was roughly whispering something into her ears, and sucking on her neck. He had his left hand between her legs playing with her clitoris, and was pounding her ass so hard that her breasts were slapping into the other guy's thighs.

The other guy was standing in front of the girl with his head back and his eyes closed as she was sucking his dick and stroking his balls. The guy standing up and having his dick sucked was groaning, and the girl was alternating between twirling her tongue around the tip of his penis and deep-throating him.

At some point the guy having his dick sucked came in the girl's mouth, causing her to gag because of how far back in her mouth it was. She swallowed the cum, then arched her back and came too. A clear liquid squirted out of her vagina and down the inside of her thigh, and made her pussy so wet that I could see the sheen on the guy that was fucking her. Her pussy looked so wet, and it must've felt really good because all of a sudden the guy that was fucking her started pounding her harder and really pulling her hair, and as she screamed out in ecstasy, he shot a load right into her. By this time, my dick was so hard that it was painful, and I had to take it out of my pants because it was bulging damn near through my zipper. I found myself beginning to stroke my dick slowly.

The couple who had been previously watching the threesome then began to move to the backyard of the home where there was a full orgy in place. There were women bent over lawn chairs with guys fucking them from behind. There were men sitting on lawn chairs with women riding them from the back. One of those women had the biggest, juiciest breasts I had ever seen and the guy sitting under her while she was fucking him was sucking each of her breasts. In that moment I would have paid money to join him in sucking those breasts and, turned on, I started to stroke my dick harder.

Another woman had her legs spread-eagle and a guy had his head buried between her legs. The girl was pushing his head deeper between her legs while breathing harder and heavier. There were women who were sucking dicks, men who were eating pussies, and a couple threesomes, including one in which the woman was sitting on the man on what looked like a park bench, and as his dick was inside her pussy another man was trying to slide his dick into her ass.

Meanwhile the couple who had walked in on the orgy had each began to participate. The woman had been grabbed by a man who had promptly bent her over, lifted her skirt and entered her with a vengeance, and the man had found an available pussy and had simply slipped inside of it and began pumping. Seeing all that, I started stroking myself even harder, and within a few minutes I came all over my pants. Both embarrassed and incredibly relieved from the stress I had been feeling, I hurried up and wiped myself off using the roll of napkins that had been conveniently placed inside the booth. I pulled my pants up, and left the booth. I paid for the viewing with my eyes downcast, and hurriedly left the store.

I sped home, feeling guilty. I was unsure why I was feeling guilty. When my wife and I first got together we would watch porn together all the time. So porn was not new to me or Stacy. But I reasoned that maybe I was feeling guilty because I had deceived my wife by not going to work, and then by hanging out all day and getting my rocks off in that booth while she sat at home with our kids. I decided to make it up to her and stopped off at the grocery store and picked her up some flowers. When I got home and gave them to her she was so surprised. She gave me such a soft kiss, sexily wrapping her arms around me. As I felt her double D's rub up against me, I was reminded of the woman with the big, beautiful breasts on the video and my dick got hard. My wife felt it, and pulled back, but not before letting me see that little gleam in her eyes that let me know it was going to be on tonight.

I gave my wife the rest of the night off. I made dinner and watched the children while she went upstairs to relax and enjoy herself. When I had finished dinner, I called for my wife and she came down in a silky bathrobe with her hair sexily pulled up and a big smile on her face. I could tell that my wife had taken a bubble bath, which is one of her favorite things in the world. She walked up to me and gave me the most sensual kiss as she softly rubbed herself against the front of my pants.

The sexual tension between us was smoldering, and as three year old Hannah giggled that mommy was all dressed for bed at the dinner table, Stacy and I gave each other looks that said what all we had in mind. We got the kids fed and we ate in record time. Stacy tucked in Henry and I tucked in Hannah. After I put my little girl in bed, I jumped in the shower in the hall bathroom. I showered quickly, wrapped a towel around my waist, peeked into my children's rooms and saw that they were fast asleep, then started into Stacy and my bedroom.

When I walked into the bedroom, Stacy had candles lit and was lying naked across the bed. I took a minute to appreciate her naked body. Her breasts were so damn beautiful. They were fuller than they had been before we had children, and as she lay there, their fullness was accentuated by her hard nipples. I let my eyes roam down her torso as I took in the "V" of her sex. She had taken the time to shave a landing strip there and I immediately felt my dick get hard and push against the towel that I had wrapped around my waist. I wanted to land right between my wife's legs. But first I had some work to do.

I dropped my towel as I walked over to my wife. She had some kind of candle lit that made the room smell tropical. I liked it. When I got to my wife I laid my body over hers and felt her warmth under me. When she wrapped her legs around me, like a hand to a glove my dick began to seek the warmth inside her. Before it could slip in, I moved my dick away from her warm pussy and began to trail kisses down her body. I stopped at her breasts and took my time sucking them. I sucked softly at first then harder and rougher as I felt her moan and move seductively under me. I was trying to be gentle and make love to my wife, but the fuck session on the porn I had seen earlier combined with my wife's movements and her warm pussy under me, pressing and rubbing against my thigh, made me want to fuck the shit out of her. But I restrained myself and began to suck her nipples softer again. I went a bit lower and kissed my wife between her legs, around her swollen pussy lips.

She tasted sweet as I licked around the outsides of her pussy. She arched her back and moaned, and as she twisted, my tongue slipped inside her wet pussy and I tasted her silky wetness. I flicked my tongue softly along the tip of her clitoris and watched as she began to breathe harder and harder. Loving the way my wife's pussy tasted, I jutted my tongue inside of her and began tongue-fucking her. I gave her feather soft flicks and licks on her clitoris, then resumed tongue-fucking her. When I felt my wife's body start to tremble I knew she was about to cum, so I pulled my tongue out of her pussy and put my dick in. It was so wet that it made squishy sounds as I fucked her harder and harder. When she came and I felt her wetness pour over my dick I released inside of her. She wrapped her thighs around me making me go deeper and deeper and my body convulsed more and more as I emptied all of myself into her. When we were done, I lay on top of her, still inside of her and closed my eyes. My wife lay under me, spread eagle, stroking my hair as it lay plastered to the back of my neck with sweat. We lay like that until both of us fell asleep.

A short time later I awoke. As I slowly moved my body from on top of my wife, she rolled over, and I settled in. I had my arms wrapped around her and my nose nestled into her thick hair. I loved everything about my wife. I loved the way her hair smelled. I loved the way her body felt pressed against mine. I loved the way she tasted. I loved how she moaned vulgar things when she was about to cum. I loved our children and the life that we shared together.

In that moment I realized I needed to do everything possible to keep my family happy and secure. Even though my job was at stake, I made a silent promise to my wife as she slept quietly beside me that I would do everything in my power to keep my job and that I would not worry her. My wife was always so busy with the kids, and worried constantly about them and about making their world perfect. As she slept beside me, her mind finally at rest, at least until she awoke, I decided that I would do all the worrying for her. I decided that I would make her world perfect the same way she sought to do for our kids. I would become that stellar employee that my company was looking for, and the provider I had always been.

I kissed my wife on her cheek, cuddled in closer to her, and prepared my heart and soul to give it my all at work. I fell asleep with thoughts of not only excelling within my company, but also eventually running the new company. I knew everything was going to be okay. In fact, I knew everything was going to be great.

After a morning quickie, I got to work extra early the next day. Before anyone had even gotten into the office, I had already lined up at least three new prospective clients and had a meeting scheduled with a fourth person. That whole morning I reviewed my selling practices and memo books, as well as expansion ideas and cost-saving techniques for the new company.

When it was time to leave the office, I called my wife to see if it would be okay if I stayed for a bit longer. I was in the middle of wooing some of my prospective clients and I didn't want to leave until I had closed at least one deal. My wife agreed, still cheerful from the night before and this morning, and back to work I went. I didn't want to stop to grab dinner, so I just ate a couple donuts from the vending machine.

At about 9 p.m. I left the office. I had closed the deal, but had missed putting my children to bed. My wife was a good sport though. Although she was asleep, she had wrapped my dinner and set it on the stove. I was too exhausted to even eat it. I went upstairs, got in bed beside my wife and went to sleep.

The next morning I awoke before my wife and my children. I made them breakfast, grabbed the dinner that my wife had made me the night before to take to work for today's lunch, left her a quick note letting her know that I was going in early, and left for work. I got off late that night as well, and just like the night before, my wife had left my dinner on the stove.

Over the next couple weeks I followed the same schedule. I found that getting there before everyone else allowed me some time to work uninterrupted, and made me much more productive. I also enjoyed staying later, because I was able to finish up my day's work, without all the meetings scheduled throughout the day. It was also around this time that I began to add weekend work. I wanted to set myself apart, and I knew that doing pharmaceutical sales on the weekend was one way to do that.

Even though I had committed myself to not burdening Stacy, I desperately wanted to talk to her about what was going on at work. A couple times I had tried to, but she was always preoccupied with the children. As a matter of fact, it seemed like the children were all we ever talked about. As I was working hard on the job, my bosses started to take notice, but my personal life started to suffer. Stacy was growing more irritated that I was leaving before the children had a chance to see me and getting back home after they were already in bed.

Our sex life was also suffering. We had not had sex in at least a month, and long gone was Stacy's cheerfulness from our evening and morning of sex. I knew the distance between us was primarily my fault, but I also resented that Stacy only seemed to have a one track mind. If she was not talking about the kids, she was playing with the kids. She never read any more, we never talked about adult things, we never talked about us. I knew as little about Stacy's life as she knew about mine. But I didn't know how to bring us closer together. I couldn't stop working as much as I had been, especially now that I had the attention of my bosses. I also couldn't ask Stacy to care less, or worry less about the kids. Especially when their care fell primarily on her shoulders.

So I did the only thing I knew how to do. I kept working hard, burying my feelings deep, and ignored the distance that I saw growing between Stacy and me. I also kept eating. Because I got in so early to work, and left so late, I was often eating out. I ate whatever was on the way to work, and whatever was in the vending machine while at work. Stacy had long stopped leaving my meals on the stove. So I basically just ate whatever I could, whenever I could.

Then one day I got some news. On my way out of the office, as I was on my way to my doctor's office to have my annual physical, I was called into my boss's office and told that I had been selected to move over to the new company. Only my coworker Leane and I had been retained. Whereas most of my colleagues had simply begun looking for employment elsewhere, and many had found it, I had been busting my butt to stay with my company, so I was not surprised that I was selected to stay. I was, however, surprised that Leane had been selected to stay. Leane had only been with the company for a few months, so I would've assumed that she would have been one of the first to go. But I didn't know a lot about her. I had only seen her a time or two. For all I knew, she could have been one of the best pharmaceutical salespersons, and obviously she was good enough to be chosen above a lot of other people.

I was told that since we were the only retained employees, we would be instrumental in bringing the new company's employees up to speed. I shook my boss's hand and left the office to head to my appointment. When I got into my vehicle, safely away from the eyes and ears of my co-workers, I let out a little yelp and a fist pump. I had done it! I had kept my job and kept my family secure. If I hadn't had to go to the doctor's, I might have treated myself to another visit to that booth in that adult store, but I knew Stacy wanted me to go see the doctor, so I went.

A couple hours later, after having a full spectrum of tests ran, I learned that I was healthy, if not a bit over-weight. Since I was tall, I didn't look heavy, but my doctor let me know that I needed to lose some weight. I knew that I did. My nights of eating "dinner" from the vending machines, and grabbing breakfast from whatever fast-food chain I passed in the morning were catching up to me. I knew I had to do something, and I knew I would figure it out. Just not today. I was way too happy to let a mildly dismal doctor report take me down from my high. One thing I knew for sure was that I was not going to tell Stacy that the doctor said I needed to lose some weight. I knew she would be hounding me and watching everything I ate, and otherwise treating me like a child.

I hated that I was getting really comfortable keeping things from Stacy. There was a time when we had shared almost everything, and talked about everything together, but lately we were on different pages. Her life was all about the kids and mine was about staying afloat at work. Now that I had kept my job, I knew that I would be able to slow down a bit. I was looking forward to a little bit of a break and to reconnecting with Stacy and my children. I knew she would be happy to spend some time and I was getting aroused just thinking about all the sex we were going to have because I'd be home more.

But it was not to be. Instead of getting a break, I got busier, and even more was expected of me. The new company was taking over the following week and Leane and I were in preparation meetings from the time I got into the office until it was time to get off. Staying late became the only way I was able to get any work done at all. Leane must have been thinking the same way, because she stayed late as well. We were tasked to work together throughout the day, so in the evenings we sometimes consulted each other on various issues that came up.

Leane was about 5'9, which was rather tall for a woman, and she had long straight red hair that came almost to the top of her butt. She also had piercing green eyes. She looked a bit like an Irish Nicole Kidman. Leane wasn't beautiful like my wife, but there was something so naturally sexy and sensual about her. I couldn't put a finger on what it was, but a couple times I had fantasized about grabbing her hair and taking her from the back. I'd had to snap myself out of it when she was in my office consulting with me about something having to do with work. It certainly didn't help things that she had the longest, sexiest legs I had ever seen.

I don't think she was trying to dress sexy, but whenever she wore a skirt to work, whether the skirt was slightly above the knee or well below it, I couldn't help but imagine how long those legs went on, or how they'd feel wrapped around my waist. Whenever I had thoughts like that I made sure to get home right away and at least lie near my wife. We weren't having sex regularly at that point in time, but I thought that if I was at least near my wife those thoughts and fantasies would go away. I was hoping they would be too afraid to come out in her presence.

Some days going home worked, some days it didn't. On the days it didn't, I would lie near my wife thinking about fucking Leane. What saved me from cheating on my wife was the fact that I loved my wife and my family and would never risk losing them, and also that Leane did not appear to be even remotely interested in me. I usually took my sexual frustrations out on my hand, or on my wife on the rare occasions when she gave me some. I knew that I would never be able to take them out on Leane. That was a fantasy that would never come true. I didn't want it to anyway, even if it could have come true.

That all changed one weekend.

I had been working steady weekends, every other weekend, since before the new company came in. I usually worked alone, and had even moved to hosting meetings out of town. Those meetings happened over the weekend and I always traveled alone. On a Friday before I was scheduled to depart on an overnight business trip, I was told that Leane would be accompanying me. To be honest I was a bit annoyed because I enjoyed traveling alone, and suddenly having company would interfere with the way I did my thing. For example, I enjoyed playing my jazz on the trips where I had to drive, and this was one of those trips. Now, instead of my jazz, I would probably have to listen to and participate in nonstop chatter the whole way there.

I nodded agreeably when I was told the news that Leane would accompany me on the trip and I went about my day. Later that evening when Leane came over to go over the trip details with me, I made sure to be cordial, and hide the annoyance I was feeling inside. I don't even think I noticed her legs that day, as I was so busy thinking about what I knew would be a long day and a long drive tomorrow. But when I got home, as the evening wore on, I grew more annoyed and became determined to enjoy my trip the way I always did. I figured since Leane was accompanying me, and I was doing all the driving, she would have to listen to what I wanted to listen to. That would be that.

The next day, on Saturday, we met at the office before starting our trip. The drive would be three hours. When we got there we were to check into our separate hotel rooms and prepare for our meetings. The meetings were in the late afternoon, after which we would take our clients to dinner. After wooing our clients, and hopefully closing the deal, we would go back to the hotel. Even though the drive was only three hours, our company always booked their salespeople a hotel room just in case dinner ran late. They wanted us focused on closing the deal and enjoying ourselves, and not concerned with wine intake and the long drive back home. After we had spent the night in our separate rooms, Leane and I were going to check out very early in the morning, and I would be home in time to attend church with my family.

When I got there, Leane was already waiting. I appreciated that she was prompt, if not early. She was dressed casually, in comfortable-looking khaki slacks, a cream blouse, and brown loafers. She had her hair pulled back in a ponytail. Even though she looked professional, she also looked a little bit like a schoolgirl with her hair pulled back and all fresh-faced. That was the first time I noticed that in addition to being sexy she was also quite pretty. Though not beautiful like my wife. I'm not sure why I felt the need to keep reminding myself of that.

I popped the trunk of the rental car and went around to the passenger side of the car. I opened Leane's door for her, and then proceeded to put her overnight bag in the trunk. She kindly but firmly replied that she "had it", and put her own bag in the trunk. She made it very clear that she wanted to be treated like an equal, and that this was all business. I felt the same way, so we were good to go.

When we got in the car, just as I feared, Leane began to talk. We exchanged pleasantries. She asked about my family. I told her I was married to a beautiful woman and had two children, and she told me that she had a live-in boyfriend. I asked her if they had been together for a long time and if they planned to get married. She told me that they had been together for nine years, and that she did not believe in marriage. She said they were happy as they were and planned to keep things just like they were.

Then she did something that surprised the hell out of me. She stopped talking. She opened a Forbes magazine and began to read. I was shocked. I kept thinking, "Is that it? Are you not going to talk to me about your childhood? About your hopes, dreams, feelings? Was that all she was going to say about a relationship? Did she not want to pick my brain about the company or about some of the previous employees?" I was truly shocked, but very appreciative of the quiet. We rode like that for about 30 miles before I decided to put on my jazz. Although I knew I should've asked her if she minded, I didn't want to risk her saying that she did. So I didn't ask. I just inserted my CD.

Within seconds, my favorite song from my favorite jazz CD began to fill the car stereo speakers. I sighed and settled comfortably into my seat, preparing to enjoy the music and let it wash over me. Just then Leane looked up from her magazine and spoke. She said, "Is that John Coltrane's, 'In a Sentimental Mood'?" I replied, "Yes, it is." She smiled, closed her eyes a moment, swayed softly, then said, "This is my favorite song." I said, "Mine too." We listened in silence as John Coltrane blew us away. After that song went off Leane further surprised me by recognizing and naming all of the other songs on the CD. When I put on a mix CD of various jazz artists, she knew most of those as well. We began to talk about the different songs that came on and what we were doing when we first heard them. The things they made us feel and think about. Without meaning to, certainly without planning to, I started enjoying talking to her as much as I was enjoying listening to the music. Pretty soon when one of the jazz CDs went off I didn't even bother to insert another. I just spent the rest of the drive talking to Leanne about jazz. The drive passed so quickly, and we were there before either of us even realized it, simply because we had begun to enjoy each other's company.

When we arrived we checked into the hotel, and because we had made such good time, we made plans to meet up and have a cocktail before meeting our clients. When I got to my room, I was dismayed and a bit guilty that I was still thinking about Leane. I just couldn't believe that the uptight woman I had seen around the office was actually really laid back and a lot of fun to be around. As I rushed to get dressed, making sure I looked sharp, I realized I had developed a slight hard-on for Leane. I got down to the hotel bar before Leane and took a seat near the entrance. I wanted to make sure she saw me. What I didn't count on was the unobstructed view it gave me of Leane as she descended into the hotel lobby.

Leane was wearing a simple black dress, but the way it fit her body and showed off her legs made me feel like a horny teenager. She had on pointy high heels, the kind of shoes that aren't worn in an office, and she looked so damn sexy that I found myself thinking about wrapping her legs around me. Again.

I shook my head to clear my thoughts just in time for Leane to recognize me and start heading toward me. *Damn, she is beautiful*, I thought. *Not just pretty, but beautiful. Maybe not as beautiful as my wife, but damn close*. I didn't stand when she came up to me, just in case I was a bit aroused, so she bent over to give me a peck on the cheek when she reached me. I think that action surprised us both and made us both feel a bit self-conscious, worried that the other might be taken aback by the gesture.

After that kiss, whatever had previously seemed to be brewing between us cooled a bit. I was grateful and aware that that was just what I had needed. My thoughts had been entering dangerous territory and I was reminded of the bible passage about one's thoughts eventually becoming their actions.

We both started to talk about our significant others more. I learned that Leane's partner was an emergency room physician and was as busy as she was. Since they dedicated so much of their personal lives to work, they always made sure to have a lazy, leisure Sunday. She told me that she was looking forward to when we checked out of the hotel because she and Martin (her partner) would be taking the day entirely off to spend it together. I told Leane all about Stacy. How she had graduated from law school, but had set aside her career to raise our children. I didn't bother telling her that Stacy had kept turning up pregnant each time she tried to go back to work.

Leane seemed to be impressed that Stacy had made the decision to become a stay-at-home mom, and she readily admitted that she could not have made that sacrifice. That's why, she said, she had chosen not to have children. She admired others who did, but candidly confessed that she did not want to be saddled with the responsibility.

I definitely understood where she was coming from as I reflected back on all the things Stacy had wanted to do but would have to postpone to raise our kids. I thought about those plans we had made so long ago to travel and see the world, and how those were being postponed if not eliminated as well. I wondered if I was being a selfish asshole by being attracted to Leane, an unattached woman who was able to dress up and look nice, while my wife sat at home caring for our kids. Was the fact that she was unattached and unencumbered what I found so attractive about Leane? Was it the lack of responsibility?

I knew I had been a terrible husband. Although I hadn't done anything, I'd had some lustful thoughts and I was ashamed. I excused myself from the table, went out into the lobby in a quiet corner, and called my wife. I told her how much I loved her and missed her, and couldn't wait to see her. She sounded surprised to hear from me and so sweet. I really did miss her. I couldn't wait to get home to show her just how much.

During our meetings with clients and dinner afterward I stayed as far away from Leane as possible. I was professional, of course, and was near her when demonstrations called for it. And I was careful to present a friendly front for the customers' sakes. But on the insides I was chanting, "You are happily married. You have a beautiful wife at home", and it seemed to work.

When dinner was over and we had, in fact, successfully closed the deal, I asked Leane how she felt about getting an early start on her lazy day with Martin. When she looked at me quizzically, I explained that I had wanted to leave right then, and begin the drive back. She looked at me for a moment, shrugged, and said that that was fine with her. We agreed that when we got back to the hotel we would go to our respective rooms and pack our bags and meet back in the lobby in 30 minutes.

Twenty-three minutes after arriving back at the hotel, I was packed and in the lobby waiting on Leane. I decided to grab a large coffee, not because I was tired, but just to keep me company on the drive back. Two minutes later, Leane came down the stairs dressed in a flowing skirt and a light blazer, grabbed a coffee as well, and off we set.

I had agreed to drive since it had been my idea to leave so late. The drive back was nothing like the ride there. We sat in silence for at least 45 minutes without either one of us saying much. When I pulled over to fill up the car, I decided to go into the convenience store to grab a snack and asked Leane if she wanted anything. It was the first time either of us had said more than a couple words to each other during the drive back. Leane asked for sunflower seeds. After using the restroom, grabbing another coffee and sunflower seeds for Leane, we were on our way again.

At some point Leane fell asleep. I heard her snoring softly. I must admit I was also getting a bit tired, despite the two cups of coffee. When I looked at the odometer, I saw that we had only gotten half the way there. We still had about an hour and a half left to go before we reached our destination. I was anxious to get home, I couldn't wait to surprise Stacy, but I always made it a point to stop driving if I felt even a little bit sleepy. I had heard horror stories about people falling asleep at the wheel and never living to regret it, or even worse, killing other people. I saw a rest stop up ahead and decided to pull over there. It was well lit in front and a bit darker in the rear. I parked in the rear, reclined my chair, and was asleep before I knew it.

I awoke about two hours later. It was almost 4 a.m. I rubbed the cold out of my eyes and looked over at Leane who was still asleep. Her flowing skirt had risen to the middle of her thigh and I was able to see those beautiful legs up close. I don't know if I was delirious from sleepiness or what, but I suddenly wanted to touch them. I sat there staring at her legs, becoming disgusted with myself. I had never cheated on my wife, and I hated myself for thinking of this woman this way. I attributed my weakened mental state to the lack of intimacy and communication between Stacy and me as of late. I vowed to myself that I was going to try harder to repair us and to get us back on the same page. Leane began to stir, almost as if she could feel me looking at her. I turned away, but not before she caught me glancing one last time at her legs. She parted her legs slightly, giving me a glimpse of her panty-less pussy before her skirt fell into the space between her legs. I looked up at her, trying to read her expression to see if that was an intentional thing or not. Her eyes were hooded as she gazed at me sexily. I shook my head in an effort to clear it. I didn't know what had just happened, but I knew we were in dangerous territory.

I put the key in the ignition and started the car. I knew that I had to do something to break the sexual tension that had suddenly swelled in the car. Leane leaned across the seat and turned the car off. She took the keys out of the ignition and threw them on the backseat. She then straddled my lap and began to kiss me with her eyes on mine.

Leane was looking at me to see if I would pull away. I could have pulled away, I certainly thought about it, but my body was stronger than my mind and I felt myself begin to kiss her back instead. On the inside I was screaming, "Don't do this Frederick, don't ruin your marriage," but my body was already responding and moving ahead with Leane's seduction. I had her ass cupped in my right hand and my left hand in her shirt. She had taken the blazer off before she fell asleep, leaving the T-shirt on underneath. I was so grateful for that now because it made it easy to unhook her bra and devour her breasts. Her breasts were not as round and full as I liked, but they were perky and stood erect, ready for my mouth. I took one of them into my mouth. Leane moaned and arched her back, pushing against the steering wheel and accidentally honking the horn. I shifted in my seat to give her more room. I had already reclined the seat and pushed it as far back as it could go when I pulled over to rest. When I shifted, Leane was able to move off the horn. The blaring noise stopped but we didn't. Leane reached into my jeans and began to massage my dick. I exhaled into her mouth as I kissed her. I tasted the saltiness of her sunflower seeds as I twirled my tongue around hers.

After massaging my dick and getting it hard and throbbing, Leane moved her hand out of my pants. She held my gaze as she lifted one of her fingers to her mouth. On her finger was some of my sperm that had leaked out of the tip of my dick and Leane slowly, methodically licked her finger clean. My dick responded and got even harder, pushing against her skirt, the only thing separating my dick from her pussy. Leane moved her skirt up around her waist, giving me full access to her pussy. I felt the wetness from her pussy on the top of my dick and, as if it had a mind of its own, it began to jut out towards her pussy.

Before I could stick it in, I came to my senses. I needed protection. Leane saw me stop suddenly, and putting two and two together told me that she was on birth control. But I could not do her raw, without protection. My wife was the only person I had ever come inside, and I didn't want to risk bringing anything back to her. I lifted Leane off my lap, whispered something about coming right back, then I ran as fast as my legs could carry me into the truck stop.

I grabbed a pack of condoms and was back in the car in record time. When I got back Leane was in the back seat. She had removed her skirt and was naked from the waist down. I got into the back seat with her, hurriedly slipped on the condom, opened her thighs and slid myself inside her.

She was so fucking tight! The pleasure was excruciating. The deeper I went the tighter her pussy squeezed me. I could hardly see straight, I was so dizzy with excitement. On the one hand I knew what I was doing was wrong, but in some strange way it made the sex even better. With my hands on her knees I drove myself into her deeper and deeper, and as she moaned I stroked harder and harder. Her juices began to pour out of her onto the back seat and the sweet aroma of us fucking engulfed the car.

Both of us were raggedly breathing when she screamed, "Shit, oh shit, I'm about to cum!" She started bucking and squeezing my dick harder. It was like her pussy had a vice grip on my dick. She screamed, "Fuck!" then came all over the back seat. She was a squirter and I felt her juices splash against me, soaking my pubic hair. As she came her pussy began to jerk and pulsate and I could no longer control myself. Her pussy was the wettest pussy I had ever felt and she was my first squirter. The wetness was unbearable and I let out a loud grunt and came, roughly, inside the condom.

I lay there on top of her, still pumping, filling every ounce of that condom, and I could feel her body quiver beneath me. I heard her mutter "Damn, that was good" as she stroked the back of my sweat-stained head. I hated to admit it, but it really was. It was the best sex I had ever had. Her pussy was already so wet, but when she came it got even wetter and I nearly slipped out. I had loved her squirting her juices out onto me. That was some freaky shit. Although I lay there spent, my energy gone, I began to get slightly aroused again just thinking about how she came. Next time I wanted to taste her. It didn't even occur to me that there wouldn't be a next time. I knew I had to have some of her again.

Consumed with my thoughts, I hadn't realized she was shifting beneath me. When I realized I was still lying on top of her and was probably heavy, I began to lift up. She wrapped her legs around me and pulled me back down onto her. We lay there kissing for a while, and in that moment I knew she was feeling the same way. I knew that this affair would continue. It was obvious we both wanted more. I knew what I was doing was wrong. Even after it was over, I was not willing to blame the heat of the moment. I knew it was the passion between us and that it had been building for some time.

As we drove back to town, Leane confessed that she had been attracted to me almost from the beginning. Because we barely knew each other and hadn't had to work together, she'd said that it had been easy to stay away. But when we began to work together it became more difficult for her to pretend. She confessed that she'd noticed me watching her and looking at her legs, so she had made it a point to wear more skirts to work. She said the skirts had gotten progressively shorter because she enjoyed the attention I was giving her.

I felt like a kid with his hand in the cookie jar. I hadn't known that Leane noticed me checking her out. I had no idea she had been wearing those short skirts for me. I admitted to her that I was wildly attracted to her and thought she was beautiful and sexy. I told her I had never cheated on my wife before, but that sex with her had been the best I'd had. I felt like I was doubly betraying my life – first by sleeping with another woman, then telling that woman her sex was better - but I couldn't help how I was feeling. I didn't love Leane or anything like that, and she didn't love me either, but neither of us could deny the sexual attraction that we felt. It was strong, and without saying a word, we had both silently acknowledged that it would continue.

When we got into town, before we went our separate ways, I drove to a remote spot and laid Leane down, rolled up her skirt, opened her legs, and ate her pussy. She had driven me crazy when she came on me and I felt like I needed to taste her. She did not disappoint. She tasted as good as she had felt, and after I had made her cum (and squirt) again, she leaned over, unzipped my pants, and put all of me into her mouth. My dick went so far down her throat that I swear I thought I could feel her tonsils. I closed my head and lay back, enthralled by what I was feeling and the pleasure she was giving me. When I began to breathe harder and told her that I was about to cum, Leane tightened her lips around my dick. That shit turned me on, and with a guttural groan I emptied myself inside her mouth. She looked up at me and swallowed my seed, in one large gulp. I didn't know where this woman had come from, but I knew I was a goner.

As I dropped her off at her car, after a kiss goodbye, I found myself wishing our weekend trip had been longer than overnight. I looked forward to the next trip, and was wishing that she would have to accompany me again. Yep, I was a goner. I shook my head, mumbling the words "shit, shit, shit…" all the way home. What the fuck was I doing? I knew I was fucking up, but I also knew that I wasn't going to stop. This was the most excitement I'd had in years and I was not going to stop.

7

Stacy

What in the hell am I doing? I thought as I sat on the sofa eating a KitKat candy bar from one of my daughter's Lunchables. I didn't even like sweets - salty foods were my vice - but we didn't have any in the house since I had cleared the pantry of all our unhealthy foods. I knew I needed to lose this baby weight, so I thought keeping only healthy foods in the house would help. But obviously where there's a will there's a way because I had found the only piece of junk in the house by raiding my child's Lunchables snack. Was that a new low?

I don't even think the appeal was the snack. I think the thing I liked most was being able to just sit and relax on those rare occasions when I managed to get both of the kids down for a nap. It was usually during those times that I looked for a nice snack to keep me company and today this KitKat would have to do.

As I devoured that KitKat, and boy was it good, I sat and watched a talk show. The topic of discussion today was restoring communication in a marriage. It made me think about Freddy and I. I couldn't

remember the last conversation we'd had. I
couldn't remember the last time we'd had sex. He
was hardly home in the evenings, and I had
resorted to pleasuring myself on those occasions
when I needed a release. For a brief moment I
wondered how Freddy was finding relief. I chuckled
when I realized that he was probably also
pleasuring himself. What a pair we made! There
was a time when we would do it multiple times per
day, and now we had gotten down to once a week,
and that was with us each pleasing ourselves.

I didn't know what I could do to change things. The
kids kept me busy from the time I woke up to the
time I went to bed. There were days I didn't get
around to having breakfast until noon, when one
(or if I was lucky both) of my children took a nap. I
didn't think my weight was a problem for Freddy. I
knew I needed to lose a few pounds, but lately he
had been gaining weight too, what with all the late
nights at work and vending machine dinners. When
he initially started working late I used to leave his
dinner out for him. But soon, one late night turned
into two late nights, and before I knew it, he was
staying late most days of the week. I didn't
appreciate that. I was with the kids all day, and that
was exhausting enough. But with Freddy now
working into the evening and sometimes later, I

had no help with dinner or getting the kids to bed. I never complained about staying at home with my kids, but I did appreciate having a bit of a break when Freddy came home, and I had even lost that.

The truth is, there were days when I wondered what my life would have been if I hadn't gotten pregnant and had been able to take that job at that law practice. I imagined that I would have been dressed to the nine's, polished, put together. At a minimum I knew that I wouldn't have been overweight, sitting on the sofa in the middle of the day eating a KitKat. I looked down at my nails and rolled my eyes. There was a time when I had kept them manicured, or at least neatly filed. I didn't need to look at my feet to know they hadn't seen a pedicure since last Mother's Day.

I was not the woman I used to be. This new, mom-version of me was overweight, dressed haphazardly, unpolished, unkempt. I didn't like it, but what could I do? I was always home with the kids, so when would I have time to go get a manicure and a pedicure? Even if I found time, I would just ruin the manicure with all the hand-washing I had to do as a result of changing diapers and cleaning up messes all day long. I would have loved to go to a hair salon and get my hair done up.

I have really thick hair that Freddy loves, and it would have been nice to get it professionally straightened so Freddy could play in it like he used to. But being home all day, taking care of two children, didn't give me a lot of pampering time. So I wore my hair in a ponytail seven days a week. Sometimes for church I would try to do something pretty with it, but mostly I went for what was convenient. I was no longer the girlie-girl or smart and savvy law student I used to be. I was a certified mom. I even had the mom jeans to prove it.

I thought about what Freddy might be thinking of me when he comes home and sees me in sweats and an old college shirt. To my knowledge he never seemed to mind. He'd even told me he thinks I'm the most beautiful when I'm in one of his old shirts. But I did sometimes wonder if he saw other women when he was out and about or at work and thought they were attractive in their makeup, heels, and dresses. Freddy has always been a simple guy, so I didn't think he cared about those things, but I sometimes wondered. Especially lately. I didn't know what was off, but I knew something was. Freddy and I had gotten so distant. We hardly talked to each other anymore. We didn't argue either. There was just a quiet civility between us, like there were things that needed to be said. Maybe things would be better if he were home more, but in addition to getting home late every night of the week, he recently started taking more weekend trips. He said that helped him stand out at the job, but I almost never saw him anymore, except at church.

I think part of the problem was Freddy's job. He recently told me that a couple months ago he had gone through a rough patch at work, and as a result he now had to go the extra mile to distinguish himself. I wondered why he hadn't told me about it at the time. I remember noticing that he had seemed preoccupied and kind of down, but since he hadn't told me what was bothering him I had assumed he just didn't want to talk. I figured he would talk to me when he was ready. But he never had, except to tell me months later that he'd had a "bit of difficulty at work but that he had worked through it." The problem was, though, that ever since "working through that difficulty," Freddy was never home anymore. Lately he was even gone on the weekends. I had to do something to build our spark again. I knew Freddy told me he was always gone because he was working hard, but I also thought that if I jazzed things up a bit, he might want to be home more. So here I was giving myself an once-over and I didn't like what I saw.

I decided that I was going to do something about my predicament. I called my mom and asked if she would fly down in two weeks to watch the children while I took Freddy away for the weekend. In two weeks Freddy was scheduled to go on an overnight sales trip. He was going to one of his usual spots, which was only three to four hours away, so I was planning to secretly meet him there. Because he made this particular trip so often, I knew where he would be staying and even the room he usually reserved (Freddy was a creature of habit). I also knew that he was usually done with his clients by 9 or 10 p.m., so I would be there by then and ready to seduce him.

I set an appointment at the new salon I had seen commercials for and I also made an appointment to get a manicure and pedicure, as well as an eyebrow and Brazilian bikini wax. I had never had a Brazilian bikini wax before, and I knew it would be a sexy surprise for Freddy. Heck, and for me too! I also went online and ordered a bunch of fun toys for Freddy and I to try. I was going to put it on my husband and give him a night to remember! I couldn't do anything in the next two weeks about the weight I had gained, but I was going to go to Macy's lingerie department to get some help picking out something that hid my love handles and accentuated my Double D's and my ass, both of which Freddy loved. I was going to spice up my marriage and I was willing to pull out all the stops to do it.

I waited so eagerly for the two weeks to pass. It was like something was in the air because Freddy was also super sweet and romantic those couple weeks. On one day he sent me a dozen red roses just out of the blue and on another day during those two weeks he came home and surprised me and the kids by taking us out to dinner. During that whole dinner we sat and talked and even laughed together. Freddy seemed so much lighter, like a weight had been lifted off him. He seemed happier than he had in months, maybe even years, and I was happy to see him that way. When I asked him about it he told me that his load at work had been lifted and he was starting to enjoy his work again. He said his job was beginning to feel fresh again. I guessed it was because of the new company, so I silently thanked God that this new company had come along. It was making Freddy a happier man.

After that dinner and Freddy's romantic gesture, we had the best sex ever. Freddy was in a frisky mood and wanted to try new things. He always liked the doggie-style position, but this time, while sexing me from the back he put a finger in my ass. At first I thought that his finger had slipped, so I jerked my body forward making his finger slip out. But then his finger went in there again, and that's when I realized it was probably intentional. It was an unfamiliar feeling, not particularly pleasurable, but not unenjoyable either, so I let Freddy do it. I figured it was something that he learned from porn.

I figured he must have been watching porn since he and I had not been having sex regularly. Freddy also pulled my hair really hard and said, "You like this, don't you bitch?" That caught me off guard. He had never called me that before. Sure, we talked freaky to each other when we were having sex, but he had never called me the "B" word. I reasoned that it was also something he picked up from porn, so I went with it, and said, "Yeah, I like it big daddy." That seemed to turn him on even more and he started yanking my hair even harder. Another thing that was different was, instead of coming inside of me, he pulled himself out of me and came on my back. He had never done that before either, but again I went with it.

Another time when we were having sex, a couple days before he was due to leave on the business trip that I was going to surprise him on, he tried to put his dick in my ass. I am his wife after all, so I let him, thinking that if I didn't then he wouldn't be able to get it anywhere else. But I have to admit that it did not feel good. Even with a tube of lubricant. He at least tried to be as gentle as possible and not pound my ass too hard, which I appreciated, but when he was about to cum he fucked me so hard that I thought I wouldn't be able to sit for a week. When we were done, after I'd had a nice hot soak, he asked me if I'd liked having anal sex. I confided to him that it had actually been a bit painful and he assured me that it would get easier. Based on that conversation I knew that Freddy had intended for all these new things we were doing to become a permanent part of our sex life.

I didn't know where he was learning all this from, but I was excited nevertheless for him to see what I had in store for us when he went out of town in a few days. Based on the freaky stuff that he'd recently become interested in, I knew that he would love our evening of sex and sex toys. I was suddenly very happy that I had ordered the butt plug, even if I didn't know how to use it.

The fact that Freddy had turned on the freakiness, and especially the charm, made it even harder to keep the surprise rendezvous a secret. But I knew that Freddy would appreciate me being adventurous and sexy. It would be like the old days and would add to the sizzle of the night.

Sure enough, on the day Freddy was to leave, I kissed him goodbye and told him I would miss him. He had decided to leave on Friday night right after work so he could get a little bit of extra prep time under his belt. He was meeting the clients on Saturday afternoon and then taking them to dinner, but apparently these were high-profile, big-dollar clients and he hadn't wanted anything to go wrong. He told me if he landed this account he could possibly get a raise, so I told him to go for it, and that he should, in fact, leave a day earlier right after work so he could get prepared.

No sooner had Freddy walked out the door that I called my mom. She had flown into town Friday, but wasn't due to arrive at our house until Saturday, a couple hours after Freddy would have departed to make the drive for his business trip. But since Freddy had left early I called her up to see if she wanted to grab some dinner with me and the kids. She loved the idea – it was much more appealing than spending the evening alone in a hotel room, especially since she had left dad at home, so I told her to come on over. I knew the kids would love seeing her a day earlier.

When mom got to my house she rang the doorbell and I let her in. As always my mom was simply stunning, even though she was "dressed down." She had on a pair of gray slacks and a soft, pink sweater that showed off her still slim figure. She hugged me and smelled of Jovan Musk, a scent she had been wearing since I was a child. I could remember for my first school dance, when I was in middle school, she had sprayed some on me and I had felt so beautiful and grown up. I had danced with Freddy at that dance and he had said I smelled beautiful. I smiled at that memory while hugging my mom and taking her overnight bag out of her hands. My mom came into the house and after giving me a kiss on the cheek, went in search of the kids. Mom was crazy about my kids, and almost knocked me down in search of them whenever we were able to visit each other.

Although mom and dad only lived four hours away, in the opposite direction of where Freddy was traveling, we only got a chance to see each other a few times each year. That was mostly on holidays. The reason we didn't get to see each other as often as we would have liked is because mom and dad hated to drive, "with all those teenage drivers out there" (even though they let me get my driver's license at the age of 15), and I was too busy with the kids. Plus it would have been so much trouble to pack up all the millions of things they would need even for a weekend trip. I knew when they got older traveling would become easier, and I planned to do a lot more of it when that time came, but for now we settled on skyping with the grandparents.

When my children saw my mom they lost their minds with excitement. My daughter, three years old, yelled, "Gamma" and my son, two years old, just let out a scream, as if he was being chased by something. I think he screamed because he was trying to imitate his sister's yell, but I knew my mom would be excited and think he was trying to yell "Gamma" too. They all hugged and laughed, and even though my mom is the cleanest, prissiest person I know, she got down on the floor and began to wrestle and roll around with them. My heart melted watching them play together, because I realized just how much my parents and Freddy's parents must miss the kids. I made a promise to myself to travel more to visit both sets of parents, despite the inconvenience. Looking at my mom roll around on the floor with my little ones let me know that the hassle would be worth it.

After prying my mom off the floor, and prying my daughter away from my mom and into her car seat, we set off to a local pizza parlor. Although I'd wanted to take mom someplace nice, she had wanted to go somewhere the kids would like. She was such a good grandmother.

After finishing our pizza we went back to the house. Henry was fast asleep, so I wiped him down and put him to bed while my mom gave Hannah a bubble bath. I smiled as I heard them laughing and giggling like two little girls. They were having so much fun, that I almost hated to end it, but I knew that Hannah had to get to bed. When I went to read her a bedtime story she begged for "Gamma" to do it, so my mom read to her. Then off to bed Hannah went. My mom and I spent the next hour or so catching up, talking about dad, Freddy, and making small talk until we eventually went to bed. I went to bed so giddy with excitement, just thinking about the exciting day that lie ahead. I could hardly sleep.

After tossing and turning all night, like a child on Christmas Eve, I woke up, got dressed, and went to my hair appointment. At the salon I felt like I was getting ready for prom. It felt great to be pampered. Heck, it felt great to simply sit and read a magazine. Actually getting my hair done was just the icing on the cake. Because it had been so long since I'd been to the salon, my already super thick hair had really grown out. I thought it would be super cute, not to mention functional, if I got it cut into a cute little bob. Although Freddy loved my hair long, and often liked to play in it, and lately pull it when we were having sex, I thought he would like the bob haircut. I thought it made me look chic and sophisticated.

After my hair was cut, colored, and trimmed, I went to get my manicure and pedicure. If felt so relaxing that I fell asleep in the chair. When I awoke, my nails were done, my toenails were done, and my feet were super soft. I was actually starting to look *and feel* like a woman again. My next stop was to go get my Brazilian bikini wax but because I felt I needed to muster up a bit more courage, I stopped in at Macy's first to pick out a sexy negligee. I found a black lace camisole that was fitted around my double D's, but looser in the waist to hide my baby fat. I also liked that it stopped short to show off my butt. I finished the look with a pair of strappy, black, needlepoint stilettos. I also grabbed my favorite perfume.

Having stalled as long as I possibly could, I finally headed off to get my bikini wax.

I only have one word for that experience: Ouch! Having had two children you would think I'd be more tolerant of pain, but there is no pain like the pain of having someone rip your pubic hair off your vagina. It stung so bad that I was actually worried I wouldn't be able to perform tonight. But the sweet little lady that did the bikini wax assured me that the stinging would only be temporary. I must admit that it looked really good down there. I knew Freddy would love it, because heck, it was even turning me on.

After completing my beauty regimen, I still had another hour or so before it would be time for me to hit the road. So I went back home to play with my children. When I arrived home I heard laughing and shrills coming from the backyard. When I peeked back there, I saw that my mom had made a fort, and she and the children were rolling all around it. My mom, prissy Priscilla, was rolling in the grass. When I went back there to try and jump in the game, they paid me no mind whatsoever. My son looked over at me for about a minute, and that was all the attention I got. As a matter of fact it seemed like I was getting in the way. My mom said to me, "Why don't you go take a nice long bubble bath?" Although I'd wanted to spend some time with my kids, I thought a bubble bath was a fantastic idea. One, because I rarely got to take one, and two, because my little ones were having so much fun with my mom it didn't seem as if they'd notice I was gone.

I went upstairs and poured my favorite bath beads and scented bath oils into the tub. I sat back and relaxed while the warm water wrapped itself around my body. I thought about tonight. I thought about how sexy I wanted to be for Freddy. I parted my legs in the bathtub, allowing the warm water inside of me. Then I took one of my fingers from my right hand and slowly rubbed it across my clitoris. When I felt my body become warm, and my vagina become moist, I moved my left hand up to my left breast and began to rub it softly, slowly across my nipples. I slid down further into the water moving my hips around and around letting the water slush back and forth across my clitoris. When the climax started to build I slipped two fingers inside my vagina and began to finger-fuck myself. I fingered myself harder and harder until I was on the brink of cumming, then I stopped. I was left hot and horny and soaking wet, and that's exactly where I wanted to be when I saw Freddy.

After I was done teasing myself and getting myself all riled up, I hurriedly bathed my body. I then moisturized my body, leaving my skin shiny and silky smooth. Next I put my favorite perfume behind my ears, inside my wrist, and between my thighs. Then I put on some comfortable slacks with a cute top for the drive to surprise Freddy. I didn't want to wear my teddy negligee yet because, for one, I did not want to walk out of my house in a teddy negligee. But I also wanted to be comfortable for the drive. After packing a small overnight bag, I went downstairs to kiss Henry, Hannah, and my mom goodbye. They were all downstairs cuddled around the sofa in their PJs with my mom reading stories to them. I ordered some takeout for them, and quietly left the house. With my favorite jams to keep me company for the drive, I set out to surprise my husband, and make tonight a special night.

Four hours later, I arrived at Freddy's hotel. I went to the front desk and explained that I would be joining my husband in his hotel room. I already knew the room number because Freddy always stayed in the same room, so I gave the gentlemen at the front desk the room number as well. After the gentleman explained to me that he could not give me a room key, I showed him my ID so he could see that I was indeed Freddy's wife. The gentleman would not budge, and explained to me that because I was not a registered guest he could not give me a room key.

I took a deep breath and reassessed the situation. I understood where the gentleman was coming from, and knew that he had to protect the privacy of guests at the hotel and ensure their safety and security, but I also knew that I had not driven all those hours for nothing. So I did something I rarely do. I pulled out my lawyer hat, and after requesting the manager, was able to finagle my way into Freddy's room. Apparently my lawyer skills were still there, because I even received an apology from the manager. The manager apologized for giving me such a hard time, explaining to me that they'd had situations where one spouse was trying to catch another one cheating and the staff members had been trained to prevent that. I told him I understood where he was coming from, and assured him that that was not the case with Freddy and I. I received the room key with another apology, and proceeded to the room.

When I got there I was not surprised to see that the bed had not even been slept in. Freddy's bag lay open at the foot of the bed, where it appeared he had grabbed a few items out, and ran out to meet with clients. Considering how big an account this was, I assumed that Freddy had probably stayed out all night wining and dining these clients.

I was so proud of Freddy in that moment. I felt so lucky to have a husband who worked so hard to provide for his family. I felt more determined than ever to make this a special night for Freddy. I pulled out my oils, massage creams, candles, and toys. Then I took a quick shower and slipped into the teddy negligee I bought for tonight. When everything was all set up and ready for Freddy, I decided to call him. Without giving myself away, I wanted to make sure that he was coming to his hotel tonight. I dialed his number and waited for him to pick up.

8

Freddy

When I got into town on Friday night, accompanied by my coworker Leane, we checked into the first hotel we could find, and fucked the night away. We fucked that night, and twice in the morning, only stopping long enough to take our showers and check into our respective rooms at the hotel the company had set up for us. Our company was expecting us to check in on Saturday, so we wanted to follow the plan as close as possible so as not to arouse any suspicion. When I checked into my room I threw on some fresh slacks, a dress shirt and tie, and met my coworker in the lobby.

On the outside looking in, we appeared to be two people on a business trip, ready to meet with clients. At least I hoped we looked that way. I hoped no one noticed the lustful looks we gave each other, the way I had to adjust my slacks whenever I stood next to her, or the way she touched my arm when she talked to me. I hoped we were doing as good a job as we thought we were, hiding our affair. On Saturday, after taking our clients out for a game of golf and an early dinner, we bid them farewell. We felt sure that we had landed the account, even though they'd said they needed a couple weeks to make a decision. I honestly didn't even care about the account. Nowadays I mostly looked forward to just being alone with Leane. Landing the account would be extra.

Leane and I decided to hit up a nightclub not too far from the hotel where we were staying. We had been there for a couple hours, drinking, dancing, grinding on each other, and having the best foreplay I've ever had, when I felt my cell phone vibrate in my pocket. I never turned it off in case anything ever happened with the kids or in case Stacy needed to call me. But because she so rarely did call me when I was on business trips, it took me a few seconds to realize that it was my phone vibrating. I showed Leane my phone so that she could see why I was stepping out, then I pressed the answer button on my phone. I couldn't make out what Stacy was saying, and then it occurred to me, "Oh shit, she's going to wonder what all this noise is." I told Stacy to hold on a minute as I trotted across the street from the club. When it was much quieter, I got back on the phone, cleared my throat, and said, "Hey baby, is everything okay with the children?" Stacy said that the children

were fine and asleep in bed, and that she was
calling because she missed me.

Instantly I felt queasy. I couldn't tell if it was
because of the guilt of what I was doing and about
to do, or because I was nervous that she had
somehow sensed that I was up to no good. But I
recovered quickly. I answered Stacy saying, "Aww
baby, I miss you too." She asked me what all the
noise was that she'd heard. I answered her that we
had taken the clients out to a little bar and
restaurant but were finishing up and that I should
be back to my hotel room within the next hour. I
asked her if she wanted me to call her when I got
back to my room, so we could talk a little bit more
without the noise. I was silently hoping she'd say
"No, I'll be sleep by then," because I knew that I
had plans with Leane tonight. I did not want to put
off getting my hands on her. My wife waited a beat
then answered, "No honey, that's okay, just call me
tomorrow when you're on your way home so that I
can listen out for you." With relief I sighed. I'm sure
my sigh came across as an "I miss you too, and
can't wait to get home," but it was simply relief
that I wouldn't have to call my wife right before I
was planning on having sex with my coworker. I
told my wife I loved her, which I truly did, and that I

missed her, which I'm not so sure was true, and then we got off the phone.

Moving slowly I walked back into the club. I was heavy with thoughts about my wife, my children, what I was doing, and how far outside of my marriage vows I had strayed. When I got back into the club, Leane noticed my change of mood. She asked me if everything was all right at home. I told her that everything was fine with my children. I didn't feel comfortable saying that everything was all right at home because I felt sure that it was not. Why else would I be out with my coworker instead of on the phone, or better yet at home, with my wife? For a brief moment I considered just ending it right then and there. I looked over at Leane, taking in her beauty, her sensuality, her fucking sexiness and realized that I would not be able to end this affair. This was the most alive I had felt in years.

Since beginning the affair with Leane, I had stopped eating so poorly. When I knew I was going to work late I stopped and bought grilled Tilapia and vegetables from the restaurant around the corner instead of stopping at the vending machine. I had quit drinking so much coffee, because work no longer felt so long and dreadful. I started hitting the gym downstairs during my lunch break and had even managed to lose the pounds that had crept on me over the last two years. But my wife had not noticed. She had not commented that I was in better shape. Unless it concerned the kids, she never had much to say to me. But Leane had noticed. She told me how sexy I was. She couldn't keep her hands off me and when she fucked me nowadays, she did it in a way that let me know how attractive she thought I was, how desirable I was to her. I was no longer desirable to my wife. She barely spoke to me, and to be honest, she was no longer very desirable to me.

Stacy was beautiful. There was no denying that. But she no longer resembled the girl I had met and the one that I had married. I felt like a fucking pig for saying this, for admitting it, but her new body turned me off. She was so flabby and out of shape. But maybe that wouldn't even bother me so much if she at least dressed like a woman. Most days I found her in the same sweatpants for days on end. She would wear her old college shirts and even though I had once found her sexy in them, now she just looked old. I could not remember the last time I had run my fingers through her hair, or smelled perfume on her, or seen her in a pair of high heels. I just didn't think of her as a sexy woman anymore.

Hell, I barely even saw her as a woman anymore. I knew I was an asshole for thinking this way, even if it was the truth, but I couldn't help how I felt. As wrong as it was, I knew I would not let Leane go. I liked the way she smelled and I liked the way she looked. I liked the way she tasted, and the fact that she always wanted to try out new positions. I liked the way she made me feel like a man. I especially liked the fact that she desired me and how good it felt to desire her.

I knew I was putting my marriage in jeopardy by having this affair, but I also knew I couldn't stop now. Come hell or high water I was not going back to the stale existence I'd had before this affair. With determined resignation I grabbed Leane's hand, kissed it slowly, and led her out of the club.

When we got out of the club I passionately kissed her and whispered in her ear, "Are you ready for tonight?" Her response was to slip her hand into my pants and massage my dick, while kissing my neck. In the back of my mind I thought, I'd be a fool to give this up. So off we walked to my hotel room, where I knew we'd spend the night fucking in every position known to man. I couldn't wait. My only regret was that I had not started to live life sooner, and my only hope was that I would get away with this as long as possible.

We got back to the hotel in record time. All the way there, Leane and I were touching, rubbing and groping each other. When we got right outside of the hotel we let each other go and walked into the lobby. Our plan was to take separate elevators up to my room. On my way to the elevator I noticed a guy at the front desk looking at me strangely. When I nodded my head at him as if to say "Goodnight" he nervously looked away from me. I wondered if he suspected that my coworker and I were having an affair. Then I dismissed his weird behavior.

To be honest, I didn't even care anymore. Even if this guy suspected something, it's not like he would tell my wife. It's not like she could find out. When I was on my business trips my life was my own. I stopped at the vending machine to grab a drink, but really it was to let my coworker go ahead of me to the elevator. When I heard the ding indicating that the elevator had arrived, I made my drink selection and proceeded over to the elevator myself.

I rode the elevator up to my floor and when the doors opened I stepped out of the elevator and headed down the hall to my room. As I turned the corner I saw my coworker standing outside my room. Because it was so late, and because no one was around, Leane had already unbuttoned her blouse. She motioned me over to her and right there outside my room we began to passionately kiss. I wrapped her legs around my waist and held her up against the wall, grinding my hardness into the warmth of her pussy. I was so wrapped up in the excitement of the moment, it didn't even occur to me that there might be cameras in the hallway. In fact, if she had been wearing a dress I would have fucked her right then and there.

With urgency I let her down and grabbed my room key. I place it inside the door, and when it opened, Leane and I started undressing each other right there in the foyer. She had already unbuttoned her blouse in the hallway, so I pulled it off and lifted her bra as I took her right breast into my mouth. I let the tips of my teeth slightly graze them, and in response, Leane released a deep groan. I started sucking harder, while moving my hand down and into her slacks.

Leane's groans got louder, and I expected any minute she would burst and order me to fuck her now. One thing I loved about having sex with Leane

Anne Drea

was that she was always so verbal and open about what she wanted and how she wanted it. That shit turned me on. So I sucked harder and slipped my hand between her legs to caress her clitoris, in full anticipation of what she would say next.

I was not expecting what happened next...

"WHAT IN THE..." I heard a voice begin to exclaim, then silently trail off. Even before I opened my eyes and released my co-worker's breast out of my mouth, I knew that voice. Those three little words belonged to my wife. I squeezed my eyes tighter, willing the scenario to change. Willing myself to be somewhere, anywhere else. I felt Leane's body tense up. I eventually looked up. I saw my coworker scrambling to pull down her bra and get her shirt on and buttoned up. Past her I saw the bed in my hotel room, covered in what looked like rose petals. I saw a few candles lit around the nightstand, and I smelled something sweet and earthy wafting around the room.

Then I saw my wife.

My wife was standing beside the bed with a look of distress painted across her made-up face. She was absolutely beautiful standing there. She had her hair kind of short and it framed her face

146

beautifully. She was wearing something short and lacey and had on the highest heels I had ever seen her in before. Her skin was glistening and I found my dick hardening again, even as it had just deflated from its previous erection.

I couldn't believe that was my wife standing there, so damn sexy. I smiled. It took me a minute to remember where we were and what was happening. That's when my smile collapsed. I was not in a hotel room admiring my wife. I was in a hotel room with my mistress being caught cheating, by my wife. I wanted to hide. I wanted to run to her, and from her, all at the same time. I wanted to apologize. But I did nothing. I just stood there. My legs wouldn't move and my mind wouldn't stop running. I wondered what she was thinking. I wondered why I hadn't yet gone to her. I wondered why I was here. What had led me to this place? I wondered where my kids were. I wondered why my wife was here. Oh God. My wife. I didn't know how much longer she would be my wife. Would I lose my kids? Why was I just standing here?

As I struggled to gain control of the situation, I noticed that my wife was just standing there too. She had tried to speak, but words must have escaped her. Instead, she stood there and took in the whole scene. Her eyes darted from me to my coworker Leane, back to me again. Then she spoke. She asked "Why?" She didn't ask the question to anyone in particular. She seemed to be asking the question to thin air. My coworker mumbled an "I'm so sorry" and fled from the room. Her movement seemed to stir the air, as it had grown very dense and stale. My wife looked at me, then looked down. I felt myself walk towards her, and she raised her hand to me, as if to say "Stop." I stopped moving toward her. My wife then turned around and in slow motion grabbed her pants from the closet, an overnight bag, and her car keys and left the room. I stood there for a minute, just taking it all in. I could not believe what had just happened. My wife had caught me sleeping with my coworker. My wife had caught me. The realization of that hit me like a ton of bricks, and I sat heavily on the edge of the bed. I put head in my hands and I cried like a baby. Fuck what I had said before about deserving this. I couldn't believe I had ruined my family over a piece of ass. I had ruined my family.

I had to save my marriage. I had to get to my wife. I hurriedly packed my bag and all the items I had in the hotel room, as well as the items my wife had left behind. My heart broke as I gathered the candles, and creams and oils my wife had brought for what looked like a rendezvous she was planning. I thought about what her plans had been for us tonight, and how great it had been that she had thought to go out of her way to make a special night for us. I wondered how long she had been planning this. I cringed when I thought about her driving back at this late an hour after seeing what she had seen.

After packing everything up, I ran over to my coworker's room. She opened the door already dressed, with her own overnight bag at her feet. She must have sensed my urgency, or maybe she too was anxious to get home and away from this mess. Neither of us looked at each other and we spoke no words. She grabbed her bag and walked slowly behind me. I walked ahead of her, still looking around for my wife. I was hoping that my wife would be nearby and had decided not to drive in such a state as the one I assumed she was in. But by the time I got to the lobby, that hope was gone. I knew she had left, and all of a sudden the shame of what I had done and the fear that I had lost my wife and family was replaced by sheer terror that something might happen to my wife while she was on the road. What if she was crying and couldn't see the road ahead of her? What if she didn't make it home?

I sent a prayer up to God, asking him to please keep my wife safe. I told Him that she had been through enough, and to get her home safe. I then gunned it home. I didn't care about getting a ticket or something happening to me. I just didn't care about anything. It was in that moment that I realized that I certainly didn't care about Leane. I looked out the side of my eye at her and wondered what I had seen in her. She wasn't even all that attractive, certainly not more so than my wife. Why had I thrown everything I had away for her? She must have felt me watching her because she began to squirm uncomfortably. I cleared my throat to clear the air, and then I did what I should have done all along. I apologized to Leane for allowing our "relationship" to go as far as it did. I told her I was sorry and would not be seeing her anymore. I told her that I was going to try like hell to get my wife back. She sat silent for a moment. Then she spoke. She asked me if I thought my wife would tell her significant other what she had seen. I could hear the fear in her voice and understood it.

Although a small part of me thought she was selfish for asking that question, I understood why she would want to make sure that her situation did not turn out like mine. I told her that I didn't know if my wife would tell him or not. Then I apologized again, partly because I didn't know what else to say. For the rest of the ride we rode in total silence. No one touched the radio, or even moved. I realized that I had been living a lie. As we sat there quietly, with me feeling nothing whatsoever for this woman, I realized the high price I had agreed to pay for such a small reward. I made a vow that if I ever got my wife back, if I got her to forgive me, I would never cheat again. I would be the husband I should have been all along, if I ever got another chance.

When we got back I dropped my coworker off at work. She slowly got out of the car, looking back like she wanted to say something but didn't know what to say. Instead of words, she walked back over to the car, leaned in, and gave me a small kiss on the cheek. I was again shocked that the kiss felt so cold. There was absolutely no passion or any feeling behind it. It became so obvious that we had both made a mistake, and I hoped to myself that she would be able to repair her relationship with her partner. I squeezed her hand and watched her walk to her car. One of the same cars we had fucked in.

I sat in the parking lot wishing I could redo the last few months. My coworker got in her car and drove off and yet I stayed there. It took me a moment to realize that I was stalling. As eager as I was to get back home to make sure my wife was okay, I was just as scared to see her face. I had already seen the disappointment, the sadness, and I couldn't stomach the words that would accompany those looks. But I had to get home. So I drove there. It felt like I was driving to my funeral. When I pulled up to the house my wife's car was there. So was her mother's. I decided to drive off. My guess was that her mom had been there to watch the children, but I wasn't sure. So I drove off. I didn't know if my wife wanted to tell her mom what had happened between us or not, so I decided to wait until morning to go home. I sat there for a while before driving off. I wondered what my wife was doing, thinking, feeling. I squeezed my eyes shut to rid myself of the image of my wife looking at me with so much hurt. Then I drove off.

When I got back to the parking lot of my job, I turned the car off, reclined the chair and willed myself to fall asleep. A few hours later, when I saw that sleep would not come, I sat my chair back up and looked out of the window. For what seemed like the one hundredth time that night I said a prayer, asking God to save my marriage. I didn't want to lose my wife, but in the pits of my stomach I felt like I already had.

9

Stacy

After Freddy told me he'd be back at his hotel room soon, I decided to light the candles and pull the oils out. I was already dressed in my negligee by then, and if I may say so myself, I was looking good. I stared at myself in the mirror, finally feeling a bit like my old self - the self who used to get regular manicures and pedicures, who slept in cute little camisoles, or boy shorts with tank tops. I felt like the old me who was sexy and sure of herself. I liked the way I looked and felt and I knew Freddy would too. I decided right then and there that I would keep this new look up. I would get regular trims for my hair, and get a manicure and pedicure at least once a month. I might even go shopping and see if I could find some cute little outfits that would still be comfortable enough to wear around the house with the children.

Feeling revived and glamorous, I lay myself seductively across the bed. After about 15 minutes of lying there, I decided to blow out the candles. The last thing I wanted was for Freddy to come back to the room and see his wife scantily dressed surrounded by a bunch of firefighters responding to a fire-in-progress call. Or better yet, I didn't want Freddy to get back to his hotel and see me standing outside in next to nothing if the smoke from these darn candles caused us to get evacuated. I chuckled to myself when I realized that even though I was dressed like a carefree sexy lady, I was still a mom through and through. Why else would I be lying here playing out every possible dangerous scenario in my mind?

I got up from the bed after blowing out the candles. I looked around the room and got an idea. I thought it would be even sexier to maybe hide in the closet so that when Freddy entered the room he wouldn't immediately see me. He would see the unlit candles and the oils and creams atop the nightstand, and then I could make an entrance. I turned the lights off, and stood in the bathroom in total darkness waiting for Freddy. The only light in the room was from the hair dryer plugged into the bathroom wall. My plan was to let Freddy get all the way into the room then step out of the bathroom seductively. Then, of course, I was going to rock his world.

I eventually sat down on the toilet to get off my feet. I was wearing six inch heels and my feet were beginning to hurt. I must have drifted off to sleep because when I opened my eyes I could hear that there were people in the room. It sounded like a bit of a commotion, and I realized that Freddy must have brought a couple of his clients back to the room with him. Maybe he had to get them some paperwork, or something. I sat there very quietly, because the last thing I wanted was one of Freddy's clients to see his wife half-naked hiding in the bathroom. I put my ear to the door so I could hear out and know when to step out of the bathroom, but all I could make out was movement and what sounded like garbled words or sounds.

I decided to be patient and wait until the others were gone. After several minutes I could still hear them, and they sounded like they were either getting closer or louder. This was not how I imagined this night going. I hoped I would not have to spend it in this bathroom. I glanced down at my watch and that's when I noticed just how late it was. Why would a client be in Freddy's room so late? I panicked. What if it wasn't a client? What if someone followed Freddy into the hotel and into his room? What if those garbled sounds I was hearing were people robbing Freddy? I looked around for something that I could use to help Freddy if it came to that. All I saw in the bathroom was a hairdryer and a bottle of perfume. I grabbed the bottle of perfume and uncapped it. Worst case scenario, I could throw the perfume into the eyes of the robber. I slowly opened the door. I peeked out and heard a definite scuffle in place. There were moans and my heart broke as I imagined someone hurting Freddy. I rounded the corner and came fully into the room. I stood next to the bed trying to make out the images of what appeared to be two people. That is when my heart sank.

Freddy was not in danger. He was in a passionate embrace with some woman. Or rather, he was in a passionate embrace with her breasts. He had one of her breasts in his mouth and was grinding himself against her. Her shirt was off, as was his, and she had a hand full of his hair in her hand. She was saying something to him to which he responded by sucking on her breasts harder. I felt the bottle of perfume slip out of my hand. Freddy must have heard it because he opened his eyes and saw me. It must not have registered who I was, because he looked at me with this woman's breast still in his mouth. Eventually she turned around to see what Freddy had seen, and was still looking at, and when she turned her breast slipped out of his mouth as a gasp left her lips. She started frantically pulling her blouse up and around her. The whole while Freddy just stood there.

I watched this whole scene through what seemed like someone else's eyes. I felt completely detached as I watched my husband – MY HUSBAND! – rush to get clothes on with another woman. I felt so removed as I watched my husband try to hide his naked body from me. After scrambling around with their clothes, Freddy stood there like a deer caught in headlights. I stood there face to face, though a room away, looking at Freddy as he looked back at me. We just stared at each other.

For a moment, it occurred to me that I should scream, or yell, or hit him. I wondered why I felt nothing. I wondered if I should slap the other woman, instead of just standing there. I didn't know what to do but I felt as if I should say something so I croaked out a "Why?" Truth is, I don't know if I was asking Freddy why he cheated or if I was asking myself why I wasn't feeling or saying anything. Since I didn't feel anything, did it mean that I didn't love my husband anymore? Was our marriage already over? Did I somehow already know that he was having an affair?

As I stood there, deep in my thoughts, the woman he was with said "I'm so sorry" and without looking at me ran out of the room. After what seemed like an eternity I looked down and noticed that I was still wearing those ridiculous heels and that teddy negligee. I hope I looked good in it when Freddy's mistress was here. I wondered if that was a weird thing to think. I realized I didn't care, that nothing made sense anymore. Here I was underdressed in my husband's hotel room, watching him make out with a stranger and yet I was feeling like the third wheel. My life had essentially been turned upside down and all I could think about was whether I looked good for Freddy's mistress and how I *should* react to this situation.

I eventually began to gather my things. Partly because I didn't know what else to do. At some point Freddy started to walk towards me and I held my hand up to stop him. I didn't trust myself to talk to him and I didn't know what he could possibly say to me to make things better. Or worse. I slipped on a pair of pants, grabbed my overnight bag and a few other things, and exited the room. I walked right past my husband like he was a stranger and not the man I had married, the man with whom I shared a family, the man with whom I shared a life.

I got down to the lobby and walked out of it with my head down. I suddenly wanted to scream. The man who had checked me in, the one who I had assured that my husband was faithful, looked over at me and I had to fight back the tears. I knew he knew, and that somehow made it worse. I walked with as much dignity as I could muster out of the hotel and back to my car. I got in the car and allowed myself to cry.

I cried for myself and for my children who were innocent but who would now be the product of divorce. When I was done crying, I dried my eyes and started my car. Then I just sat there. I didn't know what to do. I was surprisingly calm given the situation, but I didn't know if I should trust myself to drive all the way home. Yet I couldn't stay there, sitting in my car. I eventually drove off, and headed towards home, but I wasn't sure if that's where I was going. I sort of drove aimlessly thinking back on Freddy and my life. I thought about our beginning, how we started off as friends. I thought about how once upon a time I had been the love of Freddy's life. I thought about how he had been the love of mine. I knew I wasn't in love with my husband. But I did love him. I thought it was normal to not be in love after a while. I didn't know many couples who were still hot for each other after so many years of raising children, paying bills, and getting through life.

There was a time I had been in love with my husband. I wondered when exactly that had stopped. I wasn't even sure I knew what it meant to be in love. I knew that once upon a time Freddy and I could sit and talk for hours and hours, and nowadays our talks were mere sentences and brief check-ins about our children. I thought about how loved and sexy I used to feel with Freddy. I no longer felt that way anymore.

I knew Freddy loved me but I didn't know if he thought I was attractive anymore. I wondered if he'd still think I was attractive if I had not gained all the baby weight. Or if he would still be attracted to me if I had become that career woman I'd wanted to be. I hated that I had let myself go. I knew Freddy cheating on me wasn't my fault, but I knew I had to take some responsibility for allowing things to become as dull and dry as they'd become. I thought about how vibrant and full of life Freddy had been once upon a time. How he too had become sort of a functioning shell.

I didn't know what I was going to do about us. I felt hurt, and scared, and sad, all at the same time. I also felt lost. Freddy was all I had ever known. Our family was all I wanted. Yet I couldn't just walk away from what Freddy had done. How could I ever trust him again? How could we ever get back what we had, in the beginning? I didn't think we ever could.

I busied myself with those thoughts, and before I knew it, I was back home in record time. I was home so quick that I hadn't even had a chance to figure out what I was going to say to my mom. I flipped open my compact to freshen my makeup. Then I walked into the house. Because of the late hour everyone was asleep, so luckily I didn't have to tell my mom anything. I went into my bedroom and closed the door. I lay under the covers, and continued to contemplate my life. It didn't even occur to me that Freddy might come home. I imagined that after I left, he and his mistress probably met up again to resume what they were doing. It didn't matter to me what they were doing or if Freddy had left. I knew he'd better not come back here. I did not want to see his face until I figured out what I was going to do. Or maybe I never wanted to see his face again at all.

Within a couple hours the sun started to come up and I got out of bed. I had not been able to sleep anyway, so I decided to stop torturing myself lying in bed alone with my thoughts. I went downstairs and prepared breakfast for my mom and the children. I wasn't in the mood to cook anything fancy so I put on some oatmeal. When it was nearly done I went and woke my mom up. She was surprised to see me there. I had thought about what I was going to tell her so I was ready. I told my mom that I had gotten Freddy's destination confused and had driven to the wrong city. Freddy was actually in the opposite direction, so I had decided to just come back home instead of making the long drive to Freddy's. I told my mom that I had called Freddy to tell him that I'd planned the surprise but had gotten his location mixed up, and he'd felt so bad that he had promised that we would do something special today when he got home.

My mom must have sensed something was up. She must not have bought my story because she left my house in record time. After she'd gotten dressed, helped me get the kids up and dressed and fed, she made up some excuse about wanting to head back a day early because she missed dad, but I could feel that she knew something was wrong. She gave me a big hug, told me to call her if I needed anything and then she was gone. I must admit that I was grateful. I didn't want to sit around pretending to be chipper all day and I definitely didn't want to have to face Freddy with my mom there. Her leaving was best, I just wish I hadn't caused her to worry.

With my mom gone and the kids and I dressed, I decided to leave the house. I needed to take my mind off of my situation, and to be honest I didn't want to see Freddy. I knew he would eventually come home, and I wanted to delay having to see him for as long as possible. So, I went grocery shopping, and took the children to McDonald's to play in the play area. Because I still wasn't quite ready to head home, I went to the mall. I bought my children a couple of short sets, then, on a whim, I bought myself a sexy pair of shoes and a few pair of sexy panties. It had been so long since I had bought anything for myself and I decided I was going to indulge. I had no place to wear those sexy heels, and certainly no one to wear sexy panties for, but I bought them to make myself feel better.

I have to admit that shopping was helping me to get there. I decided to add a dress or two to my new buys along with a pair of earrings and a pretty purse. It wasn't name brand, because I didn't really care about that kind of thing, but it was cute and it made me feel girlie.

After I was done shopping I took the kids home, and as I feared Freddy was there. I took my time getting the children out of the car. I still hadn't decided what I was going to do. I think it depended on what he had to say. For the first time since catching Freddy with that other woman I wanted to see him and hear what he had to say.

When I got into the house Freddy was sitting at the dining room table. He looked like a child waiting for his parents to get home and discover his bad report card. He did not look up at me, but did greet the children with a fierce hug. I went back to the car intending to get my bags, but at the last minute I decided to drive off. The children were safe with Freddy, and I needed some time to get my thoughts together.

I went back to the mall, but because I had done all the shopping I could possibly do earlier in the day, I only walked around aimlessly. At some point I went into one of the salons and got a free makeover, partly out of curiosity, but also because I was just trying to keep myself busy. When I saw myself in the mirror, I must admit, I thought I looked beautiful. Even though I was only out and about so that I could stay away from Freddy, I realized that having this time to myself felt good. I made up my mind then and there, that regardless of what happened between Freddy and me, I would make time for myself.

After leaving the mall, I went over to a coffee shop and casually read a magazine. This all felt so foreign to me. I felt nervous sitting there, like I knew I should be doing something else. In the back of my mind I wondered if the laundry was done, or if Freddy had put away the groceries so they wouldn't spoil. It took a little while before I could shut my mind off and focus on the magazine. But eventually I did. I had picked up an issue of Cosmopolitan. I was really enjoying the magazine, and even beginning to enjoy myself.

At some point I laughed out loud at something I was reading, and as I looked up to see if I had disturbed those sitting quietly around me, I noticed that I had caught the attention of a tall, attractive man. I looked away suddenly, embarrassed that I might have been staring at this man. He approached me. I could feel his presence over me even before I saw him. I made sure that my left hand with my ring finger was displayed, then I looked up at him, in a somewhat rude manner. I was thinking, *He's probably someone's husband.*

Even though I didn't see a wedding ring on his finger, I was still persistent that he might be out here cheating on his wife. Before he could say a word I said, "I'm not interested." He seemed taken aback, and chuckled nervously. Then he said, "I'm sorry ma'am. I don't mean to be a bother, but I just came over to get the book that I left in the chair beside you." Then he awkwardly cleared his throat. I shut my eyes tight before slowly, and slyly, glancing over to the chair beside me to see if a book was there. Sure enough, there sat a leather bound book. I could not have been more embarrassed if I had tried.

Without saying a word I reached over, got the book, and handed it up to him. He thanked me for the book and grabbed it out of my fingers. When his hand touched mine I shuddered. He apologized again for disturbing me, mumbled something about coming here all the time, and left. Shortly thereafter I left too. I had embarrassed myself by assuming this man was coming over to make a move on me, and the only thing I wanted to do was get out of there. I had nowhere left to go but home. Ready or not, it was time to face Freddy.

When I got home it was rather late. The children had taken their baths and dinner and were just getting tucked into their beds. I went into my son's room, bent over his little bed and kissed him on the head. As I was going into my daughter's room, Freddy was coming out of it, and we nearly bumped into each other. He said "Excuse me" in a somewhat cold voice, and I said nothing as I moved over to the side to let him pass. I kissed my daughter turning her nightlight on as I left her room.

I went into our bedroom, put all of my bags in the closet, and went into the bathroom to take a nice long bubble bath. Freddy was in our bedroom sitting on the edge of the bed. He looked as if he was waiting for me to talk to him. There was almost like a "get it over with" energy in the room. But I had decided that I had no words for Freddy. I was not going to let him off the hook. I was not going to let him out of his misery. I sure as hell was not going to make this any easier for him.

I had walked right past Freddy as if he didn't exist, as if he was not there, and I'd closed the bathroom door. I poured into my bath water all of those oils that I had planned to use on Freddy, and I lit the candles that I had planned to use for our special night. My hurt and confusion had been replaced by pure anger, and I was no longer going to let my life revolve around Freddy. If I wanted a romantic night I would have one by myself. I was going to get manicures and pedicures and take care of myself like I used to. I was going to make sure Freddy got off from work early enough for me to be able to leave the house. I was going to get a life. Since he sure as hell had gotten one.

As I sat in my bubble bath with my eyes closed enjoying myself, relaxing, and for the first time not thinking about what had happened, I heard a knock on the door. It was Freddy asking to come in. I ignored him at first. But his knocking persisted. Eventually I told him to come in. But I covered myself first. This was the first time since dating Freddy that I had felt the need to cover myself. When he came into the bathroom I resumed my position of lying in the tub, but with a towel across my body. I didn't even bother to open my eyes. I wanted Freddy to see and feel just how insignificant he was in my life.

Without waiting for me to open my eyes, he began to speak. He said, "I don't know what to say. I'm so sorry. I don't want to lose my family. You and the kids mean everything to me. I don't know what came over me, it was a stupid mistake, and it'll never happen again. Please forgive me and let me make things right. Please..."

When Freddy was done rambling, I asked him to reach me my loofah, which was sitting on the sink behind him. He seemed uncertain what I meant, so I pointed behind him and he turned around and very cautiously grabbed it and handed it to me. When I got it I said, "Now can you do me a favor?" and he said, "Yes, anything, just name it, anything I can do to make things right." I said, "Could you do me a favor and get the fuck out of here?"

Freddy's eyes widened as mine closed and I sank back down into the tub. I had my eyes closed, so I couldn't see him, but I could still feel him standing there. So I opened one eye and pointed at the door. He looked over at the door and at me then back to the door again. With his head down he walked over to the door and opened it but he did not walk out of the bathroom. He waited a minute, as if gathering his thoughts or maybe in an attempt to process or understand my "I just don't give a fuck" attitude, then he spoke again. This time it was slow and calm and not at all harried like it had been when he had spoken earlier. He said, "You'll have to talk to me sooner or later" and left. I grunted. If I had my way, I wouldn't talk to him again. I was going to show him how it felt to be emotionally and sexually ignored - starting today.

Over the next couple weeks I continued to ignore Freddy. To me it was as if he was not even there. I did not cook breakfast for him in the morning nor did I cook dinner for him at night. I did not tell him anything about the children's days, or about mine. I didn't ask about his either. I assumed he had ended his affair because he came home immediately after he got off from work. But just as soon as he walked in the door, I walked out of it. I got dressed up, put my makeup on, and was always ready to go when Freddy came home. I went to that bookstore I had gone to before. I went to the movies. I went out to dinner. I even went bowling once. I did these things by myself, and even though it was awkward to go out by myself at first, I was really beginning to enjoy myself and look forward to my evenings alone. They gave me an opportunity to put distance between myself and Freddy and also to have some much needed and long overdue time for myself.

For his part, Freddy was trying to make amends. In addition to coming home early, he started bringing home dinner, and he bought me flowers. I threw the flowers away, always making sure to let him see them in the trash. I also never touched the food he brought home. A few times Freddy tried to stop me from leaving, and asked me to stay and talk. I refused. Other times he would try to plan family things in the evening, but most of the time I wouldn't participate in that either. I figured it would do Freddy some good to have some one-on-one time with his kids. God knows he had missed enough time with them while he was out with his mistress.

On the rare occasions that I did join Freddy for a family outing, I never said more than what was necessary to him. I laughed and joked and played with the kids, but I was still unwilling to forgive Freddy. In fact, the more he tried to get my attention, the angrier I became. I felt his efforts were too little too late, and I was not going to let him forget that he had hurt me to my core.

On several occasions while I was at the coffee shop, I ran into the gentleman I had seen before. The first time I saw him I turned around and left because I was still embarrassed. The second time I saw him there I stayed. But I kept my eyes down the whole time.

By the third time there, I decided to go over and apologize. It felt awkward to be there and see him so often and not say something about what had happened. It was obvious that he was a regular here and I enjoyed coming here and didn't want it to feel awkward. One evening I walked over to his table and simply said, "I'm sorry about the other day. I didn't mean to offend you. I'm not usually so rude." He said that he accepted my apology and offered me a seat. I did not want to sit, but I had already been rude enough the last time, so I accepted the seat. I thought I'd sit for a couple minutes then get going. But before I knew it, I had been there for a couple hours talking to this guy.

His name was William and he was an Independent "Indie" author. He had been a doctor but had grown tired of being around so much sickness and sadness and had decided to try his hand at writing. Six novels later he was still in love with his hobby of writing and had turned it into a profession. William had been married but divorced five years ago when he had given up practicing medicine. He confided that he and his wife had grown apart as he was trying to reconfigure his life's plan. They had two sons who were his "best buddies."

My situation was complicated, so I kept it simple. I told William that I was married with a son and daughter. I told him my husband was a pharmaceutical sales rep and I was a stay-at-home mom, but had passed the bar. He asked whether or not I planned on getting back into law and I replied that I honestly didn't know. I hadn't thought about it one way or another. We talked some more and I found that I liked William. I found him refreshing. He had thrown away conventionalism and had decided to live life on his own terms. I respected and admired that. In a way I was on a similar journey, one of self-discovery. I was trying to rediscover myself and my own interests. I looked at the time and realized I had to get going, so I said goodbye to William, and we made plans to talk again the next time we saw each other. But first I stopped off at the bookstore next door and picked up one of his books to read.

Over the next month or so, things continued to change between Freddy and I. But for the worse. We still had not talked about things and I was still giving him the cold shoulder, but now he seemed to have grown angry and was also being cold to me. I didn't care. As far as I was concerned, I was just sticking around because of the children. If not for them, I would have left his lying, cheating ass.

My days were centered on the children, and keeping the house clean. I cooked dinner mostly for the kids, since most evenings I went out. When

I went out I had the time of my life. I felt like a woman again. I had been meeting up with William regularly, and after admitting that I had read and loved a couple of his books, we had started a book club. There were seven of us now, and we'd meet up twice a week to discuss whatever book was on the list. William insisted that they not be his books, but I was still reading them on my own. He had a refreshing voice and wrote in an unorthodox fashion, and I found almost everything about him refreshing. Our relationship was platonic, and he was always respectful. I thoroughly enjoyed meeting up with him and the group and looked forward to my Tuesdays and Thursdays with the book club.

That is, until Freddy started staying out later at work. I didn't know if he was staying out because his work load had increased or because he was cheating again, or just to keep me at home, because we were not talking about anything but the children. I didn't even care anymore. As far as I was concerned, Freddy could do what he wanted and so could I. But I was pissed that he was getting home so late that I had missed two weeks of book club meetings. Before I knew it I was back at home all day and all night with the children, and Freddy was out gallivanting and doing what he wanted. I'd had enough. When Freddy came home late one night, even though it was way later than I ever went out before, I still left the house. I didn't know where I was going to go, but I wanted to show Freddy that he was not going to be the only one with a life or the ability to leave the house.

I left the house dressed to the nines, even wearing the sexy underwear I had bought. I knew that Freddy had seen the sexy underwear and in the back of my mind I wanted him to wonder and worry about why I had bought the underwear and who I might be wearing them for. So here I was, late at night, dressed to kill, with nowhere to go. Out of habit I stopped at the coffee shop and my heart leapt with joy when I saw William sitting there. I went inside and couldn't help the smile that spread across my face when William let out a gasp when he saw me. He said, "Wow, you're beautiful," and in that moment that expensive outfit was worth every dollar. Freddy had barely noticed me, and hadn't said a word to me when I walked out of the house. It was like he didn't care if I was cheating or not. Or maybe he didn't think I could or ever would.

William stood up and wrapped me in a hug. He smelled like fresh linen and cologne, and I liked it. I had never looked at William like that before, but I was suddenly in a frisky mood. I hugged him back, and probably held on a little bit longer than I should have. William leaned back and looked at me, probably trying to read me. Or, more accurately, probably trying to determine if I was flirting with him. I sat next to him and crossed my legs as seductively as I could. I was wearing a black, above the knee dress, with side-shirring. It had a clingy material, but the fact that it was black and shirred made it appear very slimming. It hugged my body in all the right places and was forgiving in all the right places. I knew I was looking good. William noticed me cross my legs and I hoped he also noticed the way I let my leg rub casually against his, as if by accident. He smiled at me in a sexy way and asked me if I would like anything to drink. I told him I wanted something a bit stronger than what they served there. He asked me if I would like to join him back at his place for a drink. I said that I would. He walked me to my car and I got in and followed behind him as he drove to his place.

He lived in a loft downtown and I loved it. It was spacious and screamed bachelor, but there were also personal touches that showed he was a father, like trophies, drawings and little boys' shoes strewn about in the foyer. I was surprised to see that I felt so comfortable being at William's place. I didn't know if it was because I had spent so much time with him over the last couple months, or because I was so angry with Freddy, but I felt like I belonged at his place - at least for tonight. I knew what I wanted to do, and judging by the way William kept looking at me from across the room, I knew he wanted the same thing. After putting on some music, William came over to me. All of a sudden I felt so nervous. I couldn't believe what I was about to do. It was true that I thought William was attractive, but more than anything, if I was being honest with myself, I simply wanted to feel what Freddy had felt when he slept with that other woman. Or, at a minimum, I wanted to get back at him.

As William got closer to me, I started to have doubts. Could I have an affair? Could I cheat on Freddy? Even though he had cheated on me, cheating went against everything I stood for. Could I sacrifice my moral code just to get back at Freddy? Unwittingly, I began to cry. I dropped to William's sofa, suddenly overcome with the grief of it all. All of the emotion that I had not allowed myself to feel, all of the hurt, came crashing down. William wrapped his arms around me and asked me what was wrong. I hesitated, but as he lifted my chin to meet his gaze I let it all pour out.

I told William that I had caught my husband cheating several months ago. I told him that before that I had already felt so low and undesirable as I sat at home watching my children and gaining weight. I told William that I felt like a failure and often wondered if I had dreamed that I'd passed the bar and was actually an attorney. That life seemed like such a long time ago. I told him how I was only here to sleep with him to get back at my husband but also because I wanted to feel desirable again, and like a woman. William just held me and stroked my head. After a moment he spoke.

William told me that I was desirable and that he had been attracted to me from day one. He confided that he had come over that first day to make a move but that I had shut him down so firmly that he had made up the excuse about coming over to retrieve his book. William said that if he had simply wanted to get the book he could have grabbed it and walked away, but that he had been attracted to me since seeing me walk in so quietly and laughing out loud so heartily. He had been intrigued to get to know the woman who seemed both shy and feisty all at the same time.

With sincerity, William told me that although he didn't know my husband, he thought that he was a fool to have cheated on a woman like me. He said that I was so obviously intelligent, and that he had enjoyed our book club meetings solely because he knew I was going to be there, and when I had stopped attending that he had stopped going too. William said that he had missed our conversations and had started staying at the coffee shop later and later in hopes that he would see me again. When I had walked in tonight, he said that I had looked so beautiful that he had thought he was dreaming.

William told me that we didn't need to make love to get back at my husband, that he was satisfied just to have my company. Then he excused himself for a moment and came back with the latest book that the book club had been reading - the one that I had missed because of Freddy. William also had two glasses of wine. With pillows on the floor, we sat up and talked about the books and explored the characters and the plot and all the ins and outs of the story. I couldn't remember the last time I'd had such an enjoyable night.

After it had gotten really late I told William that I had better get going. He offered to pay for a cab to take me home since I'd had a couple glasses of wine. I told him that I was okay to drive and thanked him for his hospitality. He gave me a hug at the front door and as I stood on the tips of my toes to give him a kiss on the cheek, he wrapped his arms around my waist and pulled me into him passionately. He held me there, firmly planted against him as he explored my mouth with his tongue. He expertly moved his tongue around my mouth, while his strong hands cupped my ass. He lifted me all the way up and I wrapped my legs around his waist and sighed into his mouth as I felt his manhood swell. William was very large and I found myself shimming my dress up my hips to get better access to it. I wanted to feel him against me and I wanted to feel all of him inside of me. With my legs still wrapped around William's waist he lowered me to the floor. He slipped off his shirt and I fell in love with the dark hair trailing down his hard abs and disappearing into the rim of his slacks.

I felt emboldened, sexy and desirable, so I grabbed him and rolled over so that he was under me. I sat on top of him with my dress above my waist allowing him to feel the warmth from between my legs. I lowered my head and took his mouth in mine. I let my hair cascade softly across his face and chest as I trailed kisses down his chest, stopping to suck on his nipples and twirl their tiny buds between my teeth.

When I felt him harden even more and use his big hands to press my hips further into his hardness, I lifted up and let our eyes meet. His eyes were half closed in ecstasy, and with unadulterated boldness I lifted his chin so he would open his eyes and see me better. When I had his full attention, I slowly and seductively lifted my dress above my head, revealing my sexy underwear. My double D's were threatening to spill over the lilac-colored, lace, push-up bra. The look he gave me made me feel like a supermodel. William's lips curled as he let one of my breasts out of the bra that was barely containing them, and put as much of it as he could into his mouth. With his tongue in the back of his mouth, he sucked my breasts while using the base of his tongue to gently massage my nipples. This drove me crazy.

I was so wet that I knew William could feel it on his stomach and through his boxer briefs as I sat on him, grinding my wetness into his hardness. He flipped me over, lay me gently on my back and went into his room to get something. Presumably a condom. I removed my panties to give him access when he returned. When he came back, he removed his slacks and for the first time I was able to see just how large William was. His was the biggest I had ever seen and I couldn't wait to feel him inside me. He slipped the condom on himself and I opened my legs preparing to feel him plunge into my wetness. What I felt instead made me sit up and cry out. William had slipped his tongue between my legs and was teasing my clitoris and sopping up my juices with his tongue.

Involuntarily, my hips started to grind against his mouth as if I was riding his face and the motion made William lick, suck and stroke my clit harder. When I couldn't take anymore, and was on the verge of cumming I forcefully lay William on his back and with my ass facing him, slid myself over his dick. I wanted to ride him backwards because I had always been told I had a perfectly rounded ass and I wanted William to have a great view of it while I rode him.

With my hands on each side of him, I began to slowly ride him. I lifted myself up and down with slow precision, coating his dick with my juices. When I felt him start to jerk and grind against me, I increased my tempo. I took as much of him into me as I could, then squeezed him inside me as I rode him low and hard. I would lift off of him only slightly then slam it back down on him hard.

William starting moaning my name and groaning and I knew he was about to cum so I let myself cum too. With a grunt William's orgasm joined my own and we both came hard. I rolled over, spent. We lay there for a bit, my head next to his foot and vice versa, and neither of us spoke. After a few minutes, William said, "Damn, girl," and rolled over onto his elbow. I rolled over onto mine too and smiled over at him sheepishly. I hated to admit it, but I had never had sex that good with Freddy. William was so big that it felt like he was in every part of me, exploring my front, sides, and all around. He asked if he could see me again, and I said that I honestly didn't know.

William looked away for a moment and I could tell that he was trying to muster up the courage to say what he was supposed to say instead of what he wanted to say. He settled somewhere in between.

William told me that although he knew he shouldn't sleep with me and should encourage me to work things out with my husband, he liked spending time with me and wanted to see me again. William said that he wouldn't put any pressure on me, but that if I could get away he would love to take me to a movie on Saturday night. I told him that I wasn't sure if I could, but that I would call him if I could make it. He gave me his number and a deep kiss, than we got dressed. Despite my protests he followed me all the way to the corner of my house before turning off and heading back home, so he could make sure I made it home okay.

When I got home Freddy was asleep on the sofa and didn't even seem to care that his wife had been out all night. It broke my heart that he didn't care and I had to be honest with myself that maybe we had reached the end of our road together. It seemed so obvious that we had. I mean, why else wouldn't he care that I had been out all night doing God only knows what?

I peeked in on my children and saw that they were fast asleep. I walked into the bedroom that Freddy and I had once shared, kicked off my shoes, and lay back on the bed. For the second time tonight, unintentionally, I began to cry. I wondered if what I had done made me as guilty as Freddy. I wasn't even sure I felt guilt. What I felt was an overwhelming since of emptiness and loneliness.

When I was all cried out, without a tear left in me, I took a shower and got into bed naked. I lay on my side of the bed with my back to Freddy's side of the bed. Even though I held Freddy's pillow to myself for comfort, it was William that I thought and dreamt about. Freddy and I were in big trouble.

10

Freddy

When I got home after Stacy caught me cheating, she and the kids were not there. I busied myself cleaning the house, cooking dinner and getting things as nice as I could for Stacy. I went to the local florist and ordered nine of Stacy's favorite flowers (nine was her favorite number). When I was all done and dinner was cooked and the house was all cleaned, I sat Stacy's flowers on the dining room table. They radiated a sweet fragrance that I enjoyed as I sat at the dining room table waiting for Stacy.

I stared off into space trying to make sense of my life. I couldn't believe I had fucked up so badly, and I wanted nothing more than the opportunity to make things better with Stacy. I had been practicing what I was going to say and couldn't wait to see Stacy so that I could express how sorry I was and how willing I was to do anything in or out of my power to prove to her that she was the most important person in my world and that I would never fuck up again. I sat there with my head in my hands, pleading with God to soften Stacy's heart and make her receptive to hearing me out and giving me and our family another chance.

Within a couple hours I heard Stacy pull up. I knew she would have seen my car and know that I was home. For a second I worried that she might pull off and take the kids and go stay somewhere else. But her car's engine turned off and I could hear her and the children approach the door. My heart began to beat so fast when she walked into the house. I looked at her but she did not see it. She seemed to be looking anywhere and everywhere but at me. My daughter ran over to me and I picked her and my son up and hugged them tightly. I was so afraid of losing them and in that moment the reality of the situation hit me like a ton of bricks and a few tears fell. When I put my little ones back down and looked around for Stacy, she was not there. When I looked outside I saw that she had placed some groceries outside the door and was gone.

I hadn't expected her to leave. I didn't know if she had forgotten something or was just avoiding me. I knew she would be back because she would never leave me without the children. If she was planning on leaving me, she would have taken the children. I was grateful that they were there. Not only did I miss them like crazy, I knew that Stacy would be back. So I patiently waited. While I waited I played with my children like I hadn't done in a long time. I wrestled with my son, I colored and played dress up with my daughter and I enjoyed them like I should have been doing all along. I finally understood what Stacy had been trying to tell me about the importance of family time and what all I had been missing. I just hoped I hadn't been too late to actually show her I had learned my lesson.

Pretty soon it got dark and I gave the children a bubble bath together, fed them dinner, and read them a bedtime story. Although it was fun playing and being with my kids, it was still hard work and for the second time my heart went out to Stacy. I realized that she did this every day, mostly by herself, and I had thanked her for taking such great care of our children and our family by sleeping with another woman. I promised myself and God and the thin air around me that I would make it up to Stacy. I just hoped she gave me a chance.

After their story I started tucking the children in for bed. When I heard Stacy pull up I was just turning off my son's light and entering my daughter's bedroom. On my way out of my daughter's bedroom, Stacy and I almost collided. I said,

"Excuse me" and she said nothing as she moved to the side letting me pass. I don't know what I was expecting but my heart sank. I went into our bedroom and sat on the edge of the bed. A short time later Stacy came into the bedroom. I saw that she'd been shopping. A couple of the bags were from women's lingerie stores and I began to get nervous wondering why Stacy would be shopping there. I knew she wasn't planning on giving me any. I hoped she wasn't planning on being intimate with anyone else to get back at me. The very thought of her being with someone else made me feel queasy, and I quickly erased that thought from my mind. Besides, I knew my wife, and she was not the type to sleep around, especially not to prove a point.

I wanted to talk to Stacy but she was uninterested. She walked right past me and into the bathroom, closing the door behind her. I assumed she was taking a bath, since I did not hear the shower running. I waited a beat, than knocked on the door. She did not answer. I knocked a little bit harder the next time. Still, she did not answer. I knew she was basically telling me to "F" off, but I needed to see her. I needed to look into her eyes and see if we were okay. I needed her to talk to me. I needed to know what we were going to do, whether or not she was going to give me another chance.

After a few seconds of knocking, she told me that I could come in. I could not read from her voice any emotion. I opened the door and the words just flew out of me. I told her how sorry I was and that I had made a mistake and that she and the kids were the most important people in my world. I asked her to forgive me, and to please give our marriage, our family, a second chance. She responded by asking me to reach her a loofah. After I did, she told me to do her a favor and get the fuck out. She was so cold and indifferent, so unlike the woman I had married.

I know I didn't deserve much these days, but we needed to talk. We needed to figure out how to move forward. But Stacy was having none of that. Since I couldn't press the issue and make her talk to me, I simply told her that eventually we would have to talk and I left the bathroom. Then I went downstairs to the sofa and tried to sleep. But thoughts of how badly I had screwed up plagued me, and I could not rest. I lie there on the sofa all night trying to figure out how I could make things better and restore my family.

Over the course of the next several weeks I did everything I could think of. I came home on time. I knew enough to know I had better not give Stacy any reason to think I was continuing with my affair.

My coworker Leane and I avoided each other like the plague. We were very careful to not be in the same space with each other. When I did get home I helped out more. I cooked dinner, fed the kids, I cleaned the house. But not only did Stacy not notice, she made it a point not to be around me. When I walked into the house, she often walked right out the door. Then she stayed out until well past the time the kids were asleep. Sometimes she stayed out so late in the evening that I fell asleep before she returned home. Even when I was still awake I pretended to be asleep, just because I didn't know what to say, or if I had a right to say anything at all.

At first I thought it was just a phase. I thought Stacy was going out to show me what it felt like to have to care for the house and the kids by myself. But after weeks of her going out and staying so late, I started to wonder if she was having an affair. She always left the house dressed so nicely. She had begun to wear heels again and as she walked by me I could smell a faint waft of perfume. Once when she left, I checked her closet, and found that some of her sexy underwear was missing. I could only assume that she was wearing those as well. Thoughts of her having an affair tried to consume me, but I pushed them away. After all, when would

Stacy have met someone to have an affair with? She never came home smelling like alcohol so I knew she wasn't out drinking. Plus, on several occasions she came home with books, so I figured she must be going to a bookstore or maybe the library. I gave her all the space and room she needed. Every day I hoped and prayed that she would stop and talk to me, to give me some idea about the state of our marriage, but she never did.

After a while I started to get frustrated. It was true that I had cheated, and I knew I deserved the cold shoulder, but enough was enough. I was not willing to play this game with her forever. Either we were going to make our marriage work or we weren't. But I refused to be left in limbo. I stopped breaking my neck to get home so early, since all she was going to do was walk right out the door. I was still careful to help out around the house and with the kids more, but I took my time getting home. I only wanted to make her talk to me. I was trying to force her hand to have a conversation with me, even if we only yelled and screamed. But that didn't work. After a couple weeks of my coming in late, she started to go out again. It didn't matter how late I came in the house, she still walked out of the door.

One time in particular, I got in so late that I thought she'd be asleep. But not only was she dressed and ready to go, she was wearing this figure-hugging black dress and those same black heels she was wearing when she tried to surprise me at the hotel all those many months ago. I got a sinking feeling in my stomach when I saw her walk out the door that night. She was so angry and outraged, that as she flew by me, I thought she was going to hit me. I almost wanted her to. Because at least then, we would have had some kind of contact. I didn't know what I was going to do, but I knew I could not go on like this. When she got back, whether she liked it or not, we were going to talk.

In the morning I woke up on the sofa. I ran to the window and saw my wife's car in the driveway. I had waited up for her as long as I could, and I never saw her come in. I didn't go to bed until well after 4 a.m., which means she didn't get home until after that. Enough was fucking enough! I bounded up the stairs furious. Our children were still asleep as I stomped past their rooms. I yanked the door to our bedroom open and saw my wife lying there, eyes open, staring off into space. The look she had on her face scared me. It was completely devoid of emotion. For what felt like the hundredth time, I felt like I didn't know my wife. In that moment I only wanted to wrap my arms around her, and hug her, and beg for forgiveness. I wanted to promise her that we would be okay, that we could grow from this. But I didn't. I had done that before, and she had not responded. Now I wanted answers. I had fucked up, but she had a responsibility to this family too. She needed to help me get us back on track.

I asked her, "Where in the hell have you been all night? And where are you going every night of the week? You are a wife and a mother! Not some single woman who can come and go as you please. I messed up. I screwed up. I am so sorry. I will never forgive myself. But if you give me a chance, I will make it up to you. But you've got to talk to me. We can't go on like this. Either we make it right, or we don't, but we have to do something."

I said all this with tears streaming down my face. The truth is, I was putting on a brave front, but the last thing I wanted her to say to me was "I want a divorce." I would rather the silence for 10 more years, than for her to tell me she wanted out. So I sat on the edge of the bed, with my back to her, so she couldn't see me cry, and so she wouldn't see my knees buckle. I held my breath as I waited.

I could feel her body quivering, so I knew that she was crying to. The air was so tense, so full of emotion, as I felt her prepare herself to tell me something. I closed my eyes willing her to tell me anything other than that she wanted out. I didn't care if she told me she hated me. Or that she didn't love me anymore. I didn't care if she struck me. But the one thing I couldn't bear to hear was that she wanted out.

I could feel her struggle. I could feel that whatever she was about to tell me was difficult for her to say. I braced myself for what I knew was coming. I also mentally prepared my response. I knew she was going to tell me that she wanted a divorce, so I prepared myself to beg. I would do any and everything if she'd give me a chance. I opened my mouth to tell her that. I wanted to get it out before she uttered those words.

We spoke at the same time. I said, "I'm begging you..." at the same time she said, "I fucked him." I kept going, sure I hadn't heard her right. I said, "I'm begging you. Please. Please don't throw away all of our good years, for one mistake. Please give me a chance to prove to you..." she held her hand up to stop me. She sat up in bed, almost as if she was willing me to see her say the words. She repeated herself. She said, "I fucked him. Last night."

Her words hung there. Like cigarette smoke in the air. I heard them, but my mind didn't process them. So I just sat there. Waiting for the words to make some sense. Softly, I whispered, "What did you say?" And boldly, having gained some conviction in her statement she replied, "I said, I fucked him last night." It was so weird to hear her use the "F" word. The only times I had ever heard her say that word – other than when she told me to get the "F" out of the bathroom a few weeks ago - was when we were having sex, and it was particularly good. So it took me a little while to get past her saying the "F" word. But then it registered. Not just the "F" word, but what she was saying. My wife had had sex with another man.

My mind asked a ton of questions. I wanted to know what man? When? But instead of asking those questions, I just reacted. It was like my hands had a mind of their own. I picked up the lamp on the nightstand and threw it across the room. My wife let out a yelp of surprise, but not before I had a chance to grab our flat-screen, wall-mounted television from the wall and hurl it to the ground. This time she let out a scream as she ran from the room. I ran after her, not sure what I was going to do. But I stopped myself when I heard my son begin to cry. He had woken up, probably from the loud bang.

Before I could lose my mind, and do something I might later regret, I ran down the stairs and out of the house. I put my fist through the window of the car, causing the glass to shatter, and my knuckles to burst open and bleed. I jumped into my car and sped off.

Going nowhere fast, I drove until I had reached the edge of town. It was only then that I noticed that my fist was bleeding uncontrollably, having soaked my shirt, pants leg, and the rug in my car. I drove to the hospital, even though I didn't feel any pain. I knew I shouldn't be bleeding like this, but I didn't even care. I drove to the hospital, more than anything, out of a sense of obligation to my children. The last thing I wanted to do was bleed to death before I'd had a chance to fix the mess I had put them in.

Sitting at the hospital being treated had a way of slowing me down and making me think. I had wanted to kill someone, and it didn't matter who. If my son hadn't woken up I shuddered to think of what I might have done. How far I might have gone. The same with my hand. I was grateful that my hand was bleeding to the point of needing to go the hospital. Otherwise, I might have run my car off the road, or found the man that was fucking my wife...I closed my eyes to shut out the image. My mind tortured me with visions of my wife up against the wall while some man touched her, kissed her, or bent her over a chair.

Fuck! If my hand wasn't getting stitches I probably would have put it through another wall. I suppose I should have felt like a hypocrite since I had also cheated, but the thought of someone else with my wife was my undoing. I cringed at the thought, and physically shook my head to try to remove the thoughts, but they persisted.

The doctor looked up at me and asked if I felt the stitches. He probably thought I was grimacing in pain from the stitches, but the pain I was feeling was much deeper, and harder to get rid of. My wife had had sex with another man. Probably to hurt me. Oddly enough, it wasn't until I thought about her with another man that I began to understand the hurt she must have been feeling. Because God knows, if it was anything like I was feeling... So what was I going to do? Should I forgive her? Should I continue to ask for a chance to restore our marriage? Was it even up to me? What if she had already moved on and wanted a divorce?

In a panic I told the doctor that was working on me that I had to get home. He raised his eyebrows and continued to sew up my hand, moving no faster than he had been before. When he was finally done, and the nurse had given me my care instructions (having been told and believed that I hurt my hand while on my job) I got out of there.

In the course of just a few hours I had gone from wondering if I was going to forgive my wife to wondering if she even still wanted to be my wife. I was in a rush to get there, but as I got closer to home I had second thoughts. My wife and I were very angry with each other, and I had already blown up earlier. I did not want to argue in front of our kids, and because of how heated this situation was, I couldn't trust myself to show restraint. I couldn't trust that my wife would either.

Once upon a time I would have sworn that she rarely raised her voice, and she would have sworn that I wouldn't hurt a fly, but it was obvious that we didn't really know each other anymore. So, as much as I wanted to head home, I stayed out until my little ones would be in bed. I drove around for hours doing nothing at all. I felt so lost and confused. I didn't know what would happen between Stacy and me, but I knew I had to give it a try. The mere thought of another man touching her drove me insane, but I knew I had to forgive her, if I expected her to forgive me. Two wrongs didn't make a right, but maybe this one time it could.

After several hours of driving around, stopping only once at the pharmacy to pick up my pain meds, I went home. It was so peaceful outside, and I was tempted to just sit there for a while and soak it up. It had felt like ages since I had experienced any peace, and I longed for those days where the most stressful thing I'd had to think about was a mediocre review at work.

When I got in the house Stacy was sitting on the sofa. She was surrounded by balled up Kleenex and it was obvious that she had been crying. I walked into the house and asked quietly, "Are the children asleep?" and she replied "Yes." I asked if we could talk, and she said "Yes." Already this was the most we had spoken in weeks. I sat next to her on the sofa, thought better of it, then got up and sat across from her. There was so much distance between us. There had never been a time in our marriage where we had been this out of touch with each other, and I was determined to try to get us back on the right track.

But first I had to know about this guy. So I asked her, "Who is he?" She answered, "Just someone I met." I asked her where she had met him from. She told me they met at a coffee shop. Then they had started a book club together. I immediately thought back to all the books she brought home over the last several weeks, and I felt a wave of nausea rise up. I asked her if she was in love with him and she told me that she wasn't. She told me they'd only slept together once, and that she had been trying to find herself, but that she had not really planned to sleep with him, that it had just happened. She said that even though in the back of her mind she had wanted to hurt me, that she had not really planned on going through with it. Then she began to cry.

I sat there for a moment trying to process the information. On the one hand, I felt relieved that it was just a one-time thing, and that she didn't want to run off with this guy. But on the other hand there was the fact that another man had been inside my wife. The image of that would be forever burned into my head and my thoughts.

While I sat there trying to process my thoughts, she asked me about the woman I had been sleeping with. I was honest and told her that I had been having an affair with the woman, who was my coworker (she winced when I told her that) for a few months. I told her it was just sexual, no feelings, and that I had no idea why I had done it. I told her that during the time I was having trouble at work and that my coworker and I had been thrust together a lot and that one thing had just led to another. She asked me if I was in love with her and if I had seen her again. I told her that I was not in love with her and although I saw her every day, I made sure not to talk to or even be around her.

I got closer to where Stacy was sitting and, on my knees, held her hand in mine, looked into her eyes and told her how much she meant to me. I told her that she was my world and that I would do anything to have my family back. I told her that I forgave her, or at least would in time, and that I wanted her to let us try again to make things better. I knew I had taken her for granted and I promised to make things better. I would come home early, would not take weekend business trips. I would give her some time away from the children. I told her that I would love and support her in every way possible.

Tears were falling from my eyes as I said this. Stacy looked at me in shock. She had never really seen me cry before. I was not an emotional man. I had been taught by my father and it had been reinforced when I was in the military that men did not cry. But in this moment my heart was aching at the thought of losing my wife and I couldn't stop myself.

Stacy hesitantly reached her hand out to me. I took it and we just looked at each other for a moment. She was looking so deeply into my eyes, like she was trying to see inside my soul. I was looking at her pleadingly, begging her to give me another chance. She had been weeping softly when I told her that my affair had lasted a few months. It hurt her deeply. I was so sorry and I willed her to see that. To see how much she meant to me. She leaned in closer and wrapped her arms around me. With that open invitation I held her strongly, tightly, to my body. It had been so long since I had heard my wife's voice, smelled her hair, touched her, or felt her body close to mine.

Stacy didn't say a word as she led me upstairs and to our bedroom. Like an obedient schoolboy I followed. When we got up to our room she closed the door behind us and just stood in front of me.

Her eyes were cast down and she looked so vulnerable. I wanted to tell her how beautiful she was to me. It was my fear that my affair had caused her to think less of herself. I wanted her to know that no one held a candle to her. That I still wanted her, every day for the rest of our lives. So I decided to show her.

I tilted Stacy's chin up to me and gave her a kiss. Our bodies were still a bit away from each other. But as I kissed her she began to slowly melt in towards me. When we were chest to chest I let her go and wrapped my arms around her. I let my hands move slowly across her shoulders and down her back before settling on her ass. God, how I loved Stacy's ass. I felt like I was home as I palmed it and ran my hands across it. She arched her back pushing her ass more firmly against my hand. I rubbed myself against her.

I was so aroused and hard that my dick was threatening to burst through my pants. As if on cue, Stacy got down on her knees and unzipped my pants, freeing me. But she didn't stop there. She slid me out of the opening in my boxer briefs and took me into her mouth. I almost lost my footing and stepped back a couple times, wobbly. The sensation of Stacy's hot mouth on my hard dick was too much and I nearly lost control. Stacy didn't usually like to give oral sex. But when she did it was always amazing.

Stacy sucked the head of my penis slow and teasingly. Flicking her tongue across the opening, then around the rim, then sucking it straight on, only to pull away and flick her tongue again. I closed my eyes and must have been holding my breath because eventually I let out an audible breath. As my semen mixed with her saliva, making my dick wetter and slipperier, Stacy took more and more of me into her mouth. She sucked soft, then hard, fast, then slow, she took all of me, then only the tip. She licked the sides and at one point even deep-throated me.

Stacy had never sucked it so good, and as amazing as it felt, I struggled not to think about whether she had learned this from the guy she had been with. I closed my eyes as tight as they could in an effort to block out the image of Stacy sucking another man. Because I couldn't take it anymore, I lifted Stacy up and lay her across the bed. I lifted her nightgown and returned the favor.

Unlike my wife, who didn't love giving oral sex, I absolutely loved tasting her. I loved putting my tongue between her legs and having her juices fill my mouth. I loved to lick between her lips and across her clitoris, feeling her body quiver and shudder beneath my tongue. It gave me no greater pleasure than to tongue-fuck her and take her to the brink of orgasm. Which is what I did.

I licked and sucked and nibbled on her clitoris until she bucked uncontrollably and screamed out my name. Then, right before she was about to cum, I slowly inserted myself inside her and began to pump long and hard. I'd wanted to stroke her softly and slowly but her pussy was so wet that I couldn't control myself. I grabbed her hips lifting her bottom slightly off the bed and slammed my dick into her pussy. I fucked her until she cried out, holding onto my chest to slow me down, but I didn't stop. I pumped and fucked her until she came hard, then I came hard behind her, emptying myself into her wetness as I screamed expletives.

Not that my wife was complaining as she lay there with a satisfied smile on her face and her eyes peacefully closed, but I hadn't meant to be so rough. It's just that I had missed my wife's pussy. I had missed the taste, smell and feel of it. But there was something else too. I had wanted to write my name on it, to reclaim it as my own. To remind her and myself that it belonged to me.

As I lie there taking in the sight of my wife's glistening body, the two of us wrapped around each other with the sweet smell of sex in the air, I realized how lucky I was to have a second chance, and I was not going to fuck it up again. This time I was going to appreciate what I had.

11

Stacy

After Freddy and I made up, it was like we were on a honeymoon. He came home from work when he was supposed to and we cooked dinner together, laughed with the kids, kissed and enjoyed each other's company. We tucked the children in together, and read them a bedtime story together.

When we went to bed, we had the most magical sex there was. Freddy was passionate and energetic and made love to me like he had in the beginning. On some occasions he seemed so hungry and eager for me, and I must admit it made me feel sexy and powerful. I had started dressing up and making an effort with my hair. I think it was paying off too. I was still primarily at home with the children, but an hour before Freddy was due to get off from work I would get dressed, put on a bit of makeup and some high heels and try to look sexy for my husband.

On the weekends we had family time and once or twice I called my parents down to stay with the children so Freddy and I could have a weekend away. Those weekends were some of the best sex we ever had, and we always came back so lovey-dovey and refreshed. We decided to get away at least once per month.

Freddy and I had also started seeing a marriage counselor. I had told Freddy that we needed to see someone because I could tell that we were both struggling with forgetting each other's infidelity. Sometimes Freddy would just stare at me from across the room, almost like he was trying to look inside me, and I could feel that he was heavy. He didn't always see that I noticed him, and when he did he always smiled and played it off, like he hadn't been staring. I didn't know what he was looking for, but I knew my husband, and I knew that he was having trouble getting the thought of me having sex with another man out of his mind.

For my part, I was also struggling with his infidelity, but it wasn't the image of him with another woman, it was the fact that he could lie to me and deceive me for so long. He had carried on with his affair for months, which meant months of lying to me and hiding things from me. That affected my trust in Freddy. I had never not trusted him before. Had never questioned his whereabouts or required that he report to me, but after the affair I found myself worrying if he took too long at the grocery store or if he stayed at work even 30 minutes past the time he was scheduled to get off. I didn't want to have trust issues with my husband, and I didn't want him to look at me the way he sometimes did, so we saw a marriage counselor.

The counselor helped us to see some things about ourselves and about our marriage. As it concerned Freddy, she helped him to see that his affair had been a cry for appreciation. He had "acted out" with his coworker, as she called it, because she had been there to share in his career aspirations and appreciate what he brought to the table. According to our marriage counselor, Freddy had felt powerful, manly, and appreciated with his coworker.

My "acting out" had not been to get back at Freddy per se, our counselor helped me see that my infidelity had been a cry for attention and validation. I had been looking for someone to notice me as a woman, as well as validate my femininity and desirability.   William had been that for me (although we never said our affair partner's names out loud). Both of our affairs had been a sign that our marriage had become stale and had stalled and we had both looked outside of the marriage to find refreshment. Our counselor showed us how to be that "refreshment" for each other.

For my part, I made an effort to ask about Freddy's job and to stimulate him intellectually. I cut back on talking about the kids all day, and tried to engage him about current events, and other adult talk. Freddy took the counseling sessions to heart as well. He always made it a point to tell me how beautiful I was, he sent me flowers with notes that said you're a great mom and wife. He gave me at least one or two weekends a month to have some me time. We were definitely getting better. Our marriage was stronger than it had ever been, and we were in love.

After getting so much stronger, we stopped seeing the counselor. She had asked us to commit to seeing her for at least a year, but we felt secure in our relationship, and ended therapy early. We definitely appreciated all the help she gave us, because we both knew without her we would not have been able to get past the hurt. But we wanted an opportunity to work through our issues together, without outside help.

We did great together for what seemed like a long time. We continued to cook together, have family time, and the sex was still amazing. But after a while, things started to slack off a little bit. Freddy had started to work a little bit later, and then a little bit later still. He explained to me that he had to stay competitive, and he worried that he would lose his edge if he continued to be the first person out the door every day. Because I wanted to show him that I trusted him, I allowed it.

At first I honestly didn't mind. But soon he began to stay late every other day, and then every day, and our time together, as well as a family time, began to suffer. I once again stopped wearing makeup, pretty clothes and high heels when he came home, because, for one, I didn't know what time he'd be home. I also resented the fact that all of the work had begun to fall on me again. How was I to keep the house clean, watch the children, prepare dinner, and still find time to wear makeup and heels for him? Especially when Freddy got home so late that all he had time for was going to bed. The sex was still good, but it was sporadic. I found myself wondering if he was getting it from somewhere else. I knew I was supposed to trust him, or at least work on it, but I couldn't help my thoughts from wondering if he would cheat again if an opportunity presented itself.

Because of Freddy's work schedule, I had not had any time for myself in several months. I didn't realize how much I had begun to look forward to that time, how much I needed that time, until it ended. I found myself bitter and resentful. Although I hated to admit it, I began to miss my book club friends, and William. I did not miss sex with William, even though it had been amazing. I simply missed having a conversation with an adult male besides my husband. William had a way of making me feel sexy, and intelligent, in a way that my husband could not. I didn't know if it was because my husband knew me in and out, and with William I had an opportunity to be mysterious, but I missed that feeling, and I found myself longing for it again.

One day as I was watching television, I came across a segment that was talking about swinging couples. I had vaguely heard about swinging, and from what I knew of it, it always sounded gross to me. Husbands and wives posting ads in the newspaper looking for any and every body to sleep with sounded desperate. I had always thought the kind of people that went to swinging events would be really out there and void of morality. But after watching this special on TV, I came to learn a lot more about swinging. For example, I learned that swinging was usually done with a core set of people, within an intimate group.

I was surprised to see that the swinging couples were all professional, and well-to-do. I was also surprised to know that the swinging had as much to do with an emotional connection as it did a physical one. The swinging couples were usually all friends, and had been for years. They supported each other and seemed to love one another.

Most surprising was learning the reported impact that swinging had on the couples. The couples discussed how swinging had restored their marriages, how it had made things spicy. A few of the wives had discussed how swinging had revived them and made them feel better about themselves, resulting in better relationships with their children, spouses, and even on their jobs.

One woman had discussed how she'd been a stay-at-home mom until she'd started swinging, and after gaining confidence and a sense of value, had gone on to college and graduate school and had become a professor. She was now successful and happier than ever with her husband, whereas before swinging she'd confided that they never really had anything to talk about and that her life had revolved around her children. With tears she had recalled feeling that her husband hadn't really valued her as a contribution to their family.

Something about that story hit home for me, and I think it was that this woman had admitted that she hadn't had any sense of value within her family. I realized that I didn't either. It wasn't that I didn't think that being at home with my children wasn't enough, or a great contribution, it was just that it was a thankless job. A job that didn't give me any access to other adults, or lunch breaks, or time to myself to develop and nurture the things that I loved and enjoyed.

Somewhere along the way I had settled into thinking that this would always be the case, but suddenly I realized I wanted more. It was true that I wanted to raise my children, and not have someone else doing it. But I also wanted to have a life of my own, one outside of just being a mom and a wife. I wondered if swinging and developing an emotional connection with other people, even men, outside of my marriage could give me that. Just as quickly as the thought entered my mind I dismissed it. For one, Freddy would never go for it, and I didn't particularly want to sleep with anyone other than my husband. I decided that there had to be a less drastic way to develop a social network and a sense of self, and I set my mind to finding one that didn't include loaning myself or my husband out to other people.

But yet, I was intrigued by this idea. It seemed risqué, and fun. And for once, I was tired of playing things safe. Here I was, a young woman, in the prime of her life, and already felt like my life had passed me by. My days consisted of the same thing, day in and day out. I was bored and uninspired. I wondered what it would do to my children to see their mom so lifeless. I had a daughter to think about. No, I did not want my daughter to ever swing, but I also didn't want her to sit around and let her life pass her by. I didn't want that for my son either.

You only get one life to live. I decided I did not want to live mine sitting on the sofa in my house waiting for my husband to get off from work. So I mustered up the courage to propose the idea to Freddy. I didn't know how he would take it. I hoped he wouldn't think I simply wanted another man. But I knew that if I did not at least ask him, I would always wonder if this could have been a possibility. So I prepared myself to have this discussion with my husband.

About an hour before Freddy was due to get off, I called him at work to make sure he was coming straight home. Sure enough, he had planned on staying at work late. I informed him that I had to talk to him about something and needed him to come home on time. I could hear reluctance in his voice, but he said okay, that he'd be home in an hour. So I started to get dressed.

I put on a cute sundress and wedge sandals, then thought better of it and took it all off. I didn't want Freddy to think that I was so eager to go out with other men. I wanted him to think about this rationally and logically, instead of seeing me all dressed up and imagining me with some other guy. So I put on a pair of comfortable jeans and a regular v-neck T-shirt. I put the steaks and baked potatoes on the grill, and played with the children until Freddy got home.

When I heard Freddy pull up, my heart started to beat so fast that I almost convinced myself not to bring it up. But as I thought about the monotony and boredom of my life, the sameness day in and day out, I felt desperate for change. Even if he said no, I was at least going to give it a try.

When Freddy walked through the door, I stopped what I was doing, went up to him, and gave him a big hug and a soft kiss. I wanted him to feel all the love I had for him. I was willing him to not get offended by what I was about to propose. He held me awkwardly as I hugged him, and looked at me suspiciously as I kissed him. His eyes were on alert as he looked around the house. When he saw the children playing on the floor, I could see that put his mind at ease some. But there was still a nervousness about him.

Wanting to put his mind further at ease, I assured him that everything was fine with the children and that nothing was wrong. I felt like I was lying a bit to him telling him nothing was wrong. But I did not want him to think that I was about to deliver bad news. I wanted him to go into what I was about to say with an open heart and mind, and not all tense and fraught with anxiety.

While Freddy played with the children, I dished up our food. Since it was still light out, and the weather was nice, I put our food outside, so we could sit on the deck. I wanted to make the environment as relaxing as possible before I asked Freddy to open our marriage to the possibility of swinging. Freddy and the kids and I sat out on the deck having dinner. Besides the children talking, Freddy and I were very quiet. I had been mentally rehearsing what I was going to say to him, and I could see that he was quiet trying to figure out what I had to say.

After we were done with dinner, Freddy gave the children a bath as I tidied up the kitchen and loaded the dishwasher. When I was done with that I went upstairs in time to read the children a bedtime story. Like old times, Freddy hung out in the room while I read to them.

For a moment I considered dismissing the swinging idea. If we could only get back to this place, this place of family time and individual time, and couple time, I would not need to have other people in our marriage. But I reminded myself that this was fleeting. I reminded myself that the only reason Freddy was home early was because I had specifically asked him to be. I reminded myself that come tomorrow and the day after and the day after that, things would go back to normal. Unfortunately, normal included me drying up at home, while Freddy got a chance to interact with other adults and have a life outside of me and outside the home.

When the children went to sleep, I asked Freddy to join me out on the deck. In the event that the conversation went awry, I did not want to wake the children. Freddy sat on the deck, and I brought out two glasses of wine. We rarely drank. The last time we had a glass of wine was on our anniversary. But I wanted to get us in a relaxed mood, and make our conversation as casual as possible. In hindsight I realize I probably should not have brought out the wine. Since we so rarely drank wine, unknowingly, I had probably already aroused Freddy's suspicions.

As Freddy sat next to me on the deck, I realized with utmost certainty and a sinking sensation in the pit of my stomach, that Freddy would not go for this. My old-fashioned Freddy would never welcome the idea of us swinging. In many ways Freddy was still that former military guy that I had married, and I knew that he would outright refuse my proposal. I already knew it. Yet, I barreled on. At the least, I wanted to ask. Even if I already knew the answer.

12

Freddy

Stacy asked me to come home from work early today, and my stomach became a knot of worry. I figured that nothing was wrong with the kids, or else she would have told me that right away. So at least that wasn't what she wanted to talk about. I reasoned that she must've wanted to talk about our marriage. I was no fool. I knew that our marriage had gone back to being boring and dull. I had started staying late at work again, partly because I had wanted to stay professionally viable, but a bigger part of it was that I was bored at home.

Although Stacy and I tried, and God knows we did, we just had nothing to talk about. She asked me about my job and I reported the same stuff day in and day out. It wasn't like I could go into detail and tell her everything, because she wouldn't understand. Stacy was one of the smartest women I knew, so it wasn't that she wasn't intelligent enough to understand, it was just that unless she was there day-to-day, it would have been hard to describe, and it got boring reiterating my day at the end of the day.

I wanted to talk about her hopes and dreams, but it didn't seem like she had any. She read the newspaper in an effort to talk about some things that were going on in the world, but I could tell that she was not passionate about any of these things. I appreciated that she took the time and made the effort to try and deepen our conversations, but they were still surface, lacking emotion and passion, and I was tired of pretending.

Everything seemed to have broken down for Stacy and me. In addition to our conversations dwindling, so had our sex life. We had sex once, maybe twice a month, and even then it was boring and rigid. Stacy had not given me oral sex in many months, and I had begun to fantasize about the way my coworker used to do it. I was ashamed to admit, but a couple times, I had made myself cum from fantasizing about the times she had swallowed it.

I would not dream of cheating on my wife again, and breaking the trust, but I couldn't help the fantasies. It wasn't like I was planning on cheating with my coworker again. Especially since she was no longer with the company. Leane had transferred to another company many months ago, and I had not seen her again. But I sure missed the way we had sex. The reckless abandon, the doing it anywhere, in every way. I missed how vibrant I felt.

Being away from my wife in the evening made me feel less guilty about the fantasies I was having and about the thoughts. I didn't want her to look into my eyes and see what I was thinking or feeling. I was never going to mess up my family again, even if it meant feeling dead inside. I was determined to keep my displeasure hidden, if it meant keeping my wife's trust and my family together.

So, needless to say, I knew our conversation was going to be about our marriage. I knew my wife wasn't happy. I had stopped giving her her personal time, because I was always at work. I know that was selfish, and I know that she was going to talk to me about that. So I prepared myself. I would promise her that I would come home early at least once a week so she could get out. I hoped that would satisfy her. Because other than that, I didn't know what all she could possibly want. I was prepared to repeat all the usual promises: I would help more with the kids, I would come home earlier and let her have some time to herself, I would do whatever it took to keep her, even if that meant suffering in silence.

When I got home, Stacy hugged and kissed me. I was not prepared for that. It instantly put me on guard. I was expecting her to be angry with me, cold. I was not expecting this warmth. I was also not expecting her to look so cute. I couldn't put my finger on it, because she was only dressed in jeans and a T-shirt, but she had an exuberance about her.

All of a sudden I wasn't so sure what she wanted to talk about. I hoped like hell she wasn't pregnant, because having more children was not in our plan. But looking at how light and easy she looked, how effortlessly she moved around the house, I started to get a sneaking suspicion that that was her news. Stacy had long ago given up any hope of being an attorney, even though I secretly hoped that she would go back to doing something she had once loved, especially now that the children were getting older. Hannah was four years old and would be starting preschool this year, and Henry was three and would be there next year. So Stacy was almost free, in that she would have her days available to pursue her career. But with a third child that would set us back at square one, and Stacy would never get back to being the woman she had wanted to be. The woman I missed and hoped was still in there somewhere.

In any case, I prepared myself to feign excitement about our impending bundle of joy. Even if I wasn't excited right now, I knew that in the coming months as I watched our child grow inside of her I would become excited. I loved my children more than life itself, and I would welcome a third, if that was what it would take to make Stacy happy. Nowadays it seemed that our children were the only thing that made Stacy happy.

When we had finished dinner, I took the children upstairs to give them their baths as Stacy cleaned the kitchen. I knew I should be doing more of this anyway, but I also hoped to score some brownie points. If I was lucky, I might even get lucky.

After Stacy finished up in the kitchen, she came up and read stories to the children. I hung out in the room watching them, enjoying my family. I was mentally trying to envision a third child in the mix. I wondered if it would be a boy or a girl. I made a mental note to start an education account for the third child. I also watched Stacy for some indication that she might be pregnant.

When we were done putting the children to bed, she asked me to join her on the deck, which I did. There, she pulled out a couple glasses of wine, and my thoughts stopped dead in their tracks. So, Stacy was not pregnant. I felt a sense of relief, but then a measure of nervousness returned. What was she going to talk to me about? I knew she couldn't know that I had been fantasizing about another woman. I briefly wondered if she had heard me pleasing myself in the bathroom a few nights ago.

My mind was racing all over the place, but I stilled it and willed it to be silent as I waited for Stacy to tell me her news. I could see that she was nervous to say it, which I must admit made me nervous as well.

After swallowing a couple times, she finally came out with it. What she said shocked me. My wife of seven years told me that she wanted to become a swinging couple. She asked me if I would be okay with us having friendships and one or two relationships outside of the marriage. She told me that we could set some ground rules, to make sure that we were doing this the right way, but that she thought this would be healthy for us. She told me that she did not desire to have sex with anyone else and was not trying to use this as an excuse to cheat, but that she missed having a life outside of us and that she needed more. She told me all this without actually looking at me. She wouldn't meet my eyes.

When she finished speaking she continued looking down as if waiting for me to blow up. My mind was racing a mile a minute. I didn't know what to think, it seemed like I was having many different thoughts all at once.

On the one hand I wondered if she had missed that guy she'd slept with and was simply asking for permission to see him again. Was the sex between them that great that I no longer measured up? Had she not stopped seeing him in the first place? I reassured myself that that was not the case because she no longer had time to see him. I had been coming home late and I couldn't remember the last time she had been out. I wondered if she was just bored with me, or with us. But then I thought about how I was bored with us. I thought back to how vibrant I had felt when I was having my affair, and how it had made me happier and less tense. I thought about how, after my affair with my coworker, I had wanted to spend more time with my family.

I agreed with my wife that we did not have to let anyone else dictate our lives. I agreed that it was our right to decide to make our marriage whatever we wanted it to be, as long as it made us happy. I just didn't know if I wanted to take it that far. What kind of man would I be if I let my wife date another man, or worse? Could I even stomach the thought of her being with someone else? And what kind of woman would she be if she wanted me to be with other women?

This was too much to think about, and I said as much to my wife. I told her that I needed time to think about this and I left the house. I got in my car and drove for a while, just letting my mind wander. I wondered if I had ruined our family. Had I been so bad a husband that my wife now longed for someone else? What if I agreed to this and it resulted in the end of us? What if my wife ran off with another guy?

I hated to admit it, but the idea of being able to be with other women intrigued me. Actually, it did more than intrigue me, it appealed to me. It was every man's fantasy - to have a loving wife at home, and a mistress somewhere else. But I had not thought about my wife having that too. I definitely hadn't thought about her wanting that.

It might seem selfish, but the fact that she wanted it too made it less appealing to me. The idea of me having sex with another woman was awesome, but the idea of her having sex with another man was scary. I played devil's advocate. What could be so bad? Well, for one, she could fall in love with the guy. So I decided if, and that was a big if, we did this thing we could only see different people and not the same person over and over again. It could not be a relationship with someone so much as an experience. So I wrote that down as rule number one on a notepad I had in the glove compartment of my car.

What else could go wrong? Well, what if she or I caught something? Like an STD or AIDS? Well, we would have to make a rule to always be careful and always use protection with the others. My wife and I didn't use protection with each other, but if we opened our marriage to other people, we would have to always, every single time, use protection. I tackled a third concern. Then another. I went through all of my concerns one by one and made a rule to accompany each one. The rules were:

1. Must be a different person, or no more than three encounters with one person. No extended repeats!

2. Always use protection.

3. Must always be honest with each other about everything (ex. development of feelings), and must give details if asked.

By the time I was done with my hypothetical list of what I called *Open Marriage Rules*, I was feeling a bit better about the possibility of doing this. I still wasn't sure, but at this point I wasn't saying no. The possibility of our marriage becoming happy and spicy and interesting again was too great to pass up. So I was at least considering it.

13

Stacy

When Freddy came home I was still awake. He bounded up the stairs with an energy I hadn't seen Freddy have in what felt like years. He silently handed me a piece of paper, and quietly watched me as I read it. It was labeled "Open Marriage Rules" and it had things such as: no extended repeat of sexual partners, always wear protection, and always be honest with each other about everything. I looked at the list, and looked back at Freddy. His eyes were glowing. He seemed, dare I say, excited about this idea.

I asked him, "So does this mean what I think it means? Do you want to do this?"

He said, "We can give it a try, but we have to set down some rules and agree on them. What do you think about the rules I've come up with?"

I told him that I thought they were well thought out and good, and to his list I added a couple more about not staying out past 2 a.m. and no sexual relationships with close friends or co-workers. We talked a bit more, and made love.

It was different somehow. When Freddy held me it was so soft and tender and I melted in his arms. We moved together so sensually and perfectly that I wondered if it was a mistake to do this. Did I want to share my husband with another woman? What if he liked her more? What if he wanted to be with her? Would this be the beginning of the end? Then I thought about the alternative. The alternative was keeping things the way they had always been.

Even though there was uncertainty about what impact this might have on our marriage, I knew for sure that if we kept things the way they were going, that we would definitely end. We were growing so far apart. I knew I could no longer exist like this. I could no longer pretend like it was okay to forfeit my life. I loved being a mom, but I needed something more. I loved being a wife, but I needed something more. I knew that Freddy and I were taking a big risk by opening our marriage, but I also knew that the potential payoff was big. For that, I was willing to take the risk.

After I managed to clear my thoughts, I decided I really wanted to show Freddy how much I loved and appreciated him. The fact that he would soon be able to have sex with another woman made me want to make it as good as possible for him here at home. I got on top of Freddy and straddled him. He always liked it when I was on top. But right when he thought I was about to begin riding him forward, I turned around and began riding him from the back. I clenched the lips of my vagina tight as I slid up and down his penis. I could feel him begin to quiver inside me and together our bodies made a squishy sound as our juices combined. When I felt the pressure build, I bent over to where my ass was right in his face and I rode him hard as I softly massaged his balls. Yelling an obscenity, Freddy came and I relished in the fact that I knew exactly how to drive him crazy and make him cum long and hard.

Although I didn't cum that time, I loved how close and connected I felt to Freddy as he emptied himself inside me then held me so close. I wondered if he too had been thinking about what we had signed up for. Was he excited, scared, nervous? Time would tell. If nothing else I knew that Freddy at least thought that this would work. Or why else would he consent to it? All we could do was hold on for the ride. And I for one couldn't wait to get started. The excitement of what we were about to do was creeping in, and I felt my nervousness give way to anticipation. We were living life on our own terms. Whether or not we opened our marriage either of us could cheat, or our marriage could end in divorce either way. At least this way we were fighting for our marriage and for each other. This was probably not the most orthodox way to do it, but it was our way. I also felt like I was fighting for myself. I was no longer going to be sitting by the wayside waiting for life to happen to me, I was getting involved and making life happen. I felt my life was just beginning.

Although we had initially talked about swinging, Freddy and I agreed that seeing each other be with other people might be too much, so we agreed to simply open our marriage to the possibilities. The possibilities could include opposite-sex friendships, or something a bit more sexual. As long as we followed the rules, respected our family and each other as number one, then we would go with the flow. We discussed feeling a bit of trepidation about our decision, but chalked it up to the unknown. Overall, I think we felt peace that we were moving in the right direction, if for no other reason than the fact that we were moving.

But then Sunday came along, and for the first time Freddy and I went to church kind of heavy. We were hesitant to face God with our decision to open our marriage. We knew, whether simply opening our marriage or becoming swingers, that we were not doing what we were taught to do from the bible. In our faith, adultery was a sin, and Freddy and I knew that we were willingly sinning by agreeing to allow the other to commit adultery.

When we got to church, Freddy and I, I guess in a subconscious effort to hide from God, tried to sit as far back away from the preacher as we could. But it was not to be. The ushers ushered us right near the front row, almost like they knew we needed some help. Or maybe I was reading too much into this. I was so paranoid about what we were doing. Did that mean we shouldn't do it?

I looked over at Freddy and his brows were furrowed. It looked like he too was in deep thought. I squeezed his hand to give him some reassurance, to let him know that we were in this together. But I was also afraid.

Luckily, when our pastor preached it was on the subject of tithing. I breathed a sigh of relief when I realized we would not be under direct scrutiny. Whatever else we were deciding to do, the one thing we didn't have to worry about was tithing. We tithed to our church and even to some charities regularly.

After church was over, Freddy and I didn't linger around to talk to other church members like we usually would have. I think we were too weighed down with our thoughts to be able to make small talk, so we didn't even bother trying.

When we got home we went about our Sunday routine as we normally would have. Freddy prepared dinner while I got the children's clothes ready for the week. When we were done we ate dinner in front of the TV watching America's Funniest Videos. This was our Sunday routine, and it was the only time we ate in front of the TV.

When we were all done with dinner, the kids sat on the floor playing games and Freddy and I cuddled on the sofa. Even though we didn't speak much, I felt so close to Freddy. I truly loved my husband, and I did not want to lose him. The mere thought of losing him made me a bit emotional. I had to do this for myself, because if I didn't, my fear was that I would lose myself, and I didn't want that to happen either.

I knew that if we called this off and went back to how things were, we would get right back on a downward ride, and I didn't know if we could survive. We had to put something in place that would benefit us both individually as well as as a couple, and I knew that this was it. I knew that opening our marriage was what we needed. I just hoped I was right. Because it would be too high a price to pay if I was wrong.

As per the schedule we put in place, I would get Friday nights and Freddy would get Saturday nights to go out. Then on Sunday, as well as the rest of the week, we would have family time. That first week went by so fast. It seemed like Thursday got here before I knew it, or before I was ready. Thanks to my previous shopping spree I had already purchased some really pretty clothes, so I had already had an outfit ready and cute pair of stilettos. My new haircut made styling my hair a breeze, so the only thing left to do was get a manicure and pedicure. I got that done on Thursday night and Freddy was nice enough to give me the extra time to get dolled up. Usually when I got my nails done I played it safe and only got a French tip, but this time I wanted to step outside of the box. Going along with what would be my newfound freedom gave me a sense of courage that made me want to live a little.

Thursday night when I got home I showed Freddy my ruby red nails and toenails and the matching red silky camisole that I planned to wear for him later. I had wanted to thank Freddy for allowing us to open our marriage and for being so sweet and so much like the old Freddy this past week. But most importantly, I think I wanted to quietly reassure him that he was the only man for me and that I had no intention of giving the goodies to anyone else. That night I pulled out our old Kama Sutra book and Freddy and I twisted ourselves into every angle imaginable. I came stronger than I had before and Freddy gave me at least two orgasms that night. It was obvious that he had also upped his game, but I think it was because he also felt like he had something to prove.

That morning I woke Freddy up to a blowjob, and when he came I tried my best to swallow it. Although the taste was okay, I never liked the texture of cum in my mouth, but I figured I would learn to love it for Freddy. My motives were pure in that I wanted to please him, but also that Freddy could easily find someone who would do those things and I didn't want any of those women to have anything over me. Freddy's body belonged to me and I wanted to remind him that I knew just how to please him and please him good. After showering, Freddy rushed off to work. Our little escapade had made him a bit pressed for time. I did my usual, which involved grocery shopping for the weekend and week ahead, as well as the weekly dry cleaning. I also took the children to McDonald's play place and to the library to get our new weekly books.

By the time we were done with all that, Freddy was due to get off in an hour. So I hurriedly put on dinner. We had agreed that on Fridays Freddy would come home an extra hour early to give me a little time to get ready.

True to his word, Freddy walked in the door 33 minutes after the hour with a dozen red roses and a cautious smile on his face. Despite my best efforts to reassure Freddy that my body was all his, I could tell he was nervous about my night out. I knew I would feel the same way about his night tomorrow, and that the only way to get through it was to do it.

I took the flowers from Freddy and gave him a long sensual kiss. Our children were enthralled watching the Sprout channel and I contemplated having a quickie with Freddy before I left. That way he would know for sure that I was going out just to have a good time and meet interesting people and nothing more.

Even though I was allowed to have a sexual relationship, I just wanted him to know that that was not in my plans, at least not for tonight. Still, I decided against the quickie because I didn't want Freddy's juices dripping from between my legs all night. It didn't matter how much I washed up after, whenever Freddy and I had sex he always left me with panties full of cum for at least the next two days. I thought it might be a little weird to walk around with my husband's fresh cum inside me while I was potentially out with, or at least in the company of, other men. It was bad enough that I was a little bit juicy in there from when we'd had sex a couple days ago. So although I wanted to give him a little bit, I decided to break our embrace and head upstairs to take a shower.

I heard him expel a long breath as I turned to walk away, and I wondered if it was because he was horny and hoping for that quickie too, or because he was dreading tonight. I decided not to think too much about it and continued walking upstairs on my way to a nice, warm, bubble bath.

When I was done bathing I went back downstairs dressed in my bathrobe. I wanted to have some time to play with my little ones before they went to bed and I headed out. My daughter saw my ruby red toenails and squealed in delight asking me if I would paint her nails the same color. I assured her that I would paint them really pretty, albeit clear, tomorrow. In my opinion, and I believe Freddy agreed judging by the look of terror on his face when she asked if she could have her nails painted red, we both thought she was too young for that.

Satisfied with the answer that she would get her nails painted tomorrow and with clear polish, my daughter came over and gave me a big hug. I squeezed her to me and inhaled the smell of her. Although she was getting to be a big girl she still smelled like a baby, and I grew sick at the thought that she would one day leave the comfort of the home that Freddy and I provided and have a life of her own. Although I complained that I never had enough time for myself, it was often the case that when I did have an opportunity to be away from my children I couldn't stomach it.

I held my baby girl tight and even managed to grab a hold of her little brother as he tried to run past, and I just held them to me. My daughter was giggling as my son was squirming and trying to get away, and in that moment I knew I couldn't do it. I couldn't go. I could not jeopardize our family or my children's security and happy home. Even if it meant I faded away, I would do it for my children because they meant the world to me. I could not believe how selfish I had been. So I decided to back out. I decided I wouldn't go through with it.

I stood up and pulled my bathrobe around myself. Freddy was looking at me as if trying to read my mind. I opened my mouth to tell him that I wouldn't, couldn't do this, but I never got the chance to say it. Before I could utter the words Freddy spoke. As if he'd read my mind and knew what I was about to say, he said, "You have to, we need this" as he looked me right in the eyes. He walked up to me and said, "I know you're scared, I'm scared too. But I really think we need this. I think it's going to help us." I realized then that this wasn't just about me, this was about Freddie too. More importantly, this was about our marriage. I was willing to give this a try as long as Freddy was on board, and as long as we both were doing this to make us better, to make our marriage work.

We had let the children stay up a little bit later so that I could have a little bit of extra time to play with them, but now it was time for them to go to bed. Freddy and I walked them upstairs and tucked them in. We kissed them good night and shut their doors, leaving them open just a crack like we usually did. Then we went into our bedroom. I went into the closet to get the dress I was going to wear, and my shoes. When I came out, I saw that Freddy was lying across the bed watching me. Although I had dressed in front of Freddy one million times before, for some reason, this time, I felt so naked and vulnerable. Maybe it was what I was wearing, or maybe it was the fact that I was about to go out and possibly meet another man.

Whatever the case, I felt so nervous dressing in front of Freddy. I slipped on a black, above the knee dress, and a pair of simple black peep-toe pumps. I was originally going to wear something a little more fitted, and certainly my stiletto heels, but I'd changed my mind. I was not going out looking for a man - that really wasn't the point of this. I was going out to have some time to myself, to meet some interesting people, and if some of those interesting people happened to be male, then that was allowed. But I was not going out specifically to find men. So I dressed accordingly.

When I was done dressing and putting on my makeup, I tucked my hair behind my ears and put on a pair of earrings. Then I was ready to go. I did not look va-va-voom, or sexy, but I did look pretty, and I felt confident, albeit slightly nervous. Freddy had been watching me the whole time, quietly, but when I was done he said, "You're beautiful." That made me blush, and I looked away before saying "Thank you. So are you."

Freddy walked me down the stairs and gave me a kiss on the cheek, I guess so that he wouldn't ruin my lipstick, and he told me to have a good time. I could see that he was trying to hide the sadness in his eyes, and to be honest I was sad too. But we both knew this would help us, so I kept reminding myself of that. Freddy told me to make sure I had my cell phone on, and to call him anytime if I needed anything. He also told me to be careful and that he loved me. I told him that I loved him too, and then I walked to my car which was parked outside of the driveway, while Freddy watched me get into it. I pulled out of the driveway as Freddy closed the front door behind him, and just like that I was out for the night, with full permission from my husband to do whatever I pleased.

As nervous as I was, the sheer fact that I could do as I pleased felt so exhilarating. In that moment I felt like the young woman I never got a chance to be because Freddy and I had married so young and had children within three years - before we had a chance to establish ourselves. I felt young, and free, and attractive, and for the first time I felt like I had the world before me. I turned the music up loud and let it pulsate through my body. Even doing that, something as simple as turning the music up loud, felt exhilarating. Because it was something I never did. I would not have dreamt of turning the music up loud with my children in the car, but tonight I felt I could do anything.

I had already researched a nice little bar I could go to. The reviews said that it was upscale, and consisted of a professional crowd. So that's where I had decided to go. As I pulled up, I suddenly felt nervous again. For the first time I thought of how nice it would have been to have a good girlfriend or two to meet me here. But because I had been home with the kids I really hadn't had any outside friendships. Thanks to Freddy and my new arrangement, however, I knew that would change soon. I had the car valet-parked so that I wouldn't have to worry about walking back to the car alone at night.

When I walked into the bar I sat at the counter and ordered a Sprite. I was not a big drinker, not even really a light drinker, plus I had to think about driving home, so I didn't want to order anything alcoholic. I nursed my Sprite for a bit, just enjoying being out, and I watched the crowd. They consisted of well-dressed, seemingly professional men, and gorgeously-dressed, seemingly professional women. A few of the tables consisted of three or more groups of women sitting, chatting, and laughing amongst themselves, and some of the other tables consisted of couples.

I people-watched for about 15 minutes, drinking my Sprite when a guy approached me. He politely introduced himself as Gregory and asked me my name. I'm not sure why, but I told him my name was Gisele, then he asked if he could sit and I said sure. Gregory was pretty short, and as he sat next to me I could feel myself looking down at him. But he was super polite, and I welcomed the opportunity to strike up a conversation.

Within just a few minutes of Gregory sitting down, I was already trying to figure out some excuse to leave. Apparently Gregory was an attorney, but I never got the chance to tell him that I was too because he never stopped talking. Gregory talked about his law practice, all the money he made, all the trips he took, and the two houses he owned, all before I had a chance to freshen my Sprite.

At one point I began to wonder if he even remembered that he was sitting next to someone, because he only seemed interested in hearing his own voice. Plus, he had really bad breath. I did not want to be rude or insensitive, so I just sat and listened to his monologue, but I was hoping and praying that it would end soon and I would be able to get away from him.

Eventually Gregory stopped talking long enough to ask me if I was married. I told him that I was happily married. He asked me very directly why my husband was not with me. I realized I did not have an answer for that, nor did I want to tell this total stranger what my arrangement with my husband was, and I especially did not want him to get any ideas. So I told Gregory that my husband was out of town. Gregory's face turned into a creepy sneer and I could tell what was on his mind. But I dashed his hopes very quickly by excusing myself to go to the ladies room. As I walked away from him I could see him checking me out, and it made me feel gross.

When I got to the ladies room I stood in front of the mirror just looking at myself. I asked myself, "What are you doing? Why are you here?" Truth is, I kind of felt out of place. I was not sitting at the table with a group of other women like some of the others, nor was I on the prowl like the single women who were sitting at the tables alone appeared to be. I splashed some water on my face and freshened up my makeup. But instead of going back out to the bar and back to bad breath Gregory, I veered right and walked right out of the bar. I had valet bring me my car, and because it was too early to go home, I went to the movies instead.

I sat in the theater with my small popcorn and small Diet Coke and laughed my butt off at the Sandra Bullock and Melissa McCarthy chick flick, and for the first time that night I was truly having a good time. When my movie was over, I grabbed some takeout for Freddy from his favorite Chinese restaurant, and headed home. When I got there Freddy was waiting up for me aimlessly flipping through the TV stations. I told him all about my night, minus the whole going to the movies. For some reason I hid that from him. I think it was because I didn't want to make him feel any pressure about his day out tomorrow. I didn't want him to feel like he'd have to pretend to not have had a good time on his night out just because I hadn't had a good time at the bar.

So I embellished a little bit and told him that after Gregory walked away, I started talking to this group of men and women and enjoyed sitting and chatting with them the rest of the night. He asked me if we had all exchanged phone numbers, and I told him that we had. I furthered the lie by telling him that we had all agreed to meet up again at the same spot next Friday.

Although Freddy seemed tense, he still appeared to be happy for me, as well as relieved that this night was over. After telling Freddy about bits and pieces of my night, I kicked my heels off and cuddled up on the sofa with him. We spent the next couple of hours just watching TV together and talking. If felt so great, just like old times.

Eventually we fell asleep, and as I awoke a few hours later, still wrapped in Freddy's arms, I realized that last night was worth it. If it meant it would make us closer and we would have more nights like the one we just had cuddled up and talking, and growing close, I knew then that I would keep this going. Even if it meant going to see a movie by myself every Friday night, I would do that, and make Freddy think I was living it up. That way he would feel free to do the same.

I kissed my husband softly on the cheek then went upstairs to shower before preparing breakfast for my family. Unknowingly, I had begun to hum and there was a pep in my step. I could already feel the positive effects of Freddy and my agreement to open our marriage. I already felt closer to him. Already, things were looking up.

14

Freddy

I woke up that Saturday after Stacy's night out on the couch. I could still smell Stacy's perfume from where she had lain next to me snuggled in the crook of my arm. It felt good to sit with her and laugh and talk. I was reminded of when we were just friends, back when we hung out and enjoyed each other's company. I stretched and yawned, willing myself to rise off the sofa. Although sleeping here with Stacy was nice, I knew my 6'1" body would pay for having slept here, unable to stretch out.

As I walked toward the kitchen I could smell the sweet smell of French toast and I knew Stacy was in a good mood. I peeked in the kitchen, watching her without her seeing me. I really loved that woman. I watched as she tried to reach something from the top of the kitchen cabinet, standing on the tips of her toes. As she reached higher her robe inched higher and I turned away to prevent getting aroused and needing a release. I knew that my day was today, and the last thing I wanted to do was go out there with sex on my mind. I was not against sleeping with someone else. Hell, what man would pass up such an opportunity when it was presented by his own wife? It's just that I didn't want to go into it thinking that way.

Unlike Stacy, who appeared to be apprehensive about going out, I was not. I was so excited to be able to get out there and socialize. It wasn't just about the sex. For me, it was more than that.

I think that's why so many men were afraid of marriage, because they felt like it would be a death sentence. A lot of men felt that getting married would be the end of their lives as they knew it. Marriage meant the end of hanging out and having guy time. It meant the end of noticing or conversing with attractive women, which was just unrealistic. Why should adding someone to your life (in my case a wife), mean I suddenly couldn't be entitled to have a life of my own? Why did marriage mean the end of individuality?

I was so happy that Stacy had proposed this, because the more I thought about it the more I realized that this would give us the opportunity to have a marriage that actually enriched our lives instead of taking away from it. Even without the sex, just the ability to go out, hang out and be essentially unrestricted put us ahead of the game. I couldn't wait to give this new life, our new life, a try.

I snuck away and went upstairs to take a shower. The kids were still asleep. I didn't know how, but those kids of ours managed to sleep through almost anything. I knew they'd be up soon though. There was no way they'd be able to resist the smell of mom's French toast. So I hurried. While in the shower I shaved and did all the little things that a man does to get ready for a night out on the town. It's probably too much information, but I trimmed the hair in my nose, clipped my toenails and groomed my man area. I'm not sure why I did that last step. I'd never done that before, but I was feeling wild and free so I just went for it. If for no other reason, maybe it would make Stacy spend a little extra time down there, since she didn't really like giving oral sex. She sure did like receiving though.

When I was all done, I threw on some gym shorts and a T-shirt. Usually, on Saturdays I did the yard work, but today I was too anxious and excited. So I didn't bother. Instead, I called up the neighborhood kid to do the yard and wash the cars, then I paid him with a big tip. He said, "Thanks, Mr. Valentin." When he noticed that I had paid him double what he'd asked for, he bounded away happily. Before he got to his dad's truck he yelled back, "Hey, next time I'll do the shrubs for free!" I was happy that I'd made that young man's day, because mine was going to be great.

As a change of pace, when we were finished with breakfast I took my family to the zoo. It had been a little while since we'd been and I was looking for a way to spend some extra time with them. Usually on Saturdays after doing the yard work I went out of town for work, but this week I decided to leave later. I had taken the day off, but I was still going to go out of town. That way if I did meet someone then at least it wouldn't be in my own backyard.

As we walked through the zoo, my son shrieked with excitement looking at all the animals, especially the ones that were extra scary-looking or dirty. My daughter seemed to take to the pretty ones, those with colorful feathers or long, elegant legs. I was just content to hold Stacy's hand and plant an occasional kiss on her lips. We had lunch while there at the zoo, and it was a good time even if a child's meal was five times what it normally cost. When we were done, the children were exhausted and fell asleep in the back of the car. When we got home, we laid them down in their beds and I went to grab my overnight bag. Stacy knew that I was going away and that this time the trip would be for pleasure and not business. I think she preferred that I not be in the same city if I was going to meet other women.

I grabbed my bag, gave Stacy a long, lingering kiss, kissed my babies goodnight and left. When I got in my car I put my jazz CD in the player and cruised along to the rhythmic music. I was definitely planning to make this a night that I would remember. When I got to the city where I usually went when I was working over the weekend, I made sure to go to a hotel well out of the way. Even though I had not been back to the hotel where Stacy had busted me with my coworker Leane, I still made sure to avoid it at all cost. I also avoided that area in general, so I wouldn't run into anyone I might know or might have conducted business with.

I checked into my room, took a quick shower, then got dressed. I was wearing some casual slacks and a button up shirt. I dabbed on a bit of cologne and surveyed myself in the mirror. I looked good. Even though I had managed to put on a few, I still knew how to dress, and despite having lost the "six pack" I used to have from my military days, I still had strong arms and legs. I grabbed my wallet and headed out the door. I wasn't headed anywhere in particular, just out to have a good time.

I walked for a little bit before I came to a club that had what sounded like jazz music floating out of its doors. I went inside and was immediately drawn to the ambience of the place. The place was decked in rich maroon fabrics with faux candles and had the sound of water everywhere. Drinks were being served by attractive women and muscular men. There was no food being served, but the entire middle of the bar was flanked by desserts of all types. The desserts along with the dark and earthy tone of the place gave the establishment a decadent feel.

I grabbed a table towards the back of the bar and ordered a drink as well as a slice of some type of cannoli. I wasn't into sweets, but tonight I thought I'd leave my mind open and try some different things. I had caught the attention of a woman just as soon as I walked in the bar and she kept watching me but I was not interested. I didn't want to just get with the first woman that I saw. If I wanted only sex, or wanted it that easy, then I could have just hired a prostitute.

What I wanted was an experience, and to truly meet some interesting women. Although I had told Stacy that I wanted to also meet some cool fellas that I could hang out with at a sports bar and catch a game, the truth was that I was only interested in meeting women. It wasn't just for sex, but I can't honestly say my plan was to get dressed up and meet interesting men. It just wasn't.

So, although I was trying to be nice to the woman who was staring at me, by smiling and raising my glass to her when she raised hers to me, I didn't want to sleep with this woman. However, judging by the way she kept licking her lips at me, crossing and re-crossing her legs, what she wanted was obvious. Although she was an attractive woman and I was really flattered, I wasn't interested, so I decided to just get up from where I was sitting and sit at the bar.

I sat down at the same time that another woman was sitting down about a seat over from me. When she sat down at least two men immediately appeared next to her, circling her and salivating like vultures. I couldn't blame them. This lady was hot. The kind of hot that makes happily married men cross the street when she walks by.

The guys openly gawked at her while simultaneously trying to appear cool and unaffected by her beauty, which they were doing a horrible job of pulling off. Still, I appreciated "Dumb and Dumber's" attempts, because as they fumbled all around this woman it gave me the perfect opportunity to watch her without her noticing.

This lady was beautiful, breathtakingly beautiful. She was of some type of oriental descent, I think, though nowadays it was so hard to tell. She seemed to be a bunch of different ethnicities all put together and blended well, adding an air of exoticism. This was probably one of the most beautiful women I had ever seen. Her hair was down to the top of her butt, and that was while it was held back in a ponytail. I imagined it would be even longer if she released it and let it fall. Her features were perfect, and her skin had a warm glow, yet another reminder that she was multiracial.

When she flipped her ponytail over her shoulder as she just did, no doubt sending her suitors mad with desire, her blouse rolled off her shoulder, revealing slender shoulders with voluptuous breasts that appeared as rounded mounds just above her blouse. Although her top was completely modest, save for revealing a bit of shoulder, she looked so damn sexy and it was obvious that she had a smoking hot body. Below the blouse, whose color I couldn't make out in the darkness of the room, she had on an above the knee skirt that showed off what appeared to be strong thighs and a rounded ass. I loved round asses. She also had on the highest heels that I had ever seen and I made a mental note to order Stacy a pair so she could wear them to bed.

Stacy. At the thought of Stacy I finally broke the spell I was under and was able to look away. I cleared my throat and for the first time the Beautiful Lady noticed that I was there. She flipped her ponytail my way as she peered at me over the rim of her glass of wine, and after she had taken a sip she looked away. I had not held this beautiful woman's attention for more than two seconds. She turned her attention back to her two suitors and I turned my attention to the drink that I had been nursing since I got there. I tossed it back then ordered another one. Although I was looking forward, I could still hear the conversation between the Beautiful Lady and the two men. Or should I say the conversation the two men were having with each other about the Beautiful Lady, who seemed bored and slightly irritated by their presence.

"Wow, you are beautiful," said man #1.

"Can I get you a drink?" said the other man, #2.

"No, you don't look like a 'drink' kind of woman, can I take you out to dinner?" answered man #1 before the Beautiful Lady could even speak or answer man #2's request.

"Hey man, won't you let the lady speak," defended man # 2. To which man #1 replied, "Look man, why are you even here? It's obvious that she is way out of your league."

Finally the Beautiful Lady spoke. She said, simply, "If you men will excuse me..." But she didn't get up. The men looked at each other quizzically trying to decide what to do, then both walked off kind of stunned. Despite trying to hold it back, a chuckle escaped me and I could not resist. In just a few words the Beautiful Lady had managed to dismiss both men without being mean and without saying much at all. That let me know that in addition to being beautiful, she was also intelligent. The Beautiful Lady appeared to be the total package.

With the two men gone, a third approached. The Beautiful Lady let out a low, though seemingly exasperated sigh. I was just as confused as the next man when it came to reading women, but even I could tell that all this woman wanted was to be left alone. After she dismissed the third man, and we were essentially alone, I didn't dare say a word to her. I could tell that she just wanted to get out and have some time to herself, and I respected that. We were alone for what felt like no more than five minutes when someone approached again. I did not bother to look up, as I heard the rustle of someone approaching. I was surprised when the footsteps stopped near me.

I looked up to find the lady that was watching me earlier now face to face with me. She asked me if she could sit to which I replied an unsteady "sure." She asked me if I was in town for business or pleasure, and I quickly answered "Business." She asked me what I did and I said pharmaceutical sales. She asked me if I was married and even though I replied that I was, and with two children, she only inched closer to me and began brushing her knee against mine.

When she offered to buy me another drink, I declined and told her that I'd had enough, and that

I would be leaving soon. When she looked up at me eagerly, I replied that I would be leaving alone. She stood up and stared me down before turning on her heels and stomping off.

This time it was the Beautiful Lady's turn to let out a soft chuckle of her own. I guess I shouldn't have been surprised that she could hear my conversation since I could hear hers too, but I was still embarrassed that she had been listening in. I hoped she didn't think I was rude, or closed off to meeting new people, since I'd informed the other lady that I was married. I opened my mouth to say something, right as she was putting down a few dollars to pay for her drinks. I couldn't find any words to say, and the Beautiful Lady chuckled again and said "Just can't get a break tonight." Then she walked away.

I ordered my brain to find something witty to say. Or to say anything that would make her sit for just a few minutes longer. Even though we hadn't been talking I had just enjoyed sitting and watching her. Or even just knowing that she was sitting so close to me. But my brain shut off and my mouth was broken, and the only thing working were my eyes as they watched her walk away. By the time I came to my senses and realized I had to talk to the

Beautiful Lady if for no other reason than to find out if she visited this spot regularly, a few minutes had passed. I hurriedly threw a few dollars down on the bar, enough to pay for my drinks and the cannoli I'd half eaten, then I rushed outside to catch the Beautiful Lady. But she was gone. Just like that I had lost my opportunity to talk to and get to know one of the most beautiful women I had even seen.

The valet looked at me strangely as I peered around the corner of the bar and stood in the middle of the street looking every which way to see if the Beautiful Lady had walked, or caught a cab, or drove away. When I asked the valet if a beautiful lady had come this way, he looked at me strangely and told me he didn't know who I was talking about. That made me wonder if I had imagined this woman, because surely any man who ever saw this woman would know that she was the Beautiful Lady I was talking about. I told the valet guy, "Never mind", then proceeded to mentally kick myself all the way back to my hotel.

How had I let that woman get away? I didn't want to marry her or anything, but I definitely wished I had gotten her number. At a minimum it would have been nice to talk to someone like her. She was definitely the type of woman I could see myself striking up a friendship with, which is what this experience was supposed to be all about. But it was not to be. I went back to my hotel room and ordered room service, then I channel-surfed until I ran across that new Sylvester Stallone movie on the Pay Per View station. I ordered the movie and sat back and enjoyed my steak. But I couldn't get the Beautiful Lady off my mind. I knew I had wasted the opportunity of a lifetime. I just hoped that we crossed paths again.

The next day I woke up early so that I could make the drive back home in time to take my family to church. I felt so down, almost like a lovesick teenager. I kept thinking about the Beautiful Lady. I looked for her when I checked out and as valet drove my car around. I even looked around my car. I was being an idiot at that point. It wasn't like she would be randomly walking around my car.

I drove home in a daze. When I got home even the mood at home was somber. When I walked through the door Stacy was still in her PJ's and the children were in theirs. Stacy informed me that we would be missing church today because she was not feeling well. Then she went upstairs to lie down.

Stacy did not ask me about my night and I didn't volunteer any information. Truth be told, I didn't think she wanted to know, and I certainly didn't want to divulge. I knew I would look like a fool if I told my wife I had spent my evening pining away behind a woman I had never even talked to, especially after Stacy'd had such a lively night meeting so many different people, including men.

Stacy had already fed the children cereal and fruit, so I took over with getting them dressed, out of the house, and out of Stacy's hair. Before I left, however, I brought Stacy up some tea and soup. She was lying in bed when I got up there. She had bags under her eyes as if she hadn't slept all night. I hoped it wasn't because I was out. I felt her forehead and she didn't feel particularly hot. I told her I was taking the children outside to burn off some energy but that she could call me if she needed anything at all. I put her cell phone next to her, kissed her on her forehead, and left the room. I hated to admit it but I was kind of happy to have the time to myself. If nothing else, it would give me a chance to think about the Beautiful Lady, which is what I did for the rest of that day.

And the following week. Before I knew it, it was Saturday again and my turn to go out. Stacy had gone out the day before and had told me that she'd had a good time. She had met up with the same group from the previous week and they had sipped wine and just talked about life. She didn't seem as cheerful as the previous week, but I figured it was just that she trying to downplay all the fun she was having. When we were growing up Stacy had always been very popular, always the center of attention, and I knew she was happy to be back out there in the crowd. Maybe she didn't want to let on how much she was enjoying herself, but I knew she was. Tonight I planned on doing the same. Without question I was heading back to that little jazz spot I had found the previous week. It was obvious that I was going there looking for the Beautiful Lady. As much as I wanted to see her, a part of me hoped she wasn't there so that I could get her out of my mind and truly seize this opportunity to meet different people, instead of sitting around thinking about one.

When I got there I checked in and met with my clients a bit earlier than I would have usually scheduled them. I was trying to conclude the business portion of my evening as quickly as possible, so that I could get to the reason I really came out here: to meet the Beautiful Lady. I got to the club about an hour before I did last time and this time I didn't bother going to a table. Instead I sat right where I'd sat before, kind of hoping the Beautiful Lady would do the same. Not wanting to tempt fate, I ordered the same drink as before and another cannoli, even though they weren't that good. I sat there for one hour, then two.

While there waiting, I people-watched as I had before. Just as before, there was the same crowd. The people weren't the same, but it was the same crowd. As had been the case the last time, there was another desperate woman sitting in the corner, and sitting a table over were two or three women chatting, trying to notice who was noticing them. I saw some of the same kinds of guys who were there last time, walking around trying to pick up as many women as possible, or at least the one woman who would let them get what they came for. I saw the young folks trying to put up the pretense of being older and more established than they were, and I saw the older ones trying to betray their years and appear to be younger. I saw a lot of people, but I didn't see the one I came for.

After three hours of being there I started talking to a woman who had been sitting at a table with her friend. I sent a drink over to them both, and when the one that I thought was attractive turned around, I raised my drink in acknowledgement. I hoped I was doing this the right way. It had been ages since I had been in the dating world, not that I necessarily was now. But I had noticed that when a guy was interested, or even when a woman was interested in a guy, they sent a drink to that person. So that's what I did. I felt a little bit like I was learning on the job. The lady that I was interested in raised her drink back to me then turned back to her friend. I wondered what I should do next. I didn't want to come off like a prowler or one of the guys looking to pick up someone for a one night stand. But I knew that I needed to do something.

As I thought it over, preparing to make my move, I saw that the attractive woman was on her way over. It still took me by surprise that women approached men nowadays. Back when I was dating it was not done that way. This new way of doing things made me feel old. But I was determined to recapture some of my young man days. So I decided to get with the program. When she got to my table I pulled out the chair for her, silently inviting her to sit. She sat down and thanked me for the drink. I went for casual and told her it was no problem. I asked her about herself and she filled me in that she was a divorced mother of three and was out for the evening with her friend. She was a high school teacher and was in graduate school pursuing her master's in education. She said she'd ultimately wanted to become a principal.

I was impressed. Here was an attractive, obviously driven and ambitious woman sitting right beside me and all I could think about was the lady I'd hardly met from before. When the attractive woman asked me about myself I told her as little as possible. When she asked what I did I blandly told her I was in sales, and when she asked if I was married I didn't answer her question. I then burped rudely at the table. It appalled her and I sort of smiled inwardly. I was hoping for that reaction.

I was trying the only way I knew how to end this conversation so I could order room service again and catch another rental movie. Maybe this time I would rent a porno and get some kind of action. I had already decided that I no longer wanted to have an open marriage. This was not going how I had thought it would and the idea of dating again, of learning new rules and playing all those games again just made me tired. I hoped I was not being unfair to Stacy by asking that we stop this and find other ways to spice up our marriage and our lives, especially since it seemed like she was having so much fun. But I was over this.

After about the third burp the attractive woman was properly repulsed and excused herself to go back to the table with her friend. I knew that she was telling her friend about my rude behavior because her friend kept turning around to look at me, and with a not so nice look on her face. I paid for my drink and sent two more drinks over to the attractive woman and her friend. That was my way of apologizing for being such a jerk. I then prepared to leave.

On my way out of the jazz club, much to my disbelief, I ran right into the Beautiful Lady - literally. When she regained her footing, after I had nearly knocked her down, she looked up at me and said, "I remember you." Those were the sweetest words I ever heard. This time I was determined not to let her get away. I spoke up and said "I remember you too. In fact, I couldn't get you off my mind."

I couldn't believe I had just said that! It was like my mind was saying exactly what I was thinking. Once again I had blown it. I knew this Beautiful Lady would think I was some kind of stalker. But instead she just smiled up at me and asked me if I was leaving already. I told her that I was but that I would like her to come with me. When she raised her eyebrows, I quickly clarified that I would like to take her to dinner. She thought it over for a bit while looking me right in the eyes, almost like she was trying to see into my soul. I looked right back, wanting her to see that I was a good guy. To my surprise, she agreed. I hailed a taxi cab and asked them to bring us to the best seafood restaurant in town. When she smiled over at me, I nervously asked, "What? Is seafood ok?" She replied, "Seafood is perfect. It's my favorite in fact."

We rode to the restaurant in a comfortable silence. Neither of us where saying anything, but my heart was beating a mile a minute. For a brief moment I wondered if she could hear it. She smiled up at me again, and immediately put my mind at ease. I didn't know why this perfect stranger that I had just met, already had such an effect on me.

When we got to the restaurant and were seated, we began to talk like old friends. The Beautiful Lady told me that she was an artist. She shared with me that she lived in the city, but also had a condo on the water, and that is where she did all of her paintings. The Beautiful Lady told me she traveled extensively, and made a habit of living her life according to her own rules. Apparently, once upon a time she had not been that way. But after going through school and becoming an Accountant just to please her family, she realized that life was too short. So she had decided to start living it the way she wanted.

Although she was a Certified Public Accountant, she proudly professed that she had never officially worked in that capacity in her life. She said she loved painting because it gave her an opportunity to create whatever she wanted to create, and go wherever she wanted to go. She never had to follow rules, or keep a schedule, and she told me she liked it that way.

I was not surprised to hear that the Beautiful Lady, whose name I learned was Serita, was a free spirit. I definitely picked up that vibe from her the first time I saw her, and that was without her saying a word. Knowing that she was a free spirit and the type of person who grabbed life by the horns made me like her even more. Perhaps that is what attracted me so strongly to her. Besides the fact that she was absolutely stunningly beautiful, maybe a part of me wanted her free spirit to rub off on me, to loosen me up a bit. I told Serita (who I still thought of in my head as the Beautiful Lady because the description fit so perfectly) everything about me.

For some reason I was totally, painfully honest with this stranger. I told her how Stacy and I met, how we'd fallen in love and married and had children soon after. I told her about my work and what I did. I didn't tell her about Stacy's work or what I might consider Stacy's business out of respect for my wife, but I did tell her about the affair and Stacy and my agreement that we would open up our marriage. I told her that I was happily married and not looking to leave my wife for anyone, but that I definitely wanted to get to know her better. I told her that from the moment I saw her that I had felt a strange connection to her and was certainly captivated, as were the rest of the men, by her beauty, but that I hadn't spoken to her for fear of being shot down.

Serita listened to me intently, ever so often taking a sip of her drink. When I was done speaking she said, "You have a beautiful soul and I'm happy I met you." She told me that she had not planned on coming out tonight but that something had made her. She said softly that she thought that "something" was me. Serita told me that she dated casually but that she was not the commitment type. "Been there done that", she said. Serita said that she would also like to get to know me better and knowing that Saturdays were my "day out" agreed to meet me back at the jazz club next week, same time. I hid it well, but when she said that I felt so joyful. I didn't know how I was going to get through the rest of the week with the excitement and anticipation I knew I would feel awaiting next Saturday.

When we left the restaurant, after having talked for hours, neither of us wanted the night to end, so we went to a local coffee shop and talked the night away. By the time we were preparing to leave, the sun was coming up and it was time for me to head back home. I kissed Serita on her forehead even though my body was roaring to feel hers against mine, and I told her that I'd see her next week. We didn't exchange numbers because she hadn't wanted to. She said that we would let fate bring us back together and if something came up and we weren't able to meet for whatever reason, then we would find each other again if it was meant to be. I hoped she would be back next week like we had agreed upon. It was bad enough that I would have to wait another week just to see her. I couldn't imagine having to wait longer than that.

I got back to the hotel and only had time to grab my overnight bag before hitting the road to head back home. I couldn't believe I had stayed out all night talking to the Beautiful Lady, Serita. I drove all the way home with thoughts of her on my mind and with thoughts of when I would see her again next week.

When I got home I asked Stacy if it was okay if we skipped church this week because I was exhausted. Stacy looked at me skeptically, and I could tell she wanted to ask about my night, about why I had come back home so tired, but she didn't. For some reason she seemed to have adopted a policy of "Don't ask, don't tell", and that was fine with me. I didn't want to tell her about the Beautiful Lady and risk her seeing how excited talking about her made me. I didn't want Stacy to see through me and see how much I was into this woman. After all, the rules stated that we were not to get too involved or see the same person repeatedly. But I was willing to break the rules for this woman, so the less I said, the better.

I kissed Stacy on the lips and kissed my little ones, then I went upstairs and climbed into bed. I fell asleep with thoughts of Serita on my mind. I woke up in a cold sweat after having dreamt that I had missed Saturday and the opportunity to see Serita again. I don't know how this happened, but I was already in deeper than I was supposed to be. The thought of that made me more than a little nervous.

15

Stacy

I didn't know what Freddy's problem was, but he came home and went right to sleep. Had he been out all night? And if so, with whom? I had promised myself I would not ask, because that was the only way to get through this, but I have to admit that I was curious.

Freddy seemed to be having a lot more fun with this open marriage thing than I was. Every week I had started going to the movies, while pretending to be out at events meeting all these people. As far as Freddy was concerned, I was the talk of the town, in the spotlight, having these wonderful experiences. When really I was just enjoying my time alone. It felt good to be out by myself for a while, without the children. Every other day of my life, with the exception of the time I had on Friday nights, I was with my children. So it felt good to just have some personal adult time away. Even if I wasn't meeting anyone.

But Freddy obviously was. He had started leaving earlier to get to where he was going. Although he got back in time to get to church, he was apparently too exhausted to go. The ease in which he rolled right into this open marriage thing made me wonder if he already had someone in mind when I proposed this? And why did he get back home so exhausted? Was he already in a sexual relationship with someone?

The very idea of it made me sick to my stomach. I mean physically ill. I remembered that first week he went out. I had spent the entire night alternating between crying and throwing up. I had stayed up the whole night wondering, worrying, and regretting sending my husband out there to potentially be with other women.

When Freddy got home I pretended that I had felt unwell so that I could be alone, but also in case he noticed the bags under my eyes or the fact that I looked like I hadn't slept. But I don't think Freddy noticed, or cared, at all. He brought me some lukewarm soup and a cup of tea and got out of the house so fast that it almost made my head spin. It was like he didn't want to be near me. He had said he was taking the children outside to burn off some energy, but maybe he had been out there on the phone talking to whomever this woman or these women were.

My thoughts drove me crazy. So I tried to suppress them. I had made it a point not to ask Freddy about what he did and who he met. The most I asked, and even that was a struggle, was whether or not he'd had fun. He always replied that he had. I'll bet he did.

I couldn't miss the boat again. I wasn't willing to. I had already sat back, unaware, while Freddy had that affair. Now here I was again, sitting back while he was enjoying this opportunity. I didn't want to wait until I was frustrated or angry with Freddy to get out there like I had done before, in response to his infidelity. I wanted to get out there now, and seize this opportunity for me. So I resolved to step outside of my comfort zone and actually put forth some effort into meeting new people. I really wanted this to work for us, so that meant I had to do my part.

For the most part, I had to admit, Freddy and I had gotten more intimate and closer during our family time. I think it was the mere fact that we knew we'd be able to have time to and for ourselves during at least one day of the week that made us enjoy our family time even more. We had started having dinner together every night, except those Saturday nights that Freddy was away, and we'd started having more family outings. Freddy and I talked more and we made love more.

The only thing seemingly negatively affected was our spiritual lives. We had missed church two weeks in a row – the first week when I was "ill" from staying up all night and the second week when Freddy came home exhausted from his night of doing God knows what with God knows who. But it didn't stop there.

Over the course of the next few months we missed more church than we attended. It was always for what seemed like a legitimate reason: one of the kids got sick, or Freddy wanted to sleep in so he'd be rested for the week ahead. But I was beginning to think this was just our way of avoiding God. I didn't think we were doing anything wrong necessarily. After all, we had both consented and the only people who could have a say-so about what we did in our marriage was us. I just think that maybe we didn't know how to make sense of what we were doing. So it made it hard to come before God, at least for us.

I resolved that we would get better about that too. So I had some work to do. The first order of business was to put myself out there. When my next Friday came around, I decided I wouldn't play it safe. It had been at least four or five months since we had opened our marriage and it was time for me to step it up. I dressed in a lace-covered top and a skirt that showed off my legs, as well as one of my best features – my ass. I went to the salon to get my hair done and I put on some of my boldest lipstick. When Freddy saw me his eyes widened and I could see him cast an appreciative look over my body. That gave me an extra boost of confidence. I walked out of the door with my head held high ready to own the night. Tonight I would not be going to the movies.

When I got to the first club I just sat back and watched. I had wanted to see how things were done. I noticed that a lot of the women were actually the aggressors, which I thought was strange and unusual, but I decided to play along. It seemed like the thing to do was to either send a good-looking man a drink, or a couple times I saw a few of the bolder women walk right up to a man. I was not that bold, so I settled on sending a drink. The first time I sent a drink to a guy it worked like a charm and he came right over. But I didn't like the way he talked to me when he came over. He was very pushy and entitled, as if me sending him a drink somehow meant that I wanted more. I was not into that. I talked to him for a few minutes, just to be nice. But then I pretended to get a phone call so I could step outside and away from Mr. Entitled.

When I got back in I decided to do things differently. I would not send another man another drink. That just wasn't me. I was an old-fashioned kind of woman. So I was going to do things my way. I took a new approach. I made up my mind to just enjoy myself and pretend the guys weren't even there. That had always worked for me before. In fact, as I looked around the club, it seemed like the ladies getting the most attention were the ones just enjoying themselves and paying little mind to the men around them. The sheer act of them ignoring the men and just doing their own thing seemed to make the men chase them more. So that's what I did.

I ordered a glass of wine and after I had taken my time and enjoyed every sip, I went to the dance floor and danced. A lot of the women were on the dance floor with their friends and I thought how it would be just as nice to meet a few nice ladies to go out with as it would be to meet a guy. But I definitely didn't know how to approach another woman and strike up a conversation, especially since I did not want to come across as gay. Most people established friendships based on common interests. That's how people became friends with coworkers, for example. But I didn't have that luxury. So I hoped that I would organically meet some nice, interesting, and drama-free women that I could go out with. But for now I was just going to dance and enjoy my night. Even if it was by myself.

Within 10 minutes of getting on the dance floor, however, I was joined by a man who had dance moves better than mine. Not that I had many, since it had been so long since I had gone out, let alone gone dancing. The dancing man was not my type. As a matter of fact, I was inclined to think I wasn't his type either, if you know what I mean, but he smelled great and I was having a good time nonetheless.

We danced to a couple of songs together, and before I had a chance to take a break, another guy came up and started to dance with me. By "with me" I really mean "on me" because the only thing he wanted to do was bump and grind. But I did that too. Even though my first instinct was to tell him to get lost and to get off my butt, I decided to just go with the flow and open myself up to new experiences. So I bumped and grinded with that guy until I felt him grow hard against my ass. That was just too much, so I excused myself to go get a drink and freshen up my makeup.

When I went back onto the dance floor, having finished off a new glass of wine, I started right back up dancing. I noticed that as the hour grew later, the dancing got freakier, and so did I. I don't know if the glasses of wine had loosened me up or if it was that I was just having so much fun, but I had gotten to the point where I was moving my ass across whatever man I was dancing with, and was even beginning to get aroused when I felt one of them grow hard against me. This time instead of shying away from it, I moved slower, more sensually. I was willing the man to grow harder, enjoying the power I had over these men. It was at least two hours past the time I was supposed to be home when I left the club. Because I had been drinking, I hailed a taxi to bring me home, which took even longer.

By the time I got home Freddy was asleep in bed. I climbed in bed next to him, but instead of falling asleep I just felt horny. I pulled Freddy's pants down, hiked my skirt up and sat my already moist pussy on him. Although he had been sound asleep, his dick began to wake up and as he mumbled, "What are you doing? What time is it?" I was already riding his dick. I rode it so hard and fast that Freddy came even before he was fully awake. He had tried to resist and hold off a bit longer, but I was relentless, pounding my pussy down on him so hard the bed squeaked and the covers fell to the floor. I felt so wild and so horny.

When Freddy came I came too, and as our juices mixed together and began to pour out of me, I leaned down and began to suck Freddy's dick clean. Freddy gasped and I could feel him getting hard again, so I kept sucking. Usually I didn't like to give oral sex, but tonight his dick tasted so good that I didn't want to let it out of my mouth. Plus I liked the way it made Freddy squirm and lose control.

Because he had just cum, it took Freddy a while to cum again so I used the time I had to practice my dick-sucking technique. I had never felt really good at it, so tonight I experimented. I did more of the things that made Freddy's toes curl and that made him almost cry out, and I paid attention to the things that got less of a response from him. I sucked the tip of his dick, which he liked. I licked the length of it up and down. I licked the sides, the front, the back, stopping only to swirl my tongue around the head and lick and swallow the thick and sticky fluid that came out of the tip. I sucked Freddy's balls (for the first time) and looked up at him – looked him right square in the eyes – as I deep-throated him. I took all of him into my mouth, past my mouth and down into the back of my throat. Then I closed my mouth around his dick and began to suck, alternating between soft and slow, long and hard.

Freddy looked down at me and unable to control himself released his cum down the back of my throat. It was so deep I had no choice but to swallow. When I had taken it all, I looked up at Freddy's face, which was washed in amazement, then I licked my lips. I made sure to get it all, and let Freddy know how good it had been to me. Freddy looked at me in amazement and said, "You are the fucking best. I love you." Then he fell asleep.

I smiled. I liked this side of me. I liked how it made me feel powerful and attractive and in control. I especially liked how it made me perform sexually and my husband's response to it. I decided I would do this every weekend. I would go out and have a good time, then come back home and fuck my husband senseless. Because I was feeling reckless and uninhibited, I thought maybe some guy out there would get lucky and I'd fuck him too. With a drunken giggle I fell asleep thinking of how this had been one of the best nights of my life, and how I planned to top this experience next week.

Sure enough, the next week, and the weeks thereafter, I got better at the whole going out and having a good time thing. I had gone shopping again to make sure I had beautiful clothes to wear. I bought classy two-piece skirt sets and A-line dresses that accentuated my figure. I definitely was sexily dressed, but also classy. I had bought a treadmill and began working out, so I had managed to lose a few pounds and was really looking good. My hair was growing out from the haircut and I let it. I liked the way having longer hair allowed me to have more styling options. I also thought it made me look sexier. I loved the way I looked and the way I felt.

I was definitely feeling more confident. My newfound confidence from going out was carrying over into everything else. I had even started thinking about starting my own law consulting firm. That way I could still practice law on my own time and not have it take too much time away from my children. Two weeks ago I had begun researching law consulting and was currently looking at some website designers to help me put up a website and get started. I was nervous about stepping back into the working world, but it was a nervous excitement.

Opening our marriage had opened my whole world and I was eternally grateful. I was no longer dying on the vine but was in full blossom in life. The only thing that was still sort of suffering was our church time. We hardly ever went to church, let alone read our bibles. When we did go, we got there late and never stayed long after church anymore. I think we had just gotten busy in our new lives.

The one thing I hadn't done yet, though, was sleep with anyone else. But I was suddenly in the mood to take things to the next level. I could tell that Freddy had already started sexual relationships with some of the women he'd met, and my decision to take it there didn't have anything to do with him so much as the fact that I was just really comfortable being in my own skin. I wanted a new man to experience that comfort.

Plus, I was curious to try out my skills on someone else. I already knew that I could rock Freddy's world, but now I wanted to see what else I could do. Tonight would be somebody's lucky night, and if I picked right, it would be mine too.

16

Freddy

"Happy Birthday to you. Happy Birthday to you. Happy Birthday, dear Henry. Happy birthday to you." We were at The Party Palace celebrating my son's seventh birthday, and were having a ball. Though probably not as much fun as he and his friends were having.

My son and six of his little friends from his first grade class were all clamoring to get the biggest slice of cake, while my eight year old daughter and her best friend were whispering and trading secrets back and forth like big girls. Whether they thought they were big girls or not, they were still eager to get their hands on some cake and ice cream.

I sighed. Three years had passed so quickly and although good things had happened for our family, it was still scary to think of how fast my little ones were growing up. Before I knew it my little girl would be moving out of the house and the mere thought of that made me feel uneasy. I wanted to keep Henry and Hannah children for as long as possible. I didn't want to turn around and they become adults right before my eyes. This made me want to slow down and enjoy my family more. I made a mental note to do just that.

Still, I liked all the changes that had happened for our family over the last few years. Both of our children were now in school, which had freed Stacy up and given her the time she needed to grow her career. She had started a law consulting business and it had done so well that she had been recruited and hired on by a top-notch law firm. Stacy sometimes commented that she missed the freedom and flexibility of working on her own and for herself, but she loved having a career and feeling so productive.

I know Stacy also loved that she was able to shop and do the things she hadn't been able to do while she stayed at home caring for our children when they were young. I appreciated the sacrifice she made of putting her career on hold, so I never complained about her shopping. She deserved it.

Speaking of Stacy, my breath caught as I saw her walk my way. She had gone to the counter to get some extra spoons for the children to eat Henry's birthday cake and I watched her, feeling so much love and lust as she swayed back to our table. She was wearing jeans with an off-the-shoulder top and her long hair pulled up into a messy bun. On her feet were heels and she looked so casually sexy.

Nowadays, since going back to work and having lost all the baby weight, Stacy always wore heels and always looked so damn sexy. Even when she wasn't trying to. I couldn't get enough of my wife. I especially loved seeing all the men check her out and eye me enviously when they realized she was mine.

I was such a lucky man. In more ways than one. I was still seeing Serita. We were legitimate friends, but we also had some of the best sex I've ever had before. I looked forward to my out of town trips like never before. Although I was growing tired of a career in pharmaceutical sales, I loved the job if for no other reason than the fact that it allowed me to work out of town every weekend and see Serita. I didn't think I loved her, but I sometimes wondered if I might be falling for her more than what was allowed with our rules.

Our marriage was still open and happier than ever, but we still had rules to follow. The rules were, among other things, that we were not to fall in love with the person or keep seeing the person over an extended period of time. We never defined what was extended, but I was sure that Stacy would not like it if she knew that I had been seeing Serita for a few years now. Thankfully, she wouldn't know. Not if I could help it. For all I knew Stacy was breaking the rules too. We had long adopted a 'Don't ask, don't tell' policy and I was not going to tell, so hopefully she was not going to ask.

After we cut the cake, we allowed the children to run around and play for a little bit longer. Henry opened his presents, and then shortly thereafter the parents began to take their children home. Stacy and I cleaned up and took down all the decorations, then we left and headed back home. Hannah's friend had already gotten permission from her mom to stay the night, so we loaded her up, along with all of Henry's birthday presents and headed home. It was a Saturday. Although I was not scheduled to work, I was still heading out of town to see Serita.

Stacy and I had kept our schedule of her having Fridays and me having Saturdays. So after I brought all of the leftover cake and the presents and party supplies out of the car and into the house, I ran upstairs to get my overnight bag. I had pre-packed it and it was ready to go. I gave Stacy a long, lingering kiss, and she kissed me strongly right back. There was no more animosity or weirdness when either of us were going out. We had long accepted and grown to respect each other's time out and away. I loved that Stacy had a life of her own and I loved the effect that it had on the rest of her life and on our life together. Stacy loved that I had my own stuff going on too. After I kissed her, I went to kiss my son and daughter. Neither of them were very interested in me as my son was playing with his new toys and my daughter was hanging out with her little friend.

I left the house after saying my goodbyes. On the drive there I texted Serita the time that I would be there and I got a little shiver of excitement when she texted me back "I'll be there. I'll be open." I knew what she meant by open and I couldn't wait. When I got to the hotel suite that Serita and I usually reserved, the suite that had become our spot, I began to set up. I had bought some sex toys and had decided to step things up a bit. I bought a vibrator (for her), massagers, anal toys (also for her) and cock rings, and because I knew that Serita was "open" to anything and everything, I knew she would be ready to try these toys.

After I had set everything up, I took a shower and ordered room service. Room service came just as I was stepping out of the shower and I opened the door with my towel wrapped around me. As I signed for our food I saw Serita approaching the door. She was in a tan brown light trench coat and her signature six inch heels. I couldn't hear them clicking on the carpet, but even without looking down I knew she would be wearing them and I immediately began to imagine sexing her in her heels. Serita liked being naked except for her heels, and I liked her that way.

When Serita got to the door as the room service attendant was pulling the cart away, another young woman starting walking towards us. I was trying not to stare but the woman was gorgeous and sexy as hell. She had on a tight, short, expensive-looking black dress and tall, super sharp-looking high heels and I found myself watching her walk our way.

Before I realized what had happened the young woman I had been watching walked right up to Serita and stood next to her. She reached her hand out to me and introduced herself as Cree. I was confused. I didn't know why she was standing there, until she gave a sly, seductive smile to Serita, then I knew. My dick got hard as Serita sidled up to Cree and told me that she would be joining us this evening. With big imploring eyes she looked up at me and asked if that was okay. I stammered, "Yeah, yes, that would be great." They giggled as they both walked into the room.

I closed the door behind them, preparing to tell them that I had ordered room service for two, so Cree could take mine, but when I turned around Serita was already on her knees. She snatched my towel off of me and in one motion took my dick into her mouth. My head dropped back and I closed my eyes. But not before seeing Cree get on her knees behind Serita and begin to massage Serita's clitoris while kissing her neck.

Serita moaned with my dick in her mouth and I could feel the warmth of her breath encircle my dick. As Cree massaged Serita's clitoris, she began to suck longer and harder and got really sloppy and wet with her sucking. I could hear her mouth make a sloshing wetness sound around my dick as she sucked and licked and then a suction noise as she swallowed the wetness. After a minute the sucking stopped and I looked down just in time to see Cree switch places with Serita and begin to suck my dick. By then I could barely take it and my knees were beginning to buckle. If they didn't stop what they were doing, I was going to cum real soon.

I eased my dick out of Cree's mouth and laid her down on her back. I lifted up her little black dress and slid down her barely there thong panties and used my tongue to give her the same pleasure that she and Serita had given me. As Cree arched her back and moaned with her legs wrapped around my neck, she and Serita kissed. Serita sucked Cree's breasts as Cree grinded her pussy into my face. She tasted so fucking sweet that I took my time lapping up her juices. I let my tongue move up and down her clit, then I moved it in slow circles around the bulb.

Cree got wetter and wetter. As she cried out, Serita tapped me on the shoulder, gesturing for me to let her have a go. When I moved to the side, she bent down and buried her face between Cree's legs. As she bent over, her skirt was hiked in the air and I could see that she was panty-less. She grabbed my hand and pulled me closer to her, to the point where my dick was right behind her pussy.

I knew that I should probably leave to get a condom, but I was enjoying watching Serita eat Cree's pussy right in front of me. The wetness of Serita's pussy against the hardness of my dick was intoxicating. I kneeled behind her, grinding my dick as close to her wetness as I could get it. I wanted so badly to just put it inside her raw, but I didn't. I grinded it against her and as her wetness began to drip down my dick, I pulled her hair back and ground it next to her harder.

As I bucked against her, she moaned and Cree moaned and all the moans began to get to me. I couldn't help myself. I began to push myself harder against the back of Serita's pussy and before I knew it the tip of my dick had found the entrance of her pussy. Even as something inside me said to wrap it up, I let my dick ease, effortlessly, into Serita's dripping wet pussy.

When it got inside, it was so wet and slippery that I lost control. I began to fuck Serita so hard, grunting like an animal, that she could not continue to eat Cree's pussy. Cree got up and bent over next to Serita making her pussy available to me. I had never had a threesome before, but I relished the opportunity to fuck two beautiful, sexy women at once.

With Cree's ass up in the air, I withdrew my dick from Serita's pussy and put it, raw, into Cree's pussy. Cree was just as wet as Serita and I fucked her just as hard. I pounded Cree's pussy, from the back, hard and rough and only stopped long enough to pull out of Cree's pussy and back into Serita's. I fucked them both, hard, and with a loud and hard grunt I came deep inside Cree's pussy, holding her ass steady while I poured all of myself inside her.

When I was done I collapsed beside the beautiful women, body shivering and pulsing in ecstasy as I watched Serita drink my cum out of Cree's pussy. I couldn't believe that this was my life. I couldn't believe how lucky I was. I pinched myself, just to make sure I wasn't dreaming, then fell asleep lying across Cree's breasts with Serita's head resting mere inches from my spent dick.

I was the luckiest man alive. I couldn't imagine ever having to give this up. Rules be damned. Anything other than what I wanted to do, when I wanted to do it, be damned. I would never go back to the life I used to live. I was living every man's fantasy and I was never giving it up. Ever.

17

Stacy

We met at a bar.

He was wearing black slacks, a black linen shirt, and instead of the traditional black loafers one might have expected, he had on camel-colored gators. I thought that set him apart, gave him an edge, and it immediately made me want to get to know him better. I was in a bold and frisky mood, so I sent him a drink. When he received it, along with the hand-written message I had sent via the cocktail waitress, he raised his glass in acknowledgement of the drink, but he did not immediately come over. Normally, I am a southern belle, but tonight I decided I would be "that woman" and I allowed myself to be the pursuer. I watched him as he flirted with the other women. I watched as they shamelessly flirted back with him. All the while he watched me watching him, and I decided that I was enjoying this game we were playing.

At some point I decided to take it up a notch.

I went out to the dance floor and started to dance seductively. This whole show was for him, and he knew it. I had already changed clothes after work, and instead of my conservative navy blue pencil skirt and blazer, I was wearing a short and tight little black dress that showed off my natural double D's, even as the dress accentuated my tight ass. My ass had always been my secret weapon. I wielded it tonight like a sword.

I worked my ass around and around and grinded it up against the first man who had the nerve to dance up on me on the dance floor. I moved it around his dick until I felt its stiffness, then I abruptly left the dance floor to get a drink. But really I left to reassess my position in this little cat and mouse game we were playing.

When I got to the barstool and looked over my shoulder, I saw that I had Mr. Man's full attention, along with the attention of about five other men. This time Mr. Man sent me a drink. Instead of raising my drink to him as he did me, I declined it and sent it back. I had decided that I wanted to be pursued. I declined the next three drinks that were sent to me from three different men, all the while rocking on my barstool as if I was grooving to the music. But really I was letting Mr. Man get a glimpse of how good I would ride his dick when given the chance.

Luckily, the chance came quickly.

I saw him approach me out of the corner of my eye, but I pretended not to notice. I was prepared to play coy and extend this little game of cat and mouse, but a quick glance at my watch let me know that enough time had passed and I needed to speed things along. When Mr. Man approached me, he smelled as good as he looked and I was instantly wet. I was so wet that my thong was plastered to the swollen lips of my pussy. I wanted this man now.

He leaned over and whispered into my ear, "Can we dance?" I countered and whispered back, "Can we fuck?" He leaned back, almost in shock, as if taken aback by my boldness. Yet I could see the shift in his pants, as if his dick had responded to my request, and I knew he was down even before he did. He led me out of the bar.

I could see his confusion when he glanced back at me, and I knew what he was thinking. As he held my hand leading me out of the bar I knew that he could feel the huge 4.5 carat, cushion cut diamond and platinum wedding ring sitting on my left hand that signified my marriage commitment to another man. I could sense that he wanted to ask me if I was married, but that he didn't want to know the answer. Or rather, that he already knew the answer, but didn't want to ask the question, for fear that he might remind me of what he assumed I had forgotten. Or didn't want to remember. I could see all over his face, and in the bulge of his pants that he didn't want to ruin his luck. So he didn't ask the question, and I didn't supply the answer.

When we got to his SUV he asked, "Your place or mine?" I looked at the spaciousness of his Lincoln Navigator and said, "Neither." Then I opened his truck and entered the backseat. I could see Mr. Man begin to thank his lucky stars. I must admit I was making this very easy for him. It's just that I had to be home by 2 a.m. That was the rule, and I had already wasted enough time with our little game of seduction in the bar.

When Mr. Man got in the backseat, his dick was hard as stone, and as much as I wanted to feel it throbbing inside of me, I couldn't resist the urge to taste it first. I used to hate giving oral sex, but now I loved the taste of a new dick. It was like exploring an unknown flavor of ice cream with a blindfold on. The taste and the texture would all be new and that drove me crazy. When I'd had my full, and Mr. Man was on the brink of cumming, I pulled away and allowed him to come back down as I prepared his dick and my pussy for the next part of the evening.

When his rapid pant had decreased to a steady breath I slid my wet pussy over his cock and mounted it, tightly clinching the lips of my pussy over the head of his dick. He moaned with delight, and a small tear escaped out of the corner of my eye. I didn't usually allow guys to go in raw, but I was pressed for time and something about this one made me feel deliciously reckless.

I started to establish my rhythm, and I could swear I heard Mr. Man exclaim that he loved me. That's when I knew I was giving him the good stuff. Not to be outdone, Mr. Man clamped his big hands around my hips and began to slam me down real hard on his dick. The sex was so fucking good that I wanted to keep it going for a while, but when he reached down and began to tease my clit with his thumb while steadily slamming me down on his dick, I couldn't help myself and I began to cum all over him. Within seconds he came too and I could feel the warmth of his cum spread inside of me and come dripping back down the sides of his dick and out of my pussy.

We sat there for a while, just enjoying the silky wetness all around us, both of us throbbing, panting, smiling. Until finally I spoke, "I gotta go" I said. Mr. Man looked like he had lost his first love. I was touched by his sadness to see me go, and definitely wanted another taste of this fine, handsome stranger, so I gave him my business card. Not the business card that listed me as an attorney in a prestigious law firm, but the one I'd had made for occasions such as this, with my "alternate name" and my google phone number so that we could keep in contact while I maintained my confidentiality.

I stepped out of Mr. Man's car and declined his offer to walk me to my car. When he had driven off, still looking back in his rearview mirror, I pulled out my travel size mouthwash, gargled and spit. I removed my panties and tossed them into the nearest dumpster. Then I headed home.

When I got home I decided to park on the street so that the garage wouldn't wake my husband and children.

I opened the front door, disarmed my alarm, and crept slowly up the stairs.

My house smelled of sweet goodness, and I could tell that my husband had baked some cookies with the kids.

I stopped into my children's rooms and watched them sleep for a moment, and then I slowly closed their doors being careful not to wake them.

I tiptoed down the hallway into my master bedroom.

On the left side of the bed, his side of the bed, lay my beautiful husband, sound asleep.

I removed my clothes and stepped into the shower. I stood there in the water for several minutes savoring the hot water as it slid down my body. I allowed it to remind me of the evening I had spent with the tall handsome stranger I'd met at the bar. I remembered how he'd touched me and made me cum, and I felt myself grow moist again. I hurriedly finished my shower, resisting the urge to pleasure myself and obtain one final release. Done with my shower, I rinsed off, put lotion on my body and slid into bed, naked, with my husband.

Feeling the warmth of my body, my husband nestled up next to me and whispered, "Did you enjoy your night?" I whispered back, "Yes." He then asked, "Will you be seeing him again?" I sighed, "I surely hope so." My husband gave me a soft peck on the cheek and off we went to sleep.

I awoke to Freddy already inside me. He was pushing himself in and out of me so sensually, that even without me being fully awake my body had already begun to respond. I must admit, this was a good way to wake up, and as always Freddy knew just how to work my body. This was not the first time Freddy had woken me up this way. Since opening our marriage, and especially within the last several months, Freddy had become insatiable. He wanted it day and night, sometimes several times a day. It was like the more sex we had the more he wanted. He and I were having sex almost every day of the week and I knew he was also having other sexual relationships, but he always wanted more.

As he moved inside me, my body quivered and shook as I came. It wasn't a strong orgasm because I had worn myself out from last night. But it felt good nevertheless. Freddy came too and filled me up. It spilled out of me and pooled below my butt. I made a mental note to change the sheets, especially since I had probably leaked a little bit of the stranger from last night's cum.

I cringed when I remembered last night. It was true that I'd had a lot to drink, but that didn't excuse me being so reckless. I made a mental note to get an

STD and HIV/AIDS test. Freddy and I had a rule to always use protection, and I had thrown that rule out the window. I knew Freddy would freak if I told him, so I kept it to myself for now. I wanted to get checked out and make sure we were okay.

I didn't want to alarm Freddy, especially since I had no plans on doing that again. Freddy had broken some rules, including staying out later than we had agreed on, and I knew that he had been seeing the same woman at least a few times, but I was willing to bet that he had never been so reckless as to have sex with anyone else without protection. Freddy was disciplined if nothing else, and he wouldn't go there.

I was so angry with myself that I had done that. I just hoped I hadn't picked something up from the stranger and passed it on to my husband. I couldn't live with myself if I put Freddy or our marriage in jeopardy. I would get the test first thing in the morning.

When the next day came and I called the local clinic (since I didn't want to see our family physician), they informed me that it was best to wait about six weeks to three months before I took an STD and HIV/AIDS test. They said it could take that long or longer before a potential STD would show up on tests. I figured it was my punishment to have to wait that long to get the results. The six weeks of waiting and worrying were gruesome. I had stopped going out during that time since the last thing on my mind was seeing other guys. I couldn't concentrate on any of my cases and I took a brief leave of absence.

During my leave I spent some time doing some of the things I used to do before I got so busy at work. I woke the children up with a homemade hot breakfast instead of the usual cereal and fruit, or toaster-ready waffles and juice. I talked with them about their day instead of dropping them off in a mad dash to get to court on time. When I picked them up from school we baked cookies, went to the library to check out books like we used to, and even went to see a movie one day. We cooked dinner together, or I cooked dinner and enjoyed them talking to each other. I even enjoyed their bickering.

It was such a difference from how things had become. I was so used to our new schedule and my new fuller life that I hadn't even realized that I missed some of how things used to be. I missed spending time with them and being a big part of their day, and I hadn't even realized it. Before I knew it the six weeks had passed and I took the STD test. I was told the results would come by mail in another two weeks. About five days later I was surprised to get a call from the clinic. I missed the call as I was in a deposition. When I checked my messages I saw that I had a message from them asking me to call them back at my earliest convenience.

My heart raced as I wondered why they might be calling me. Did I have something? Was something wrong? I didn't feel sick, maybe a little bit tired, but I figured that was because I had recently gone back to work from my brief leave of absence and I thought the long days were just taking a bit of time to get re-accustomed to. I had gotten spoiled by all those days of leisurely getting the kids up for school, then being able to come back home and take a nap if I 'd felt like it. So I reasoned that my fatigue was from that. But other than being exhausted, I felt fine.

I hurriedly called the clinic and after being on hold for a few minutes was put on the phone with a nurse who delivered some news I was not expecting. I was six weeks pregnant, and as the nurse excitedly gave me the news that I was healthy as a horse and expecting a little one, I got a bit excited too. I hadn't really thought much about having another baby, especially with my career being back on track. But the time I had spent with my children made me realize how quickly they were growing up and how much I missed having a baby in the house.

The nurse told me congratulations, reminded me to start my prenatal vitamins as soon as possible, then got off the phone. I sat there for a moment in a stunned, happy silence, trying to process the news. I was pregnant. I was actually pregnant. I thought about Freddy. I wondered if he would be excited. I wondered how I would tell him. I started thinking of witty ways to tell him that would involve the whole family. I wondered how the children would respond. I knew my daughter would want a sister, and I didn't think my son would care. Just so long as whoever came didn't bother his toys.

I smiled at the thought of my children. They were so perfect, and I began to imagine what the third child would look like. Would it have my personality or Freddy's? Would it be a daddy's girl or a momma's boy? Would it look like me or like Freddy, or like its older brother or sister? I smiled at the idea of my son being a big brother.

Financially we were good. My job paid great, and for the first time I was already in a career instead of waiting for one to start. I imagined it would be a lot easier to stay career-minded with a career already in place instead of trying to establish one after my child got here, like I'd had to do when Freddy and I had our first two children. Things would be perfect now. Maybe we'd even buy a bigger house. I took the rest of the day off and rushed home to wait for Freddy to get off so I could tell him and the kids the good news.

It wasn't until I got home that the reality of the situation hit me. I was six weeks pregnant and it was almost exactly six weeks ago that I'd had sex, unprotected, with another man. To make matters worse, I'd had sex the very same day with my husband. There was absolutely no way to know for sure if this child was my husband's or the other guy's.

I sank down in Freddy's chair and began to cry. What had I done? Why had I been so stupid? I couldn't tell Freddy I was pregnant because then I'd have to tell him that it could be someone else's, and if I had to tell him that it could be someone else's, then I would have to tell him that I'd had unprotected sex with another man.

Freddy would never forgive me. Even if he forgave me for having unprotected sex with another man, he most assuredly wouldn't forgive me for getting pregnant, even potentially, from another man. I didn't even know if Freddy wanted another child. I definitely knew he wouldn't want another man's child. I was screwed.

I cried again as I thought about the hole I had dug for myself. And maybe even for my family. Had opening our marriage really made us better? If I was being honest, at least at first glance, it would seem that way. We were happier and more sexual with each other. I had a career and it was better than I could have ever imagined. Even though Freddy had grown tired of his job, he was still overall satisfied with the direction that our lives were going in.

But on the other hand, we had made some definite sacrifices and had grown weak in some other areas. My time off from work had already shown me that one of the areas we were weak in was family time. We had not been spending as much quality time with our children. Especially since both of us had increased our days out. We had gone from having a date out one night a week each, to having two or more days out a week.

Our children were still happy and energetic, and never wanted or needed for anything. So I think I had begun to mistake that for quality family time. But the truth is, we were not spending time so much as we were buying them things. Without realizing it, we had become *those* parents.

Another area that was suffering was our spiritual lives. I cannot tell you the last time we had gone to church. At first, we would miss only a few Sundays. Then it got to a point where we only attended a few Sundays. Nowadays, we didn't even do that. We didn't even bother going to church anymore. Most of the time, Freddy got in so late from his date night the night before that it would've made us too late to attend church. I guess on those occasions I could have just taken the children to church by myself. But I didn't. That was my fault.

Other times, it wasn't about Freddy getting home late. I just didn't want to go to church. Being in church made me feel guilty, like I was doing something wrong. I didn't feel like I was doing anything wrong at the time, and I didn't want to go to church and be made to feel guilty. But now I wasn't so sure. Now I felt like I had been wrong. How else would I explain being pregnant and not knowing who I was pregnant for?

I was better than this. I no longer wanted to be this woman. I made up my mind right then and there that this open marriage thing had to stop. Perhaps it had already served its purpose. Sex between Freddy and I was the best it had ever been. I had a career now. Both Freddy and I were in shape and taking better care of ourselves. We had both learned how to enjoy our lives, and even more importantly, we had both learned that we could enjoy our lives. We now knew that being married didn't mean we couldn't still be individuals. So I no longer saw a need to open our marriage.

If Freddy wanted to keep his days out he could. But I would no longer permit him to sleep with other women. I would also no longer sleep with other men. I might still go out every other Friday night or so, but other men were off-limits. Plus, I made up my mind that on at least some of those Friday nights I would take my children out.

I had learned a hard lesson. But I was grateful that it wasn't too late to turn things around. But first things were first, I had to decide what to do about this baby. Should I keep it, since it could have come from Freddy and me, or should I get an abortion in case it was from the other guy? That would involve doing something I didn't believe in. I cried thinking about the fact that I might be killing Freddy and my own child. I had always believed that it was a woman's right to choose. I still do believe that. But for me, it was never something I thought I would do. Yet here I was thinking about doing it. I cried the rest of the day.

When Freddy came home, despite my best efforts, I could not stop crying. When he asked me what was bothering me, I lied on the spot and told him that I had lost a case that was very important to me. He understood that and offered to let me go lie down while he took care of the children. I was grateful to Freddy. But that also made me even sadder to realize I had betrayed him. I did not deserve him and he did not deserve this.

I made up my mind to be better. I would be a better wife, a better mother, and a better person. I would get back into church, and being the kind of woman I could be proud of. The kind of woman I would want my daughter to be. Whether or not I got this abortion, I was going to get my life in order. I prayed my family would not suffer any more than we already had. Then I prayed about what I should do.

The next several weeks I was somber and tearful, and thankfully Freddy just assumed it had to do with the case I had lied about. Despite having a baby growing inside me, I felt so empty. I plagued myself with thoughts of whether my child would be a girl or boy. Would this child become a doctor, a lawyer, or teacher? Could they become the next president, a Nobel Peace Prize winner? What If this child was conceived by Freddy and I? Could I kill a child that Freddy and I had made within the sanctity of our marriage? Was our marriage even sanctified anymore? I had decided that I was done. Even with all the good that had come out of us opening our marriage, none of it was worth what I now had to deal with. I was done with this lifestyle. Now it was time to tell Freddy that I wanted him to stop too.

I didn't talk to Freddy about quitting our open marriage lifestyle for a couple of weeks after finding out I was pregnant. I wanted to give myself a chance to collect my thoughts. I knew Freddy could tell that something was up because we hadn't been having sex and I hadn't been going out. I continued to play it off like I had a full plate at work and was still bothered about the "case I'd lost." I did try to throw hints that I was at the end of the open marriage stage of our lives.

On Friday night, when it would have been my evening to go out, instead I ordered in from Freddy's favorite restaurant and rented an action flick. I was trying to show him that I would rather spend that time with him. We watched the movie and had a good time. Freddy even commented that this was like old times. I was hoping that the next night, when it was his night to go out, he would reciprocate the gesture and also try to find something for us to do together. But he did not. Instead, he went out that night just as he had the week before and probably would also do the week after.

I also tried to point out to Freddy that we had not gone to church in quite a while. To that he responded that just because we had not been inside of a church in a while didn't mean anything. He said that as long as we still loved God it didn't matter where we were on a Sunday morning. When I brought up the fact that we did not have as much time with our children as we used to, he reminded me that that had changed right about the time I took on my new career.

Freddy was not making it easy for me to tell him that I wanted to close our marriage and just be with him. So I realized I was going to have to take the direct route and just tell him. I made sure to do it on a Friday, technically my night out, so that he could see that I too was going to be willing to give up my night out with other guys. I wanted him to see that as far as romantic or sexual relationships went, I only needed him.

When Friday came around I took Freddy and the kids out to eat. I wanted him to see that being out with me, or even me and the children could be just as much fun as being out with another woman. I wanted him to see that he could have everything he wanted right here with his family.

While out, we all had a good time. We all talked and laughed, and at the end of dinner the children convinced us to all share a huge ice cream sundae. We were so stuffed and full that we all groaned on our way back home, and the children were so exhausted that they fell asleep before they could even take a bath. We laid them down in their beds, then went outside to sit on the deck and talk.

I knew that now would be the time to tell him, especially after having such a fun family day. So I prepared myself. I didn't think it would be a big deal to stop. After all, I had been the one to propose it. So I expected that when I asked Freddy to stop, he would. Boy was I wrong.

When we got on the deck I told Freddy that I loved him and had come to realize that I missed him and our family. I told him that I wanted to be the only woman for him and wanted to close our marriage to other people. When I said that, Freddy looked at me with a smile. He told me that I was the only woman for him. I smiled at that. It had gone great, and just as easy as I had envisioned it would. I then asked, "So, you're okay with stopping any sexual relationships you're having with anyone else? In answer he replied, "Wait, I didn't say all that."

I looked at him confused as he began to explain. He said to me that I was the only woman for him, but that he very much enjoyed having an open marriage. He said that he felt whole and like he hadn't had to trade in his identity just to be a husband. He said that he didn't want to go back to the way things were. I told him that I did not want to go back to how things were either, and that was why I wanted us to continue to have our own free time, but that I didn't want us to share that free time having a sexual relationship with anyone else. He frowned and told me that a part of what made the time feel free was that we could decide what we did with it. I told him that we still could decide to do what we wanted with it, and he countered that part of what he wanted to do with it was to have sexual relationships. He said they invigorated him and often reminded him of what he had at home, and made him want to be a good husband.

Getting angry now, I told him there were other ways he could be a good husband that didn't involve fucking anyone else. I reminded him that this was supposed to be about developing relationships and not just having sex. Yelling at this point, he told me that it wasn't just about sex for him but that sex was a part of it and that he would continue to do as he had before. He told me that we'd had a deal and that it was not my right to just cancel it without getting his input. He yelled that I could do what I wanted to do and stop seeing others or not, but that he was going to continue. Then he stormed off.

I could hear him grab his keys and shortly thereafter his car started up and I could hear him angrily drive away. I had no idea this would go like that. I was not expecting that response from Freddy. I thought my biggest worry would be trying to figure out whether or not to keep this baby. But trying to close our marriage would prove to be very difficult, as I realized that Freddy was deeper into this than I had thought. As a matter of fact, he was deeper in than I could have ever imagined. Little

did I know this was just the beginning for us.
Perhaps, the beginning of the end.

18

Freddy

Stacy must be out of her fucking mind, I thought as I grabbed my keys and got the hell out of there. There was no way in hell that I was giving up my life. It was true that this started out as a new lifestyle for us, but now it felt like it was my life that was at stake. What the fuck did she want? Did she want me to go back to working all day and night? To using my weekends as a glorified landscaper? Did she want the only time I had for myself to be when I was in the bathroom? On the fucking toilet? She had introduced us to this life. Why was she trying to take it back now?

I drove onto the freeway, speeding slightly, going nowhere in particular. I was trying to calm down, but I was so angry. I had come alive since we opened our marriage. I was more confident. I took better care of myself. I even think I was a better father and husband. Because I knew I would have time to and for myself, it made the time I spent with my family that much more special. When I was with my children, I gave it my all. When I was with Stacy I tried to be the best me I could be. I tried to be the best sexual partner she could ask for. After all, I knew she could get it elsewhere and I never wanted another man to show me up with my own wife. I tried to be the best provider I could be and had been the only breadwinner in our family until Stacy began working three years ago.

Stacy had never wanted or needed for anything, and that is because I had worked my ass off to make sure she and the kids had everything they needed. Hell, I didn't even really like my job anymore, but I still stayed and I worked hard because I wanted my family to have it all. Didn't that matter to Stacy? I had sacrificed, and sure, she had also. But didn't my sacrifice mean anything? Didn't the fact that I worked hard day and night and carried our family - was the sole provider for the vast majority of our marriage - mean something? Didn't it mean that I should be entitled to have something I wanted, or did I have to just provide and that's all? Was I not allowed to enjoy my life too?

I got off the freeway and in the distance was a sports bar that was famous for its wings so I decided to stop in there. I ordered some wings and a beer and people-watched as I waited for my food to arrive. I noticed several good-looking young women, most of which were underdressed and I stood back and enjoyed the view. One young woman looked to be college-aged and had the biggest, highest breasts I had ever seen. They were struggling to stay in a barely-there top that also showed her tight and toned abs. Every time she bent over the pool table to take a shot, almost every guy in the spot watched her excitedly. I think more than a few of us were hoping that she'd pop out of her top. Not that she needed to, because her top left very little to the imagination. I was enjoying every second of watching them bounce around.

The woman with the bouncing perky tits was playing pool with three of her friends and they all looked like they had stepped off the cover of a Maxim magazine. One of the girlfriends had on low-rise jeans that cupped her ass beautifully. She didn't have as much ass as I liked to see on a woman, but her ass was perfectly rounded and her jeans were just low enough for me to see a rather intricate tattoo going from the top of her jeans and disappearing down below. I found myself wondering how low the tattoo went, and whether it curved around the front. The other two of her friends had on short dresses that barely covered their asses, and as one of them played pool with the one with the bouncing tits, I found myself longing for a peek. At one point one of the friends in the short dresses laid her body across the edge of the pool table, angling to get a better shot, and I could see just a bit of her pussy. She was not wearing any underwear. A few guys cast appreciative glances at her, and one or two sighed. Those women at that pool table would be the undoing of more than a few men here.

Eventually my food came. I had been enjoying watching the four beautiful young women so much that I had nearly forgotten that I had ordered food. I ate my wings and enjoyed my beer, making a mental note to come back to this place. I had found a new hangout spot. I ate my wings in silence, casually watching the four beautiful women and a couple other attractive women walking around the sports bar. They kept walking, never staying in any place too long. So I figured they were there to get attention. Which is exactly what they were getting.

I tore my eyes away from the Maxim Four and looked around. I saw an older woman sitting at the bar watching the game. She was tossing back beers and eating nuts and yelling at the screen along with the guys. She was cute in a natural kind of way, and despite the half-naked four women demanding the attention of all the men in the sports bar, I couldn't take my eyes off her. She was wearing a pair of jeans so fitted that I couldn't figure out if they were jeans or tights. She had on a ball cap, so I couldn't see her hair and she didn't appear to have on any jewelry that I could see. She was cute though, and seemed like she'd be fun to hang out with.

When I finished my wings and beer, I went to the bar, close to where the lady in the ball cap sat. She nodded her head at me in acknowledgement of me sitting down, then she went back to the game. She would yell when there was an upsetting play, than she'd clap and hoot when there was a good play. I just watched in silence, until she pulled me in. She shot out arbitrary questions, like, "Can you believe this shit? And what the fuck are they thinking? What kind of play was that?" She had a potty mouth that initially made me cringe, because I wasn't used to any of the women I knew talking like that, especially not Stacy. Heck, I barely talked that way myself, unless I was really upset. But I liked it on her.

Even though I wasn't attracted to her in that way, I knew without a doubt that she would be a firecracker in bed. Nowadays that seemed like the place my mind always went. Yet Stacy expected me to go back to being damn near asexual. But this was who I was now and she would have to get used to it.

Bored with just sitting there, I started getting into the game that the lady in the ball cap was watching along with a few of the other patrons. Pretty soon we were yelling at the players together and high-fiving when they got it right. The lady in the ball cap's team won, and she celebrated by sending everyone who was watching the game a beer. She and I and a few other patrons sat laughing and talking and enjoying each other's company. I learned that Janice was married with one son and her husband traveled a lot with his job as a sports agent. She was an executive assistant and loved sports. We talked about sports, children, and marriage. Before either of us realized it, we were the last two remaining as all the other people who had been watching the game had either left or had moved on to playing pool.

Janice and I talked about her and her husband's career, and my wife's and my career. Janice told me how much she hated her job. She said being an executive assistant was like being a glorified gopher. Her husband, however, loved being a sports agent. Janice admitted that she wished she could do it too. I suggested to her that she become a sports agent and join her husband, maybe even start an agency together. She sounded so excited and intrigued by the idea but admitted that it would never work because her husband would never allow them to work together. Janice said her husband liked having the spotlight all to himself, and liked being the famous and well known sports agent. She disclosed that her husband would never allow her to get in on the action, even though he often looked to her for advice and for her opinion on decisions he made with and for his clients.

When she told me who her husband was I couldn't believe it. I had seen this guy on major sports networks. He was a household name. I was almost star struck and couldn't believe I was sitting here with his wife. When she told me who he was, I realized money couldn't have been a problem, so I asked her why she stayed in a job she hated. She told me that she worked so she could have something of her own. I immediately thought of Stacy. Stacy had said the same thing to me right before she started her law consulting business. Even before that, the idea of having something of our own was the reason we had opened our marriage.

I don't know if it was all the beer I had in me, or the fact that I simply didn't care anymore. But I told Janice about my open marriage arrangement. She sat there, mouth wide open, while I told her that my wife and I had an agreement that we could see who we wanted on our designated day and could even have sexual relationships if we wanted to. I told her how I'd had threesomes and some of the best sex of my life while in this arrangement and how I had become a better person in every way. I confided to Janice that my life had improved in every way since starting this arrangement with my wife. All except for my job, which I hated, but other than that this arrangement had greatly improved my situation and my wife's.

Janice sat there, in shock. She blinked several times and took a couple sips of her beer, probably trying to wrap her mind around what I had just said. After what seemed like a few minutes, but was surely just a few seconds, Janice spoke. She said, "Man, shit, you talk about me needing to make money doing what I love, but you may have found a gold mine." I was confused and asked her what she was talking about. She said, "Can you imagine how many other men and women would want to take part in an arrangement like this? Hell, you could quit your job and make this open arrangement thing a service you offer to others." She said it wasn't her cup of tea, but she knew people who would jump at the chance. She confessed that based on what her husband told her about some of his players, they would too (along with their wives). I laughed at that. That was the funniest thing I had heard all year. Janice didn't appear to be drunk, but she must have been to propose such a crazy idea. I couldn't tell if Janice was serious or not, because she laughed too. But I couldn't stop laughing.

When I finally caught my breath, I jokingly told Janice that we should go into business together. She would open a sports agency and I would supply her customers with alternative sexual experiences. I continued laughing at that, even as Janice's eyes lit up. She seemed serious at first, that is, until I got her laughing too. We both laughed long and hard and continued to toss around ideas for our alternative sexual experiences sports agency. In between bouts of laughter and more drinks we decided we would name it A.S.E. Sports Agency. The A.S.E. would stand for Alternative Sexual Experiences, and even though it would be pronounced "ace," which is defined as "an expert in a given field," or as in the case of sports "a person who excels at a particular sport or other activity," we and our players would know what it really meant. Everyone else would think we were just playing off the word "ace" and its reference to superior athletes.

Janice and I talked and laughed about this until both of us realized how late it was and decided it was time to go. We exchanged numbers, agreeing we had similar personalities, and it would be cool to hang out again, platonically. Janice winked at me when she said platonically, reminding me that the whole open marriage thing was not her thing. But then, seemingly in all seriousness, she told me that she would continue working on our business idea and would call me when she figured some things out. I laughingly replied "Okay", then walked Janice to her Jaguar. I offered to call her a cab but she stressed that she was not drunk and was a big girl that could definitely handle a few beers. As she pulled off, yelling "It was nice to meet you" I curled up into the backseat of my car and fell asleep.

Unlike Janice, I apparently couldn't handle all the beer I had consumed and needed to sleep it off. I fell asleep thinking about and laughing at our little Alternative Sexual Experiences Sports Agency. "A.S.E. Sports Agency" I said out loud before feeling myself fall into a deep alcohol-induced sleep.

"A.S.E. Sports Agency, making your dreams come true on and off the field..." I mumbled as I drifted off to sleep.

The next day when I awoke, realizing I had slept in my car, I hurriedly rushed home. I knew Stacy would be pissed, thinking I'd had sex with some woman just to show her that I didn't agree that we should stop our open marriage arrangement. I got home in record time. Bracing myself for Stacy's wrath, I walked in the door. But not only was Stacy not upset, she was pleasant and sweet. She asked me what I wanted for breakfast, and when I replied that I was not hungry, she whisked me over a hot cup of coffee and told me I needed to eat something.

I sat at the dining table, slightly afraid. I didn't know if Stacy had snapped or if she was somehow planning to try to hurt me. I had heard of stories of women seemingly just fine, then turning around and losing it on their husbands. I watched Stacy cautiously. She went about the kitchen cooking breakfast and humming a tune. I wanted to ask her if she was okay or if she had wanted to talk, but I didn't want to risk changing her mood, since she seemed so peaceful right now. I figured she was saving her wrath for me for later, so I just kept my guard up and ready for the verbal lashing that I knew was coming.

But it never came. After breakfast Stacy dressed the children and herself and told me that they were going skating. She asked me if I would like to come along. On the one hand I wanted to go and spend some time with my family, but I also wanted to avoid any confrontation. I decided to go, still waiting for the shoe to drop. I didn't want to decline and have Stacy thinking I didn't want to spend time with her and the kids. We went skating and had such a great time. My daughter was already a natural, and I watched her with pride as her little body glided around the ring, keeping up with the big kids. My son was uninterested in skating, so he and I hung out in the arcade, playing games and eating junk food. Stacy and I didn't usually let them have much junk food, but since we were having a fun day, I thought it would be okay.

After a couple hours there we ordered a pizza. When the pizza came out both children stuffed a slice or two into their mouths and rushed off to finish skating or playing in the arcade. That left me and Stacy alone. But she still didn't yell or scream, or even appear upset. She watched the children play with a smile on her face and hardly seemed to notice that I was even sitting there. At some point she looked at me and said, "We are so blessed." I nodded my head in agreement. We truly were and I knew that. I hoped I wouldn't lose my family, and then I realized that that was what Stacy was trying to get me to see. She wanted me to see how blessed we were and how much our family meant. But I already knew that. Still, I felt I should be honest with Stacy and tell her that I had decided that I would not stop seeing other women. I hated to ruin the peace between us, and I certainly didn't want to argue again. But I had to tell her the truth.

I opened my mouth to tell her that I wanted to continue with our open marriage, but before I could speak, Stacy raised her hand, effectively silencing me. She looked me in the eyes and told me that she loved me and wanted our family to get back the strength we used to have. She told me that she would not be seeing any other guys, but that she would give me space to figure things out on my own. Stacy said that she knew it was unfair to make me stop simply because she had decided to, especially when she had been the one to get us started in the first place, but that she was hopeful that I would come to the realization that closing our marriage was best. Until then, she would pray for us, get back into church, and continue loving me like she always had. Then she gave me a sweet kiss, and turned back to the children.

I sat there in stunned silence. I knew I had heard her. But I wasn't at all sure I had heard her right. Had my wife really just told me that I could continue to see other women and didn't have to stop because she was going to? I said there quietly, confused, trying to figure out if there was some ulterior motive for my wife's behavior. But after watching our children skate and play for a little while, my wife glanced at her watch, then said we should get going so I could have time to get dressed and head out. That's when I knew she was serious. My wife was really going to let me continue with this lifestyle, even though she no longer wanted to do so herself. I did not know what to make of that.

On the one hand I was happy that I could continue to do what I loved to do, what made me feel happy. But on the other hand, I was skeptical. I couldn't make sense of why my wife would allow me to continue this. A part of me just sat back and waited for the proverbial shit to hit the fan. I knew that it would. But in the meantime I decided I would go along with our arrangement.

When we got home it was early evening. Because my wife was being so cool I gave the kids a bath and ordered some Japanese food from a local restaurant so she would have dinner there for when she was ready to eat later. I took a shower, and partly to test my wife to see if she was serious about letting me continue on, I offered to stay at home. I told her we could eat and play scrabble. To be honest, although I was trying to see if she would truly be okay with me leaving, I would have still been absolutely okay staying home with my wife.

Having the time with her and the children had actually been a lot of fun, and I was really feeling very close to her. She seemed tempted at the offer for me to stay. But then, almost with force, she shook her head no and told me that she wanted me to enjoy myself out. She said she would wait for me to get this out of my system on my own, just like she had.

Stacy then kissed me on the lips very softly and sensually and told me to have a good time. Without looking up, she sat back on the sofa and picked up the book she had been reading, "Testimony: 10 Stories Detailing Supernatural Miracles, Blessings, and THE POWER OF PRAYER" by A. C. Ross, and quietly dismissed me. I gave her another kiss on the lips, and went upstairs to give my children a kiss even though they were already fast asleep. Then I left the house, still bewildered at my wife's decision. I was honestly the luckiest man in the world. No doubt about that.

As was my usual, three to four hours later, I was at Serita and my hotel of choice. I had made the drive so often that I seemed to get there on autopilot. It was like I blinked and was there. Although I slept with other women, Serita was still my lady of choice. She was, by far, the freakiest woman I had ever slept with and I looked forward to whatever new things she wanted to try. I was always game to try anything, and I had told her so. The only thing I had said an absolute no to was involving other men. That was a "Hell no." But other than that, she could bring anyone or anything into bed with us. As always, tonight she didn't disappoint.

Tonight Serita had another woman join us again. Her name was Anya and she looked as eager to join us as I was to join them. Serita also had a pair of handcuffs and a box of children's candy called Pop Rocks. I vaguely remembered Pop Rocks from when I was a child, but I had no idea what Serita and Anya were going to do with them. Pop Rocks, if I remembered correctly, were candies that "popped" in your mouth when you ate them. It was almost like fireworks in the mouth. I didn't know what Serita had in mind but I knew it was going to be good.

After lying in bed kissing, touching, and rubbing on each other, Serita and Anya ordered me to sit in a chair. I was so deliriously excited that I would have done whatever they said. So I didn't even raise an eyebrow when they put handcuffs on me and restrained my hands while they tied me to the chair. After they had tied me securely, Serita lay Anya on her back, spread her legs and began to lick slowly, softly, and sensually between Anya's legs. Anya moaned, softly at first, then got louder and her moans grew longer and stronger as Serita licked harder and faster, making longer and deeper strokes against Anya's clit. As Serita sucked and licked between Anya's legs, she also fingered herself with equal intensity. I watched as her ass lifted up and down as she inserted first one, then two fingers into her pussy. Her head bobbed up and down between Anya's legs as she licked and ate her pussy and her ass bobbed up and down as she finger-fucked herself.

By then my dick was so hard that it shot straight into the air and had begun to leak semen from the tip. I wanted to join them so badly. I wanted to fuck the shit out of the both of them, but they made me sit there, restrained, watching them give each other and themselves immense pleasure. As Anya's moans turned into shrills and shrieks my dick grew harder and harder, and for a moment I thought I was going to cum just from watching. But then Anya came and let out an "Ooooh," as her pussy erupted into what looked like a stream of water. As Anya came and her body quivered and jerked, she squirted into Serita's face and mouth. I sat there awestruck. I had not seen a woman do that since Leane so long ago. I was amazed and envious. Fuck, I wanted to cum in her face and mouth too, I thought.

When Anya came down off the high of what seemed like a strong-ass orgasm, and as her body began to quiver less and her stream of cum dried up, Serita still lay there, licking Anya's clit and drinking her cum. After Anya had gathered herself, they switched positions, and this time Anya licked and sucked and ate Serita's pussy. Just like Anya had, when the pressure became too much to bear, Serita wrapped her legs around Anya's head burying her face deep into her pussy then came with force, squirting her juices into Anya's hair, her face and her mouth. Just like Serita had done, Anya licked it all up. When they were done with each other, they turned to me.

I didn't know what they had in store, but my body tensed with a delicious anticipation. They crawled over to me, on their knees, with their pussies still gleaming from the wetness of their cum and each other's saliva, and while taking turns they each licked, sucked and stroked my dick. They never rose off their hands and knees as first Anya then Serita, then Anya again, and then Serita again took my dick into their mouths, sucking, licking, swallowing, massaging. It was like they were fighting over my dick, and neither would let the other get more than a few good sucks before grabbing my dick from the other and putting it into her own mouth.

I sat there, unable to move, eyes half open, in pure ecstasy watching these two beautiful women give me the best head I had ever had before. My toes curled and my dick throbbed and leaked but they wouldn't stop sucking. I moaned expletives and talked so fucking dirty to them but they would not stop.

My body began to quiver and despite my best efforts to hold in my orgasm I felt the pressure build uncontrollably. At that point, Anya put my balls in her wet mouth and begin to suck them while Serita trailed her tongue along the sides and tip of my dick. I shuddered and let out a guttural "Awww fuck" and came, hard, down the side of Anya's face.

As the cum poured out of me, Serita took my dick into her mouth and let the cum fill her mouth and run, with ease, down the back of her throat. Not to be outdone, Anya took the tip of my dick into her mouth as she massaged my balls, almost like she was trying to get some of the cum for herself.

I sat there shaking like a leaf. I had never had such a strong orgasm and I was spent. My body sat there, lifeless, but in heaven nevertheless. I couldn't speak, could barely move as I sat there absorbing the aftershocks of that powerful orgasm. After a minute or two had passed, I vaguely wondered why the women hadn't untied me yet. All I wanted was to curl up in bed with these two women and sleep. I felt I would need a few days of sleep to recuperate from the strength of that orgasm and restore my energy. But I hadn't realized that Serita and her friend Anya weren't done with me yet.

As I was drifting off, I saw Serita approach me with something in her mouth as Anya looked on slyly. I couldn't make out what was in her mouth, but as she closed her mouth over my dick I felt the sensation of mini explosions going on around my dick, and just like that, despite having absolutely no energy at all, my dick woke right back up and stood as close to attention as it could.

The warmth of Serita's mouth coupled with what I assumed must have been the Pop Rocks candy sent me into a tailspin and I gasped for air as I watched Serita suck my dick and make it feel like it was literally exploding. Then Anya took a turn. She filled her mouth with the Pop Rocks candy and closed down on the tip of my dick, before slowly easing her mouth down my shaft and finally around the bottom of it. Anya was deep-throating me, with the Pop Rocks, and it was too much to bear.

The sensation of the Pop Rocks coupled with the warmth and wetness of Anya's mouth felt too good and in less than five minutes I had cum again. This time it was Anya's turn to swallow whatever cum I had managed to make in the fifteen minutes since I had cum last. She swallowed it all, complete with licking her fingers when she was done, as Serita looked on with amusement.

When they were finally done with me, I lie across the bed, lifeless and limp, having been drained of all my energy and all of my cum. I must have fallen asleep, because as I opened my eyes I saw Serita and her friend fully dressed and smelling great. They were dressed in different clothes from what they had been wearing when they first got here. It was apparent they had showered. They had on fresh makeup and they had each styled their hair. They looked like they were heading out clubbing or something.

They both gave me a kiss on the cheek and Serita said that she and her friend were going out to enjoy the rest of the night. Her friend smiled and told me that it was nice to meet me and just like that they were gone. As I drifted back to sleep I vaguely remember wondering if they had showered together, and thinking of how nice it would have been to witness it. Maybe next time...

When I woke up only a few hours later I was in shock. I was shocked that I had only slept just a few hours despite the epic orgasms I had just had. And I was shocked that this was my life. For what seemed like the hundredth time, I thought of how lucky I was and how other men, and maybe even women, would probably love to live like this. What if Janice was right? What if this was every person's fantasy - married or otherwise - to live like this?

Having your every sexual fantasy and desire come true? What if it was effortless, not requiring you to scour the streets looking for the person or people who could make your desires come true? Could I provide that service? Could I really make a business out of what had become my life?

It was true that I was incredibly lucky to be able to do this. But if given the choice, would others want to do this too? I thought back to the incredible ecstasy I had felt just hours before, and realized that each and every person should get the chance to experience that, or something like it.

With renewed energy and enthusiasm I swung my legs out of the bed and sat up. I decided I would do it. I would partner with Janice and we would open a sports agency that would cater to our clients' every need and desire. Janice would operate the sports part, because although I followed sports I knew nothing about running an agency or representing anyone or much about what went on behind the scenes. But I would be responsible for the other part of our agency. That part that made us special. The part that made ALL your dreams come true.

I grabbed a pen from the hotel nightstand and on the sketch pad provided, wrote that down. That would be our slogan. Despite the late, or should I say early hour, I called Janice and told her that I wanted us to go into business together. She said, "What took you so long", and responded that she had been waiting for my call.

With unbridled excitement Janice explained that she had gone as far as to start on a business plan. We talked about it for a few hours then got off the phone with plans to meet next week on my night out to go over the business model and business plan. After getting off the phone with Janice I sat back in bed. With pure unadulterated elation I realized that the Alternative Sexual Experience (A.S.E.) Sports Agency had just been born.

Open Marriage: **A.S.E. Sports Agency** (Book 2)

Sneak Peak...

A.S.E. Sports Agency...

Making your dreams come true on and off the field

Let A.S.E. Sports Agency represent you and cater to all of your needs

Call us today!

(Ph) 800-555-0409

(Fax) 800-555-1127

Email: info@asesportsagency.com

Website: asesportsagency.com

1

Client: **Mitch Berg**

Profession: Ice Hockey

Position: Center

ASE Code: Orgy

Client Profile: *Mitch Berg; Ice Hockey player, plays Center for the Canadian Crusaders; Agency client since 2011; ASE member since 2014; Prefers young blonde coed women, small in stature, with bisexual preferences; Requirements: Multiple, female partners (three or more) that are sterile.*

I am legendary in the world of ice hockey as well as in the world of sports in general. I am even well-known in celebrity circles. But it's not necessarily because of my skills on the ice. Though my skills on the ice have garnered me some records and titles, they do not compare to what else I am known for. I am Mitch Berg, an ice hockey Center for the Canadian Crusaders, and I am the father of 13 children - with rumors that there could be more out there. It was a running joke that I was creating my own sports team with all the children I have. Oh, and they are all by different women.

It is also well known that I like to party. I am often in the news for throwing parties that make my other wealthy and high-profile neighbors upset. I have been cited with noise complaints and lawsuits for destruction of neighbors' property. I've also had the cops called to my various properties because of my parties on so many occasions, that at one of my parties I just eliminated the middleman and invited the cops to the party as guests. That had made national news and when I was interviewed about it, I just laughed and joked that since they would be called anyway, I might as well just invite them to the party. That's just the kind of guy I am. I am a fun-loving, party-throwing type of guy, with emphasis on the party part.

Admittedly, I have slept with as many celebrities as could fill a football field. At this year's VMA's, the host had joked that my conquests could fill the location where the VMA's were being held. Many gasped at that, but I just laughed. How could I not? It was probably true. I never took myself, or life, too seriously.

There were two things, however, that I was very serious about, and that was my game and not having any more children. As it concerned my game, whether I partied hard or not, I was always the first at the rink and the last to leave. I practiced in and out of season, and always made it a point to lead my team to victory. I never tried to dominate the game from my teammates, even though I was easily one of the best, if not the best on my team, as well as in ice hockey in general. I shared the spotlight with my teammates, and made sure to share the attention. As long as it was positive.

When the attention was negative, I took the blame. When the team had a win, as captain of the team, I shared the credit and pointed out every team member that had contributed to our win. I always emphasized team. But when we lost, or displayed unsportsmanlike conduct, I took the blame, faulting my lack of leadership as the reason for the loss or the bad behavior. I have been told that I am a fan favorite, a team leader, and an all-around great guy.

The other thing that I am serious about, dead serious about, is not having any more children. I love sex, especially with multiple women, and usually all at once. I sometimes joke that "orgy" is my middle name. But those orgies and wild sex parties had landed me with a number of paternity claims, and all so far, with the exception of one claimant, have proven to be true. I paid a very

Anne Drea

generous portion of my very generous earnings
every single month to my 13 children and their
mothers. I didn't complain, and the money was not
the main reason I didn't want any more children.

The reason I really didn't want any more children
was because I had realized, at around child number
nine (my son Crescent) that I could not possibly be
there for all of my children and was bound to miss
important events in their lives. That, I knew, was
not fair to them. I had helped to make them,
whether on purpose or not, and I knew it was my
job to take care of them. I also knew that it took
more than money to take care of children. Taking
care of them meant being there for and with them.
With the number of children I have, as well as my
strenuous and time-consuming game and practice
schedules, I knew that would be impossible. It
saddened me daily that I wasn't being fair to my
children and I didn't want to subject any more
children to my lifestyle.

In all fairness, I had tried to stop at child number
nine. It was then that I realized that I was missing
first steps and basketball games and ice hockey
games, and little princess birthday parties. My
second son, Mike, had called me on the phone one
day and asked if I would be able to swing by and

teach him and his teammates a few tricks. Mike was on the ice hockey team and his friends along with his coaches thought it was the coolest thing in the world that I was his father. They wanted me to come to their practice and teach them some of my legendary moves. But no one wanted it as much as Mike. When Mike had called and asked me if I could swing by, I'd had to break his heart and tell him that it would be impossible. The truth was, I could not just swing by Mike's house because Mike's mom lived 2000 miles away from where I lived.

I had met Mike's mom at an after-game party, and we'd had a one night stand. That night I had slept with her and a couple other women whose names I did not know, all at the same time. Three months later, Mike's mom had gotten in contact with my coach to have him tell me that she was pregnant. Mike's mom had been in college, and upon getting back to school to start her fourth semester, had realized that she was pregnant. She admitted to me that she had been a party girl. But that she thought the baby was mine. I decided to do the right thing, and had supported her throughout her pregnancy. But I'd also had a paternity test to make sure that it was my child. When I found out that Mike was my son, I had not only supported him, but had also paid Mike's mom's tuition so that she could finish her degree. When Mike's mom finished college she moved 2000 miles away to take a job, and I had only been able to see Mike a handful of times throughout the year. I wished it was more.

Still, I fully supported Mike financially, including having set aside full tuition for each of my children to attend college and beyond should they decide they wanted to. I had always wished I could see more of Mike, and my other children as well. So after I had my ninth child I became more vocal about not having children. I knew that I was doing my children a disservice, even if they were all rich. The truth was, I had never planned to have any of the children I had. But I hadn't exactly been careful.

After number nine, I starting telling the women I was going to sleep with, even before it got to that, that I didn't want any more children. I used protection, and I also asked them if they were on birth control. If someone ever said that she was not on birth control, I didn't even take the chance. I wouldn't sleep with anyone not on birth control, and it didn't matter how fine she was.

But still women kept turning up pregnant. The reasons varied. Once or twice the condom had broken, and another time I suspect that the girl I was sleeping with had slipped it off. Another time I had forgotten to put it on after receiving the best oral sex ever. It had been so good that I hadn't been thinking and had just plunged myself deep into the woman. It wasn't until after I had cum inside her, as I watched it slide back out of her as she lay there, that I had realized the mistake I'd made. Not even four weeks later the woman had called me, giddy with excitement, to let me know that all three of the pregnancy tests she'd taken had shown up positive. That was my 13th child, and the last one that I knew of.

Some of my buddies joked that the women kept getting pregnant because they knew how generously I took care of all my other children, and to an extent their mothers. Still, I knew that it was as much my fault as it was theirs, so this time I was taking extra precautions. One of my buddies had suggested I have a vasectomy, but I didn't want to do that. The last thing I wanted was someone "cutting my balls off" or even cutting anywhere near them. Plus, like I told my buddy, I really believed that having a vasectomy would de-masculinize me and water me down on the field. The last thing I wanted was to lose my aggression and my edge on the field. So a vasectomy, or any cutting of any kind, was out of the question. I went to A.S.E. with this dilemma.

I had been with A.S.E. Sports Agency for a full three years before using their Alternative Sexual Experiences services and that was because I hadn't felt like I needed any help in the "getting laid" or "fulfilling my sexual desires" department. I knew how to party. The ladies liked me, and I liked them, and I had no problem whatsoever in that department. But A.S.E.'s reputation preceded them, and long before I became a client of their sports agency I had heard that they could and would do anything for any client of theirs at any time. As long as it was legal, there was no job too hard or too big for A.S.E., so I had boldly approached Frederick with my dilemma.

Sitting across from Frederick in his L.A. office, I came right out with it. I was never one for mixing words. I told Frederick that I loved sex, and loved having it with as many women as I could fit in a bed, or hot tub, or back of a limo. But that I wanted to make sure I never had any more kids. Ever! To be thorough, Frederick had asked me about having a vasectomy, to which I had replied, "Hell no!" So Frederick had gone back to the drawing board.

Frederick had notated all of my concerns and what my desires were and had told me that he would get back to me within 24 hours. I was pleased with the fast turn-around of Frederick's promised response, especially since I had a party coming up in a week. I shook Frederick's hand and exited his office. Not even an hour had passed before Frederick called me back with a solution. It was a good one, albeit seemingly far-fetched.

Frederick had suggested to me that I have my orgies and sex parties with only women who were sterile. When I laughingly replied, "Yeah, sure, awesome! But how can we make that happen?" Freddy had assured me that he could make it happen. Frederick had even gone as far as to say that he could arrange it for that night. As intrigued and amazed as I was, I asked Freddy to just send the women to my beachfront home on the night of my party. I warned Frederick that I didn't want any knock-knee, lazy-eyed women simply because they were sterile, and that I still wanted them to be blonde, young, beautiful, sexy and hot. Frederick had responded with ease. As if finding young, hot, beautiful, blonde, co-ed, college-type, sexy, and STERILE women was not a tall order.

I got off the phone in amazement. I was half curious about who the women would be and how they'd look, and amazed that A.S.E. could pull something like this off. All I had to do at that point was wait for my party and my guests of honor to arrive. I had heard that there was nothing that A.S.E. couldn't do. But, as it concerned this, I wasn't so sure. I found myself anticipating this party more than I had any of the others before.

When the day of the party rolled around, I was excited. I gave one of my boys some money to grab some alcohol and wings for the party. I occasionally had teammates over to my parties, but I mostly still hung out with my boys from the neighborhood that I grew up in. When I'm throwing a big party, I put my party planner Gayle on it. But tonight would be different. Tonight, instead of having a blockbuster party, I was just having a few friends over and the ladies that A.S.E. found. Those sterile, hot, blonde, bombshells.

I went to my barbershop and got my hair trimmed. I always liked to look good for the ladies. I wasn't movie star good-looking, but I made sure that I kept myself clean-cut and dressed nice, at least for parties. An hour before the ladies were to arrive, my boys Jeff, Cesar and I were sitting back, drinking, and talking. I hadn't told them about the special services that A.S.E. offered, but I had told them that I had some special guests coming tonight and that they would be all mine.

Usually I shared the ladies, and I made sure there were plenty of hotties to go around. But before I exposed my guys to these ladies, I wanted to make sure they passed the hotness test. The last thing I needed was a bunch of horse-looking ladies showing up and running my boys off. Or worse yet, ruining the reputation of my sex parties. My boys had been told that they could stay and mingle with the ladies, but towards the end of the evening, when it was show time for the ladies, they had to go. My boys understood, and just joked that the next time I needed to make sure I hooked them up with my special honeys. I assured them I would and we were good to go.

We were at my beach house and enjoying the view. I had been blessed in my career and always took the time to appreciate all that I had been so lucky to attain. Near the start of the party I left my boys and hopped in the shower. When I was coming out and throwing my gear on, I heard the doorbell ring. I didn't rush down because I knew my boys would let the ladies in. But I was a little anxious to see them. Worst case scenario, if the girls were atrocious, I could always kindly send them on their way. Then I could go find some ladies on my own and hope like hell that the condom didn't break or that they were actually on birth control when they said they were. So I had a "plan B" and either way the party would go on. I just wanted to see if A.S.E. would deliver.

Deliver they did! When I got downstairs, the ladies were already outside sitting around the pool with my boys. There were three ladies and they were all drop-dead beautiful. I mean I actually had to do a double take when I saw one lady more beautiful than the next. I walked over and introduced myself to each girl one at a time. I also used that opportunity to get up close and see just how attractive the girls were. I also wanted to make sure they had something going on upstairs.

The first girl that I walked up to was Sandy. She was about 5'6", and had long, beautiful legs and blonde hair that fell to her waist. She said that she was attending college and was a nursing major. She informed me that she was 21 years old, as of yesterday. I gave her a hug and told her that it was nice to meet her, and happy birthday. Then she discreetly slipped me a piece of paper. I opened it, and it was a medical report certifying her sterility, with her name, social security number, and a picture of her photo ID on the page. I smiled at her, she winked at me, and I moved on to the next girl. So far so good. It certainly looked like A.S.E. was delivering on the impossible.

When I got to the next girl she was also blonde, but with some flecks of brown in her hair. She had the prettiest sea-green eyes and was absolutely beautiful. Her blonde hair was in a pixie cut and she had on a short denim skirt and fitted tank top that showed off her athletic body. She introduced herself as Lesli and told me that she was 22. She also told me that she was a graduating senior from college majoring in broadcast journalism and had been a cheerleader throughout high school and college. Her body surely reflected that she had been a cheerleader, and I couldn't wait to see some of her moves. As Sandy had, Lesli also handed me the same type of medical report. Again, I was shocked and pleasantly surprised to see that A.S.E. had pulled it off. Un-fuckin-believable!

Lastly, I got down to the third woman. She was a bit taller than Lesli and Sandy, about 5'8". Her hair was the longest and fell down below her butt. She was wearing a black top with tight jeans and black needlepoint heels. She was stunning. She introduced herself as Riley and hugged me before I could even give her the same hug I had given the other two ladies. She handed me the same paper the other two had, and as she was walking away, offered to get me a drink. This was shaping up to be a great night.

After Sandy, Lesli, Riley, and my boys and I'd had some drinks, we all got in the hot tub and played truth or dare. At one point, Sandy was asked to make out with Riley and they had. Sandy had gotten on Riley's lap and kissed her, intertwining her tongue with Sandy's and pulling Sandy's hair to bring her closer. Finally they had pulled themselves apart, but it was obvious they weren't done with each other. I couldn't wait until they resumed, with me in the middle, tonight. Sandy had also made Lesli give Cesar a blowjob, and she had. She had bent over in the hot tub, pulled Cesar's shorts down and had given him five or six long strokes that had made him hang his head back in ecstasy. After that brief blowjob, Cesar had been smiling goofily at Lesli the rest of the night. I had to admit that I was a little jealous that Cesar had had first dibs on Lesli.

By the end of the night, having played truth or dare, we had learned that Sandy had a girlfriend, Lesli watched porn more than most guys, and Riley was pierced down below. I couldn't wait to see it for myself later. We also learned that Cesar had a crush on Lesli, Jeff had never had a threesome, and that I suspected that I had a few more children out there somewhere. This was the realest game of truth or dare I had ever played. We had also seen Sandy and Riley make out, Lesli give Cesar an express blowjob, Jeff finger Sandy, and Cesar suck on Riley's breasts. I hadn't really been involved in any of the dares, but that was okay because I knew I would get a chance to participate later. I just sat back and let my boys enjoy themselves until it was time for them to head out.

An hour or so later, I started giving my boys the eye to head out, and slowly, kind of reluctantly, they did so. Then it was just me and the ladies. I invited them all up to the sitting room next to my bedroom, and there I had whipped cream, strawberries, chocolate sauce, edible underwear, a pair of dice with one that listed a body part and the other that listed what to do with that body part, as well as a ton of porn. Lesli smiled when she saw the porn, as she had confided that she loved porn and watched it at least once or twice per day. She walked over to my collection, shuffled through a couple of the DVDs before selecting one and popping it in.

I don't know if they were turned on by the porn in the background or if they just wanted to continue what they had been doing before, but Sandy and Riley started making out almost as soon as they sat down. With Sandy and Riley making out and Lesli watching porn, I just sat back and watched. Sandy and Riley had gone from kissing to stroking each other. Riley's hand was between Sandy's legs and Sandy's eyes rolled back in ecstasy before also putting her hand between Riley's legs. Riley lay on top of Sandy as both girls rubbed each other between the legs and tongue-kissed passionately.

I was so caught up in what Sandy and Riley were doing that I hadn't noticed that Lesli was sitting by herself on the sofa in the sitting room, playing with herself. When she looked up and saw that I was watching her, she motioned me over with her finger. I sat beside her. She replaced her hand with mine, slipping my hand down and into her underwear. I could feel that she was already wet. I slipped one finger inside her and used another to stimulate her clit. She moaned and turned her body in closer to mine. I continued fingering and stimulating her and her moans increased.

When I couldn't take it anymore, I picked her up and put her on top of my lap. I slipped off her top and put one of her breasts in my mouth, sucking it gently, slightly tugging on her nipple with my teeth. She arched her back and let her head fall back, grinding, making my fingers go down deeper into her.

By now, Sandy and Riley were naked, and as I glanced over to the sofa where they were, I could see that they were in the "69" position. Sandy was on her back, with one leg bent, and the other open and slightly cocked to the side, and Riley was on top of her, her face buried between Sandy's legs and her pussy open over Sandy's face. Sandy had her hand on Riley's thighs and her face was turned up as she licked Riley's pussy. I pulled Sandy up from the sofa we were on, and walked her over to the sofa that Sandy and Riley were on. I wanted to be close to the girl-on-girl action. I laid Lesli on her back, pulled down her panties and buried my face between her legs. I sucked her pussy, making her body jerk. After a while she was dripping wet, and I lifted my face out of her wet pussy, slipped on a condom and stuck my dick in it. I fucked her hard on the sofa, catching the attention of Sandy and Riley who had finally stopped eating each other's pussies.

Sandy and Riley bent over the sofa, their asses in the air, and on cue I slipped my dick out of Lesli's pussy and into Sandy's. I fucked Sandy, then slipped my dick into Riley, fucking her too. By then Lesli had gotten on her knees too, so that all three women were bent over the sofa. I went to each of them, fucking for a few strokes before slipping into the next one and then the next. We fucked from the back, in the ass. I ate each of their pussies and all of them sucked my dick. At one point I had one of them sucking my balls, the other sucking my dick, while the other one ate between the legs of the one who was sucking my balls. Orgies were the best because there was always someone pleasing someone else, with each person getting licked, sucked, or fucked. Everyone was winning.

As I always did when I was fucking multiple women, I came and I came hard. As my cum squirted out of my dick and into the face of one of the girls and near the pussy of the one that was bent over eating the third girl, I sighed with relief that I wouldn't have to worry about any of my sperm getting inside her pussy. As the girls moved into the bedroom to spend the night, and sleep off the sex power-session we'd had, I rested easily. I had no worries of unplanned pregnancies or paternity letters coming in the mail.

As I drifted off to sleep it was with visions of some of the wild things Lesli, Riley, Sandy and I had done and also with thoughts of how on the money A.S.E. Sports Agency was. I had to tell a couple of my teammates to switch to them. A.S.E. Sports Agency had been one of the best decisions I had made in my life, and tonight's escapade had confirmed that.

About TTP Publishing

"Providing short and sweet books you can enjoy, when you're ready to enjoy them, that WON'T take all day...

...BECAUSE YOU HAVE THINGS TO DO"

TTP Publishing is a book and media publishing company that specializes in publishing short books. It was founded by an avid reader who, after becoming a mom, doctor, bill-payer, and errand-runner, realized she had little to no time left in a day to sit back and enjoy a good book.

What's more, this busy mom was also impatient, meaning she not only wanted to sit back and enjoy a good book with her limited "me" time, but she also wanted to reach the conclusion of that book - without having to wait days or even weeks before she had more time to read again.

This busy mom had an "aha" moment as she thought of how awesome it would be if good books were shorter and lasted the length of say, a good movie, or dinner out.

That's when ***TTP Publishing*** - "TTP" stands for ***to the point*** - was founded.

 TTP's books are sometimes funny, sometimes controversial, sometimes spicy, and sometimes tell-it-like-it-is, but they are almost always short and to the point...*because you have things to do.*

 For information on submitting your book for publication, please visit us at www.ttppublishing.com, or send us an email to info@ttppublishing.com.

Happy Reading!!!

TTP Publishing Books

Act Like a CEO, Think Like a Millionaire: Why You Should Care LESS About What a Man or Woman Thinks About Love, Relationships, Intimacy and Commitment and MORE About GETTING WHAT YOU WANT OUT OF LIFE

What You WON'T Expect When You're Expecting Because This is The CRAP They Don't Tell You: ABC's of a Sucky Pregnancy

Confessions of a Surrogate for Celebrities

TESTIMONY: 10 Stories Detailing Supernatural Miracles, Blessings, and THE POWER OF PRAYER

Open Marriage: An Erotic Trilogy (Book 1)

Open Marriage: A.S.E. Sports Agency (Book 2)

*Open Marriage: Behind the Scenes (Book 3)